THE DAY ENDS AT DAWN

Praise for the Valentin St. Cyr series

Chasing the Devil's Tail

"A beautifully constructed, elegantly presented time trip to a New Orleans of the very early 1900s. The characters are memorable and the period is brilliantly recaptured."

—*The Los Angeles Times*

Jass

"Another voyeuristic tour of Storyville, New Orleans's red-light district during its heyday at the turn of the 20th century. Fulmer's dialogue adds its lyric voice to the gutbucket sounds and ragtime rhythms pouring out of the bars and up from the streets."

—*The New York Times*

Rampart Street

"The sense of place is so palpable you can almost hear the music. Fulmer's writing is crisp and nuanced. Valentin is a hero for whom it's easy to cheer."

—*The Detroit Free Press*

Lost River

"David Fulmer's evocative prose captures the sights, sounds, and smells of 1913 Storyville in his superior Lost River."

—*USA Today*

Eclipse Alley

"Fulmer...adds plenty of texture to keep things fresh. An always satisfying historical mystery series that deserves more readers."

—*Booklist*

THE DAY ENDS
AT DAWN

DAVID FULMER

New Orleans, LA

Joseph S. Phillips and Susan J. Wood, Ph.D., Publishers
www.blackwidowpress.com

Cover Design: Kerrie L. Kemperman
Text production: Geoff Munsterman

ISBN-13: 9780998643199

Printed in the United States of America

To Valentin, Justine, Buddy, Evangeline, Each Carter,
Frank Mangetta, Tom Anderson, James McKinney, Lulu
White, Miss Antonia Gonzales, Reynard Vernel, J. Picot,
and the sundry others who populated my Storyville books.

Thank you, my friends, for allowing me to bring you to life.
And farewell.

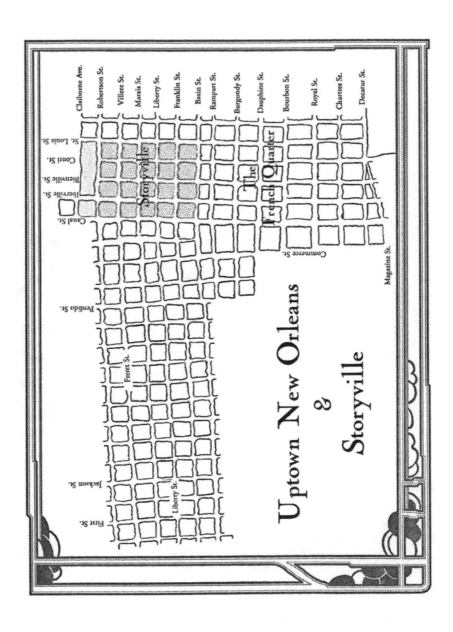

Uptown New Orleans & Storyville

THE DAY ENDS AT DAWN

ONE

Chief William Reynolds began the last morning of his life as he had every working day for the prior seven years, slipping into police headquarters on Tulane Avenue through the rear door and riding the elevator to the fourth floor. He chose not to enter by way of the main lobby because he preferred that his officers not know exactly when he was in the building.

"Keeps them on their toes," he would say.

On this first Thursday of August, 1917, he was an hour later than his usual eight o'clock arrival, having come from a breakfast meeting at City Hall that had left him troubled. His aide and driver Sergeant Daley trailed behind as he walked down the hall, anxious to get to his desk. But he heard voices as they drew closer to his outer office.

When he arrived at the door, he all but threw up his hands. Captain Sallis and Lieutenant Dimitry were in the midst of a three-sided argument with a hulking giant of a man dressed in khaki trousers and a blue work shirt. His name was Kenneth Mullens.

Reynolds said, "What are you doing back here? You were given orders." He was exasperated. Problems with patrol officers like Mullens were supposed to be handled by someone on the first floor. And yet here he was, with his six-foot-and-four-inch, two-hundred-and-twenty-pound self half-filling the anteroom. His gaze was bleary and the scent of sweat came off his clothes. The chief waved a dismissive hand as he passed through. Daley stopped to block the doorway so Mullens couldn't follow him inside.

Glowering, the tall man looked over the aide's head to address the chief directly. "I need to be back on my shift. I need my pay. I got to eat."

Reynolds spoke without turning. "I told you. You go back when Dr. Barnes says. He gets the final word. Now that's all."

The chief crossed to hang his coat on the rack, letting the officers deal with Mullens, who went by "Big Kenny." He had been a thorn in the department's side ever since he was hired on. Over time, it became clear that he was half-mad and not New Orleans police material.

The chief moved to his desk and was deciding how to rid himself of the cretin when he was startled by sudden shouts and the sounds of a scuffle. Now truly irked, he wheeled around to see Mullens thrashing in a tangle of arms and legs with Daley, Dimitry, and Sallis. He was about to bark, "All right, stand down!" when the pistol appeared in the big man's hand.

Each Carter heard the news before it reached the street and his first call was to the house on Dumaine Street.

Valentin St. Cyr had been up late and when the telephone chattered he pulled a pillow over his head. Then he felt his wife's finger poking his ribs and surrendered, rolling out to reel down the hallway to the foyer. He lifted the receiver and heard a shout: "Mr. Valentin! Jesus and Mary. Some fucker shot the Chief of Police!"

Valentin snapped out of his daze. "Did what?"

"Chief Reynolds," Each said. "He was shot dead not an hour ago."

The detective said, "Shot by who?"

"Some copper. That's what they're saying."

"All right, well..." Valentin rubbed his forehead with his free hand. "Find out what you can and call me back." Each burbled something he didn't catch and the line went dead.

When he returned to bed, he heard a muffled "Now what?" from beneath the covers.

"That was Each," he said. "Chief Reynolds was shot dead."

Justine pulled down the blanket and sat up to stare at him.

The speed at which the news made it from one end of New Orleans, from Marigny to Carrollton and from the river to the lake, was astounding. A walk down any street was accompanied by the sound of telephone bells and buzzers ringing from inside every house. The citizens who were not already on the way to early mass or work stood on galleries sharing what little anyone knew. Of course, much of it was gossip that sprouted into rumors, and within an hour of the tragedy, tongues were flapping over the murder of not just Chief Reynolds, but a half-dozen other officers and the mayor, too. These wags then went to announcing that the killer was on the loose, possibly heading for that very neighborhood. The chatter rose, hung for a while, and then fell apart under its own weight.

The first calls from police headquarters arrived no more than ten minutes after the smoke had cleared at the Annunciation Street home of Tom Anderson. Lucy, the housekeeper who had been with Mr. Tom for four years, took the call, listened in startled silence, then whispered, "Thank you. I'll tell him when he wakes up."

Justine and Valentin were at the kitchen table when their phone chirped for the second time that morning. This time it wasn't Each on the line, but James McKinney.

"Did you hear?" the lieutenant said.

"I did," Valentin said. "Is it true?"

"Yes. He's dead."

Valentin asked how it had happened.

"The chief had Mullens suspended because he'd been acting crazy," James said. "He's been nothing but trouble. He went in this morning to ask Reynolds to put him back on duty. A fight started right there in the office. He drew a weapon and started shooting. Reynolds was hit twice. One of the wounds was to the face. It was fatal."

"Damn," Valentin said.

"Then Mullens got loose and shot another copper on the stairs. He ran out onto Saratoga Street. One of the officers gave chase and put one in his leg. He gave himself up. They're holding him in Parish Prison."

Valentin said, "I imagine it's chaos at headquarters."

"Pretty much."

"What about the appointment with the mayor? You think it's off now?"

"I'll find out." The lieutenant promised to call with an answer and broke the connection. Valentin dropped the handset in the cradle and went back to the kitchen to tell his wife what little more he had learned about the murder of Chief William Reynolds.

The bedlam the lieutenant described had been a swarming of policemen and doctors and general confusion on the fourth floor and in every part of the building. Word of the shooting went out the front door minutes after it happened and found its way directly to the *Times-Picayune* building on Poydras Street.

Reynard Vernel had just settled at his desk and was pulling a new roll of yellow paper into his Underwood when he caught a buzz of voices from his editor's office. A few seconds later, Kassel emerged to call out to the half-dozen reporters in the newsroom.

"Chief Reynolds was shot dead at police headquarters a little while ago," he announced, his broad face florid. Those scribblers who had been in their chairs stood up, gaping. "They have the fellow who did it in custody. That's all we know."

The reporters fell to whispering amongst themselves.

Kassel pointed a finger at Reynard and said, "You. Go."

Mayor Martin Behrman sat behind his wide oak desk, stunned by the news that Major Sont was relating. The major had been assigned to City Hall as a liaison between the city's two public powers. The men were a good fit in terms of temperament, both regarding the foibles of the offices they represented with cynical eyes. Sont was a tall, wicked whip of a Lothario, the mayor short and stocky. While they were not friends, both looked on their work together with satisfaction.

"We still don't know if he was trying to shoot the chief or if it was an accident," Sont said.

"Hit twice does not sound like an accident," the mayor commented.

"No, sir, it doesn't. But I'm told it was a wild scene. Mullens lost his temper and the officers were trying to restrain him when he drew a revolver. He got off four shots. One killed Chief Reynolds. And another policeman was shot dead."

"What other policeman?"

"Mullens' uncle. Charles. He was a desk sergeant."

"His *uncle*?"

"He's the one who got him hired on in the first place. He was on duty and when he ran up to try and stop him, Mullens shot him in the chest. They carried him to Mercy. He didn't survive."

Behrman said, "Good lord."

"Mullens was taken down outside. He's in lock-up."

The mayor said, "This city..." and shook his head. "Is everything at headquarters under control?"

"Yes, sir."

"All right. We need someone in the chief's chair right away. Who's next in line?"

Sont said, "Assistant Chief Cook, Mr. Mayor."

Behrman stopped and rolled his eyes. Major Sont kept his expression neutral. The mayor said, "Well, it's temporary. Let's get him in here."

After Sont left the office, Mayor Behrman summoned Mr. Pettibone, first instructing him to contact Assistant Chief Cook and then to review his schedule for the day. One by one, the assistant marked appointments to be postponed until the city could calm. When he reached the eleven-thirty meeting with Lieutenant McKinney and

Valentin St. Cyr, the mayor said, "No, I'll keep that one." When Pettibone raised an eyebrow, he said, "It's important. November is only three months from now." He turned and so did not see his assistant casting a cool glance his way.

Valentin and Justine were drinking their second coffees and reading over the morning paper when Evangeline stepped into the kitchen, dressed for mass in a white blouse and gray skirt. She murmured a good morning on her way to the stove, where the pot was warming. She leaned against the sideboard and spent a moment regarding the couple at the table.

She had been in their home—now her home—for a year and she wondered if they knew how much they were growing to resemble each other in small ways even in that short time, with Justine a quadroon of French, African, and Cherokee and Valentin a Creole-of-Color on one side and Sicilian on the other. Her eyes were deep black, his a gray-green shade. She was a fair bit darker than he. Indeed, Valentin St. Cyr cast such a rare profile that most people did not know where he belonged and so he could walk in any door.

Now looking between them and their matching troubled looks, she said, "Did something happen this morning?"

Valentin was no longer surprised by this mysterious woman's ability to read what was unspoken. He was also not surprised that she took the news about the murder of Chief Reynolds with no more than the absent lament, "The poor man." She looked at him and said, "Does this have something to do with you?"

Justine said, "Probably."

"No, not directly," he said. "James McKinney and I have an appointment at City Hall, that's all. It will probably be postponed."

"But you'll go downtown anyway." Justine's tone was only faintly accusing. She stood up, said, "I'll take my bath now," and left the room.

"Well, at least it doesn't have to do with Storyville, does it?" Evangeline said.

He was saved from having to correct her by the ringing of the telephone. McKinney was calling to tell him that the mayor would expect them at eleven.

Reynard Vernel knew of Chief Reynolds' routine and when he reached police headquarters, did not join the scrum of reporters who had cornered Assistant Chief Cook on the front steps and instead hurried around to the back of the building just in time to see the stretcher being carried to a waiting ambulance. He spotted Lieutenant McKinney standing just outside the door and joined him to watch as the body was loaded, the door closed, and the vehicle rolled away with motorcycle escorts in front and behind.

The lieutenant shared the details in a quick minute. "The man is out of his mind," he finished. "So we won't be surprised if he ends up in Jackson." He treated the reporter to a sharp look. "But don't quote me on that. On any of it."

"Will 'police sources' do?"

"That's fine. You can get the rest from Cook."

Reynard closed his notebook and walked away, leaving the lieutenant with his thoughts.

Two

J. Picot had left New Orleans and his post as police captain with a brief note of resignation to the chief, delivered from parts unknown. He had gone into hiding and created a new identity to cover his tracks. The money he had put aside from two decades of graft served him well and he was able to sink into a safe if dull life on the outskirts of Little Rock.

There he spent his monotonous days seething over the fate that was mostly his own doing. His fixation with destroying Valentin St. Cyr had clouded his mind, bringing him within a breath of losing his own life. As it all fell apart, he had been forced to scurry away from the city that he had been feasting on for the better part of twenty years.

Little Rock's red-light district was a pale shadow of Storyville, two blocks of rundown houses and a few dozen mostly ugly trollops staffing them. The days of Captain J. Picot using his power to sate his fleshly hungers were gone because of one man. He wished to repay the favor, but a return to New Orleans was too dangerous. If the Creole detective didn't get to him, the courts still had charges waiting. All so he sat and fumed and dreamed bloody scenarios that ended with St. Cyr dead on the floor.

That lasted until the morning he opened his copy of *The Arkansas Gazette* and saw the blaring headline:

THE END OF VICE
Famed New Orleans Tenderloin to Close
by
Reynard Vernel

What he read brought a rare laugh from his fleshy throat that caused the closest diners to turn and look his way. He bent over the page. So it had taken the U.S. Navy to achieve what the upright citizens, the churches, and Captain J. Picot could not. Or so the story claimed; Picot knew it wasn't that simple. And so he now began to mull a last visit to the city to share in the death dance.

Assistant Chief John H. Cook had been in his third-floor office for fifteen minutes when he heard the crack of gunfire and then a rumbling commotion, first overhead and then on the stairwell at the end of the hallway. Shouts followed and then policemen were running past the door.

The assistant chief was slow to move, leaving his desk only after the two other officers had exited to see what was happening and then waiting another minute.

By the time he got to the fourth floor, it was all over. The corridor in front of the chief's office was crowded, but he was able to catch a glance at Reynolds lying on the floor in front of his desk with Captain Sallis and Lieutenant Dimitry bending over him, one side of his face covered in blood and his dead eyes staring at the ceiling. Someone shouted that a doctor was on the way. Cook listened to the snippets from this mouth and that. Big Kenny Mullens had arrived in an angry fit, had shot the chief, and then escaped.

A police sergeant appeared from the stairwell with the breathless news that Mullens had also shot his uncle, who had been working at a desk on the first floor and had rushed to help.

Sensing that no one had noticed him, Cook retreated to the other end of the hall, descended the stairs, and returned to his office, where he stood at the window and considered what the chief's death might mean for his official duties. A half-hour later, he received a summons from Mayor Behrman.

By the time Valentin reached the District, it seemed the whole city knew what had happened at police headquarters. He realized this when he stopped for the light at the intersection of Roman and St. Louis streets and caught excited chatter from the gaggle of men standing on the northeast corner. There was no mistaking the shouts of "Reynolds!" and "Chief!" and "Big Kenny!"

It brought to his mind the memory of a time almost thirty years before when another police chief was murdered. He had been a boy then, but he remembered how New Orleans had raged in the aftermath. And how that rage had been visited upon his family. That had been a dark, dark time and he never—

He heard a shout from behind and realized that he had been sitting with the Ford at an idle.

The men on the corner had turned to stare. He shook off the images that had been floating in his head and pulled away, turning left on St. Louis and then right on Marais four blocks down.

It was still early enough that he was able to park right in front of Mangetta's Grocery and Saloon. He entered on the store side and found the usually noisy crowd of shoppers even noisier as they chattered back and forth in English and Italian, with "chief" and "shot dead" mixing with "*omicidio!*" and "*morte!*"

The proprietor spied the new arrival moving around the edge of the mob and offered a bare nod of greeting. Valentin passed down the short hallway that connected the grocery to the saloon, stopped at the brass urn at the end of the bar and carried his coffee to the corner booth. It was a daily ritual and yet it felt skewed on this morning. To take his thoughts off Reynolds' murder, he spent some time mulling all the days and nights he had spent on the premises.

He had lived in a room upstairs for a time when he and Justine were on the outs. His friend Buddy Bolden had played on the low stage. Almost every one of his big cases had ended with an early morning aftermath of hashing out the last details over one of the saloon tables. And the proprietor Frank Mangetta, *Zio Franco*, Uncle Frank, had been a kind part of his life since his childhood, having arrived in New Orleans from the same Sicilian village where his father had grown up.

As if summoned by these reveries, the *zio* himself appeared, filled a cup from the urn, and joined him at the table. "*Che cosa*, eh? The Chief of Police?"

Valentin allowed that it was an awful tragedy. William Reynolds had been a fair-minded type who had kept his hands off Storyville unless there was some pressing reason for a unique police presence. When such special circumstances arose, he would direct James McKinney to seek the Creole detective's assistance—with the permission of Tom Anderson, of course. The mayor, the business community, and a good share of the churches were satisfied with his leadership. None of that made a difference when a crazed gunman showed up at the chief's door. Whoever was to replace him would have substantial shoes to fill.

Frank wanted more details. Valentin said, "I don't know anything else." He noticed a figure at the front window, pointed, and said, "But he will."

The saloonkeeper looked around, then got up to open the door. Each walked in, looking his usual sly and satisfied. Valentin understood; he had been out scooping up news from the streets. It was a hustle he'd been playing for the fifteen years since he ran away from the Waif's Home, showed up in the red-light district, and began following a certain Creole detective around, using the moniker "Beansoup." As the years passed, he stayed close, and now at twenty, had become a genuine Storyville rounder who now went by "Each," a moniker taken from the initials from his true name, Emile Carter.

He had been a ragged squirt in the old days and had carried that same bony-framed, silly-faced, wild-haired picture into his manhood. It seemed that he was wearing the same derby, only five sizes larger. That his attempts to present himself as a seasoned Storyville sport did not work was not for lack of trying.

Valentin and Frank waited while he fetched coffee and crossed to stand next to their table. "So what's the word?" the detective said.

Not to be hurried, Each sipped his coffee. "The coppers have been talking, so it's out how it happened to the chief," he said. "They don't know so much about the fellow shot him, though. Big Kenny." He winked. "At least not as much as I do."

"So?" Valentin said.

"Sick in the head, is what. One day, he's on his beat and he's fine, the next, he's off acting crazy as hell. Not making sense. Talking all this shit no one can understand. Saying he's going to arrest some sport for something he didn't do. Yelling at things that ain't there. And the next day, he's back to normal. A couple months ago, he got religion and was preaching to these poor fools. And then he quit it." He pointed a finger to his temple. "You ever see one of them soldiers come back after they got shot in the head? He's like that. Lately, he's been around Fewclothes, telling anyone who'll listen about the chief putting him off the force."

He took another sip of his coffee, eyeing the effect of his information. Both men at the table appeared properly impressed.

Frank drained his cup, slid out of the booth, and said, "I got to get back in the grocery."

Each said, "And I got some business…" He gestured toward the street.

Valentin watched as he made his exit. Who knew what "business" he had, as long as he stayed out of trouble?

By the clock on the wall, he had another half-hour before it was time to leave for City Hall. So he slouched down and fixed his moody gaze outside.

Kenneth Mullens had first been taken in shackles to the infirmary at Parish Prison, where the wound to his leg was treated. A City Court judge arrived at the room to arraign him and order him held over for trial. He did not speak a word to the doctors, the judge, or any of the officers on hand. Afterward, he was moved into the bowels of the building and placed in a cell separate from the others and reserved for the most dangerous prisoners. Two guards were posted at the steel door.

Both had disappeared when a lone man in an overcoat and a fedora in a style worn ten years before walked slowly along the cells and came to a stop at the last one. His features were hidden and the guards knew better than to cast even a single glance his way. He spent a silent moment gazing between the bars at the prisoner, who was crouched on the steel cot.

"Mr. Mullens," the visitor said. Mullens turned his head. "You've committed serious crimes. If you go to trial, you will be found guilty and you'll be hanged right out in the yard." Mullens didn't move or speak. "I'm here to tell you that it doesn't have to go that way."

Now the prisoner rose to his full height and made a turn and faced the bars, standing as if at attention.

"You can escape that penalty," the man said. "Escape execution. But you must listen to what I'm going to say."

Mullens held himself at an even tighter posture and said, "Yes, sir."

The visitor said, "Very well, then," and waved him closer.

Valentin left the saloon and made a slow stroll south to Basin Street. The mansions were quiet and only the janitors and maids arriving to prepare them for the day passed along the banquette. The houses would stay as such until two o'clock. By that time, the girls on duty would have awakened, had their baths and their breakfasts and then lounged about until it was time to dress for the day's first visitors.

Business would be light but steady through the afternoon hours and into the early evening. And then Storyville would truly come alive.

At eight o'clock, a second shift of doves would flutter down the stairs to greet the more important clients, men of means who could spend on the champagne and wine and the favors offered in the upstairs bedrooms. The best of the houses would feature professors playing pianos in the parlors. Even on a weeknight, the mood was festive and would last until the early hours. It would all wind down as the morning approached. There would be some eight quiet hours and then it would start all over again.

Storyville had stood for twenty years as a square mile of legally-sanctioned sin, though it had existed as such in one form or another since the time when red lanterns were hung in the windows of the rough shacks that lined the basin that was dug to provide the soil upon which families of means could build their fancy French Quarter homes.

Beginning in the early part of the prior century, the shacks became houses and later mansions; and by the time the ordinance of 1897 had declared prostitution illegal in all other parts of New Orleans, the quarter now called Storyville (named after the author of the law) was employing as many as two thousand sporting women, from the elegant octoroons of the first-class bordellos down to the ragged crib whores of Robertson and Claiborne streets. Along with the flesh trade came restaurants, dance halls, gambling parlors, and more common enterprises like Mangetta's Grocery and Saloon located for almost thirty years on a mostly quiet block of Marais Street.

These days, much of the talk around the bordellos had to do with the news of the District closing after those two decades of legal protection. The papers reported this was a result of pressure from a Department of the Navy that did not want young sailors stationed at the new base downriver exposed to the temptations of a red-light district so close by.

But like everything else in Storyville, there was more to it; and so on the very morning that the chief of police had been murdered, Valentin St. Cyr was on his way to a meeting with the Mayor of New Orleans.

Mr. Pettibone ushered Assistant Chief Cook into the mayor's office. The exchange of greetings was perfunctory. Pettibone had explained that they were waiting for the arrival of Police Commissioner Williams and so Martin Behrman and Chief Cook spent ten uncomfortable minutes talking about nothing in particular. Both men sighed their relief when the assistant announced the commissioner's arrival. Williams' aides remained outside.

The mayor and the commissioner had spoken on the telephone and now Williams, a tall and gruff man, addressed Cook directly. "We require someone at the helm. I mean today. The police department requires it. The city requires it. So you'll take on those duties immediately. Out of respect for Chief Reynolds, you'll conduct business from your current office."

"Yes, sir, I understand," Cook said. His voice was low and dry.

The mayor, watching and listening, thought it odd that he showed no surprise at the news. "The chief's aides will be assisting you," the commissioner went on. "They're good men. Good officers."

This time, Cook didn't reply, but nodded slowly. When Commissioner Williams asked him if he had any questions, and he shook his head, the mayor sat back, thinking that the man either didn't grasp what was happening or he knew exactly what had transpired and was putting up a stony front. Whatever the case, it was another puzzle. He had been planning to have Cook stay for his meeting with McKinney and St. Cyr, but now decided against it.

The commissioner spoke up again. "Anything you wish to say, Mr. Mayor?"

"Not at this time," Behrman said.

"Well, then." Williams and Cook got to their feet and left the office.

There were administrative matters to be addressed and the commissioner and the Acting Chief of Police rode the elevator down without exchanging a word. When they reached the first floor, Cook was surprised to see Lieutenant McKinney and the Creole detective Valentin St. Cyr crossing the lobby. He guessed where they were going.

Mr. Pettibone opened the door for Valentin and the lieutenant and Mayor Behrman waved them to the two chairs facing his desk.

Valentin had met with the mayor a few times before and found him not an easy man to figure. At times, he showed principles, at others he was craven, like two months before when he had put his race-baiting stripes on display by preventing a colored schoolgirl from taking first place in a spelling bee which she had clearly won and thus preventing her from going to the national bee. On the other hand, he controlled a city that boasted citizens of every shade from coal-black to lily-white more fairly than any other southern mayor. Valentin was sure Behrman knew he carried a dose of African blood in his veins and yet still employed and trusted him. It was the kind of dance that had always caused him to detest politicians.

"First order of business," the mayor was now saying. "Assistant Chief Cook is now Acting Chief Cook."

Valentin had heard the name but had never crossed paths with the man and knew nothing about him.

James said, "Yes, sir," in an empty tone of voice that announced that he *did* know Cook and that what he had just heard was not good news.

The mayor caught this, too, because he said, "He was next in seniority. He'll fill the position until we find a permanent replacement. And that's all I have on that issue." He addressed Valentin. "What do you have to report?"

"To begin, the Department of the Navy's request that—"

"You mean the order," Mayor Behrman said.

"Yes, sir. That Storyville be shut down before they finish construction on the new base appears legitimate."

"Appears?" Behrman said.

"Well, there's much that doesn't make sense."

Behrman sat forward. "That's what I've been saying. People who support this have made a lot of money in Storyville. The properties they own continue to earn. They'll lose hundreds of thousands of dollars over the next few years. And the city will lose millions. Not just individuals, but the churches, too. And they'll give that up because some sailor boys might take pleasure with a woman."

"Yes, sir."

"Then, what's really going on?"

"I'm getting some information that points in another direction," Valentin said. "It has to do with Washington. But not the Navy exactly. It could be that some of those people are managing this for their own purposes."

"You mean money?" Then: "Of course, you do. Who are they?"

"I don't know that yet."

The mayor said, "I see. And where are you getting this information?"

"I have someone up there. He's been digging around."

"Does anyone else know what you're up to?"

"The lieutenant and Major Sont."

"And your wife."

Valentin sensed the lieutenant smiling. "Yes, sir. I have cover with a case I'm working."

The mayor turned his way. "The riverboat business?" Now Valentin smiled; Martin Behrman did not miss much.

Valentin said, "But things are moving fast, Mr. Mayor. I don't know that there's time to have what you need before November."

"I understand." Mayor Behrman stared at nothing for a few seconds, then said, "Do you think this business has anything to do with what happened this morning?"

Both Valentin and James looked up in surprise. The Creole detective said, "I don't see how."

The mayor continued to gaze out the window. "But you can't say that it couldn't."

"No, sir, I can't say that."

Behrman turned around again. "At this point, I don't expect I'll be able to stop what's coming. But I don't want anyone getting away with malfeasance. Understood?"

The two men said, "Yes, Mr. Mayor," in succession.

"All right. What else do you need from my office?" The detective gave a slight tilt of his head and Behrman. "Oh, yes, of course. Mr. Pettibone will take care of that. I'll see you out and you can get something now. Anything else?"

The mayor was true to his word. Valentin left City Hall with ten twenty-dollar bills in his pocket, on his way to the Western Union office to make the call to the nation's capital and Mr. Patrick Geary, formerly of the Pinkerton Agency.

Acting Chief Cook had just finished with the paperwork and was enjoying the respectful looks the officers cast his way. No doubt the boot-lickers would be knocking on his door directly.

He was crossing the lobby with his two aides in tow when he happened to see Lieutenant McKinney making his way to the street door and made a note to find out what business had occupied him on the fifth floor.

THREE

The mayor's fears were confirmed as the steamy August passed into September. Construction on the base at Belle Chasse continued with two shifts running. The newspapers and scandal sheets ran stories on a daily basis of a Storyville grinding to an eventual halt in November, along with editorials that mostly praised the demise of the tenderloin at long last, though there were also sober voices that asked if anyone believed that closing the District was going to stop the scarlet trade in New Orleans.

Chief Reynolds was laid to rest with full police honors in St. Louis Cemetery No. 4. His murderer Kenneth Mullens was judged insane and remanded to the East Louisiana Hospital in Jackson. Acting Chief Cook settled into his duties and quietly managed the department.

Meanwhile, the world went on. Most of the headlines concerned the Great War. Earlier in the year, Congress had allotted millions of dollars for the war effort after Germany failed to cease aggressions. This was followed by President Wilson issuing a Declaration of War and shortly after that, a military draft was instituted and preparations for sending American troops into battle were completed.

Another battle was being fought on the home front with suffragettes on the march from coast to coast. In less trying and more local news, "Livery Stable Blues" by the Original Dixieland Jass Band became the first recording in that style, distressing many but delighting more and within weeks, the bubbly strains of what had gone from *jass* to *jazz* were floating out of windows all over the city and soon across the nation. It was one blessing.

As the days cooled, the wires between New Orleans and Washington D.C. grew hotter from the calls back and forth between Valentin and Patrick Geary, sometimes two and three times a day. The one-time Pinkerton did not disappoint; he had burrowed into the back channels of this department and that, his task made easier by Washington's laxity in everything, including secrecy. Men who were as addicted to power as others were to a bottle, a pipe, a needle, or the lewd favors of a wanton woman could be twisted into giving up anything. Geary said that one Louisiana congressman looked especially promising.

The details came bit by bit, and the more Valentin learned, the more he understood that they were encountering a dangerous game. The lordly politicians could crush a man, ruin his life, and batter his family by shuffling papers. At the other end in New Orleans, the violence was just as devious but far more direct. Week by week, he came to realize that the machinations were like the scrabbling of rats in a dark alleyway.

Little of this reached the meetings Mayor Behrman called with Lieutenant McKinney and Major Sont on the first and third Mondays of September and October. St. Cyr's information would arrive in time to forestall the District being shut down. It was now a matter of avoiding calamities.

On the first Monday of November, the two policemen stepped into the mayor's office to find Acting Chief Cook in attendance for the first time. There was no explanation as the three guests settled in, the officers in chairs that faced the desk and Cook standing to the mayor's left. The aides who had accompanied him took a seat next to the door.

The mayor began by saying, "The acting chief has police business to attend to. So can we go ahead, Major Sont?"

The major had a writing pad on his lap and glanced down at it as he reported. "Eviction notices have been served on the addresses that haven't been vacated, which is about half of them. We believe another quarter will move before the twelfth."

"And the rest?" Behrman said.

"The rest will likely wait until the last minute to leave. If they don't go voluntarily, they'll be removed that morning."

"What problems will they pose?"

Sont said, "We won't know until we get to it. I don't think anyone will get violent. Just troublesome."

The mayor looked at the lieutenant. "This is what you've seen back there?"

"Yes, sir. It will be a crazy twenty-four hours. But I don't guess anyone is going to hole up in some house and try to shoot it out."

Behrman said, "No, that's not Storyville." He rocked in his chair for a moment, then turned to Cook. "Chief?" he said. "Any questions or comments?"

Cook's eyes had been shifting from one person to the next and sometimes to the air in front of him, as if nothing he was seeing or hearing pleased him.

"I believe the major and his people have everything under control," he said in a tone so bland that it expressed exactly zero. "My people will be monitoring the situation over the next weeks and then through that last day."

The mayor waited for more and when nothing else came said, "All right, then..."

The acting chief rose from his chair, uttered something no one caught, and left the office, his aide trailing behind him.

After they were gone, Mayor Behrman lost himself in his thoughts for a few moments. Then he addressed the lieutenant. "Does he have any idea what St. Cyr has been up to?"

McKinney glanced at Major Sont, then said, "It's hard to say, sir."

"But he has to be guessing," Sont said. "And wondering why he's not in these meetings."

"I'm sure he is. I'm going to say what we've all been thinking." He jabbed a finger at the door. "Something's not right about him." He took the two officers' silence as agreement and he looked past them.

"He bears watching." He let that sink in and when Major Sont nodded, he said, "The second Monday in November is not far off, gentlemen. And I want to be ready."

Lulu White was lost in a dream, a shadow-play that carried her back ten years and a glory to behold. She was enthroned at Mahogany Hall, her girls gathered around like a bevy of colorful, chirping birds, her male guests standing by in their finest three-piece suits. A professor sat at her white piano, but his back was turned so she couldn't make out if it was Tony, Jelly Roll Morton, or one of the others. Of course, her fancy man George Killshaw was there to attend to her needs. He'd do a different kind of attending later on, after the last of her customers was gone and they retired to her heavy four-poster. The way they all looked upon her was like the glow from the heavy chandeliers over her head and some bowed when they approached her.

In the next still moment, her mind shifted, telling her that none of it was real. She fought the cold light, but it was no use. She opened her eyes and it was all gone, leaving only the dingy room that was now her home. The bottle on the night table still held an inch of rye and she sipped it as she stared down at the bare floor with dull eyes.

How had it happened? How had she fallen so far and so fast? Storyville had been going downhill for some time, true; but Saturday nights were still a riot of bright colors and music, the champagne flowed, and the rooms upstairs still reeked with the musk of women and echoed with the sound of bare flesh slapping behind the closed doors. Miss Lulu White sat atop it all, second only to Tom Anderson, and he had all but vacated his throne.

Then, in a matter of what seemed minutes, she lost her crown. Someone had decided that she was the next domino to fall and she faced a petty arrest that was blown up through legal wrangling that her own attorneys were powerless to stop. They used up all her money and the landlord—a good Christian man, to be sure—decided that after eleven years, Mahogany Hall was no longer available. She was then threatened with an old charge should she try to open another establishment. Just like that, it was over, and she sold off the furnishings and used the money to escape the city.

The next few weeks were a blur as she made her slow way north, visiting five hundred miles of saloons before being deposited in St. Louis by a rounder who then took most of what money she had left. She had never been without wits and so found a house and four healthy girls, but after a few weeks she realized that her heart wasn't in it. She left both the house and the girls behind.

The bottle was empty. She heard footsteps in the hall and a tap on her door and came out of the reverie to murmur, "Is that Justine?"

She heard a small laugh from the hall. "Is it *who*? No, ma'am. It's Corinna. There's a telephone call for you."

"Oh. Corinna." Miss Lulu sat up.

"Yes, yes," she said, feeling her head clear and though she couldn't think of who would be rousing her at that hour, said, "I'm coming." She pulled the kimono from the hook on the wall as the girl's footsteps padded away.

She was halfway along the corridor when she remembered that the day was drawing even closer. Like everyone else in Storyville, her hopes had risen when she heard about the new Navy base at Belle Chasse, not ten miles down the Mississippi, and the young sailors it would bring to those scarlet doors. But times had changed. Tom Anderson no longer had the will to stand up for the District he had created. When the drumbeats about the immorality and diseases that would be lurking there started anew, a stake went through the sinful heart of those twenty blocks.

She reached the stand and picked up the telephone, only to find that the line had gone dead. "Corinna?" she called. The girl appeared from the kitchen at the end of the hall. "Who was it?"

"Don't know, ma'am. She didn't say."

"She didn't..." Miss Lulu was baffled. She thought about it some more. She didn't know who had telephoned her. But she knew where the call had come from.

The young lady in the grand bedroom broke the connection before the woman came on the line and crossed to the window that looked out on Esplanade Avenue. She wondered what in God's name she was doing. She had spent time and money on information and then picked up the telephone after overhearing an earlier phone call the family attorney had made from their study. It was a conversation about Storyville in which the name "Valentin St. Cyr" had been mentioned.

Acting Chief Cook left the mayor's office and walked back to headquarters with two of his men five paces behind him. This arrangement had not been ordered. On the very first day of his new assignment, the aides realized that he did not want them or anyone else close to him unless there was a very good reason; and if that happened, he would simple mutter a curt word or wave a sharp hand.

He spent the fifteen-minute walk in discussion with himself. He had not been fooled in the least by the masks that the mayor, Sont, and McKinney had worn. They were telling him next to nothing about the closing of Storyville. Not that he had shown much interest. The place had run itself under the hard hand of Tom Anderson and with the help of the detective St. Cyr. Now it could end the same way.

He stopped at the corner of Tulane and the aides did the same. It brought a smirk that he carried to the other side.

What did concern him was the silent conversation that was going on between those three. He was not a stupid man. He had risen through the ranks to land on the verge of being named Chief of Police by laying low and playing smart and that meant keeping his mouth and face closed and holding fast to what he knew. They didn't want him in on the plans? He had attended meetings that were far more secret than the sessions that Behrman was conducting and he was ahead of whatever St. Cyr had been trying to dredge up since August.

They had reached headquarters. Acting Chief Cook did not follow the late chief's routine of entering from the back. He also didn't walk in the front door, instead taking the side entrance that was closest to the elevators. The aides knew to let him ride to the third floor alone.

When he reached his office, he sat down at his desk and mused for a few minutes. Things had to be done. He picked up his telephone to make the first of three calls.

The Saturday sun was going down over Little Rock and J. Picot was staring out the window of the rooming house on Second Street, once again lost in his memories of New Orleans, when his telephone shrilled, bringing a moment of confusion. The ringing was real. He lifted the handset, listened for thirty seconds, and hung up without having spoken a word.

"Christ, Almighty," he whispered. He looked over at the mirror and saw on his face the same smile he had presented to those who fell under his power in that other time and in a place four hundred miles down the Mississippi. Now the former captain picked up the phone and called the station to inquire about the schedules for trains to New Orleans.

FOUR

An hour before dawn on Monday, November 12th, the Southern Crescent pulled into Union Station and drew to a stop at Platform 1. The engine rumbled and creaked for a half-minute before heaving a wheezing, steamy sigh and fading into iron silence.

Instead of rising and moving down the aisle, the lone rider in the last car turned in his seat to survey Basin Street. Through the fog off the river, he could make out the facade of Anderson's Café, once the centerpiece of the District, the doors now chained and the tall windows shuttered with rough planks, the history of that address as the anchor of that once-famed quarter finished after the better part of twenty mostly glorious years.

The passenger leaned closer to the glass to survey the mansions that inhabited the blocks "down-the-line," the few that were not lost in the mist displaying feeble lights through dusty panes. The rest stood as blank as tombstones. The only souls traveling the banquettes at this hour were the minions who attended to those houses that had managed to stay in business, moving in a ghost parade. And where would they be tomorrow? Gone along with Storyville, New Orleans?

The rider rose, made his way to the door, stepped onto the platform, and walked outside to find the street that had for decades been a riot of music and revelry hushed beneath the chill of the lingering night. It reminded him of the feeling that soaked the air when someone or something had died. Though in this case, the last breath wouldn't be gasped for another twenty-four hours, after which the train would pull out, carrying him back east.

He walked to the corner of Canal Street, where two Ford jitneys were parked at the curb, their drivers asleep in their seats. He rapped a knuckle on the hood of the first machine and the small-boned, wild-haired mulatto behind the wheel came awake and sat up, blinking.

The man murmured an address and reached into the pocket of his gray coat to produce two gold dollars. At the sight of what was twice the standard fare, the mulatto rolled out of the seat and hurried around to open the right side door. Once his passenger was settled, he stepped to the front of the machine and cranked the four cylinders first to a gurgle and then to a steady idle. The second driver stirred. Large and dark and groggy as a bear, he peered from under his riding cap, watching the Ford bounce onto the cobblestones and turn north.

They left the District behind and were crossing Galvez Street when the driver said, "You know what day this is, friend?"

His passenger offered a bare nod and said, "Who doesn't?" They didn't speak again.

With the last of the night fog hanging in wisps about the bare branches and the single streetlamp casting a cone of veiled white, Dumaine Street was a tunnel passing through a cloud. The shadows hid the houses from the banquette and almost from each other, the air so laden that it dampened the twitterings of the night birds, the lowing of distant ship horns, and the rumble of the trucks traveling up Broad Street.

It was odd, then, that in this symphony of the dark, Valentin St. Cyr came awake to what sounded like footfalls on the wet cobbles. He sat up, swung his legs off the bed, and stood to cross to the window while his wife slept on.

It had not been his imagination: a figure posed at the corner, half-silhouetted in the cone of amber light from the lone streetlamp.

He could feel the probing stare from over thirty paces and was considering that he was mostly invisible in the dark room when the figure raised a hand in a motion he recognized in a sudden instant. He turned to throw himself over the sleeping form on the bed. Justine gave a start and then let out a small cry when the shot cracked, shattering the windowpane and throwing a burst of shards across the floor.

"Stay down," he said, then rolled off the bed and ducked into the hallway.

Evangeline opened her bedroom door, her brow stitching. "Did I hear—"

Valentin took her elbow and drew her away. "It was a gunshot," he said.

The sleepy eyes went wide. "A...what?"

"It came through our window." He answered the next words out of her mouth before she could voice them. "She's fine. I don't know what happened. It could have been an accident. Someone getting wild with a pistol."

She was coming more alert now and peering at him, another question forming. But Justine appeared, wrapped in a shawl. "Valentin?"

He looked between her and the woman who shared their house. "Stay in the foyer," he said. "Call James. I'm going outside."

The telephone chirped before dawn so often that, as before, Lieutenant James McKinney began moving while still half-asleep, slipping from beneath the blanket and making his stiff way to the stand in the hallway. Though he was not surprised by a call so early, he was startled at the sound of the voice on the other end. "Miss Justine," he said. "What is it?"

She described what had occurred without a wasted word. Just like her husband, the lieutenant mused.

"Where is he now?"

"He's gone outside to see."

The policeman's head was clearing. "I'll send a patrol and I'll drive out as soon as I get dressed. You and Miss Evangeline stay put." He placed the handset in the cradle, wincing over his last words. As if she needed instructing.

Anna Mae sat up in bed, ran her fingers through her red curls, and said, "What is it?"

"A small problem at Mr. Valentin's," he said. "Go back to sleep." The mattress creaked and he shuffled to the kitchen, yawning. When he switched on the light, his eyes were drawn to the calendar hanging next to the door with this day's date the only one circled in red.

Valentin pulled Justine into the hall, then slipped back to throw on a jacket and trousers and for the first time in almost a year, crouched to open the bottom drawer of the dresser and reached in for the Iver Johnson .32 in its oiled cloth. He could hear the women whispering in the foyer.

After a spin of the cylinder, he stood up, crept to the kitchen, and made a silent exit across the back gallery and into the garden, using the time to still his anger. Had he not seen the figure, he would have written the gunshot off to some drunkard on a tear. These things happened, even on quiet streets of modest houses. But the hand that lifted the pistol had been steady. Someone who knew how to handle a weapon had arrived to place a shot into Valentin St. Cyr's bedroom and possibly into Valentin St. Cyr.

Nothing was moving on the street. Whoever had fired the weapon was either lurking in the darkness or had fled. Had he been on a case, he would have lingered there for an hour, watching for some sign of him. But this was his home and his family and he couldn't spare the time.

Huddling in the foyer, Justine was once again struck at how composed Evangeline remained whenever there was menace about. The older woman had already moved past her surprise and settled into the odd event of a bullet coming through one of their windows. Such was life with the Creole detective Valentin St. Cyr and Evangeline was not fret-ting; indeed, Justine felt the gray eyes studying her for signs of worry and the question that had been circling her brain for a year returned: Who are you?

"He'll be on his guard," Evangeline said, offering a kind smile and a gentle hand.

Valentin made a slow creep around the side of the house to a shadowy spot by one of the jacarandas and scanned the street, eyes and ears perked for anything that didn't belong. His years first as a policeman and later as a private detective had only confirmed his distrust of coin-cidence, especially when the pieces were so uncommon, like a gunshot through a windowpane at the beginning of the day when a landmark that had stood for the better part of a century and had been a part of his life for almost a dozen years was being shuttered forever.

Yet at the moment, nothing was moving and he heard no untoward sounds. He stood very still, watching and listening, until far in the distance, a train whistle sent a piercing note to end the night.

FIVE

The leaves had just begun to fall on the grounds of East Louisiana State Hospital and gusts of wind sent random flutters over the tall wrought-iron fence, as if they were seeking escape before being trapped and turned to dust.

The man who had been raking stopped to watch as the most delicate of these reached the narrow asphalt road that meandered past the hospital and through the town of Jackson then turned south. He could hear the name of the place that lay at the end of the road in his head: *New Orleans.*

It brought an image to a mind that held fewer with the passing of time: streets of lights that dazzled through the night, gentlemen in fine suits, both rounders and tramps streaming this way and that, and painted hussies beckoning from galleries and open doorways and windows. Now came the sounds: sweet enticements from painted mouths, the laughter of men at their pleasure, and the music. Always, the music, dark blue, delirious, as loud as Judgment Day and as soft as a sweet woman's moan, but never-ending.

He could not play it anymore and it wasn't often that he could hear the echoes in his head. He could see, though, and on the sky above he made out splayed notes winging like flights of birds, breaking the flitting shapes into pieces and putting them back together another way, and then he *did* hear, but at first it wasn't wild horns, swirls from clarinets, the *bump-bump-bumping* of the bass fiddle, the *chuck-chuck* of the guitar, or the happy rattle of the drums. It was a sound that was as clear as the wind and the rowdy beauty of it brought him such joy that the white-clad men and the nurses in blues stopped, all their eyes curious at the life they rarely got to see in him.

Now a chorus of bubbling brass and drums and bass fiddle and guitar rose in a sudden swirl that passed from one ear to the other, a private concert from the bandstand inside his brain. And who was that tall fellow stalking back and forth, leading all of it with a silver wand? It was—

"Buddy? Hello, Buddy!"

The cyclone died, tumbling into silence.

A man in the white coat was peering at him through glinting spectacles. "What in the world was you *smiling* about?"

After Valentin located the shell—a .25 rim-fire—and pried it from the plaster, he found a square of scrap lumber to cover the broken pane. With a last survey of the street, he moved along the hallway and stepped back outside into the half-dark morning. After he had walked two blocks in all four directions, his pistol at the ready, he arrived back at the nearest corner just in time to meet the patrol car James McKinney had sent. He and the two uniformed officers made another round of the quiet streets. The coppers knew St. Cyr's reputation and kept their comments to a minimum and thoughts to themselves.

With the first blades of dawn lightening the sky, they returned to the spot where the shooter had stood, and the detective had one of the coppers shine his flashlight over the soil. Dirt had been brushed where footprints might have had been and no empty cartridge had been left behind.

Valentin gave the plot of earth another brief survey before the three men started away. They had walked only five paces when the glare of headlights swept the wet earth. He stopped, said, "Wait," and bent to the ground.

———

Evangeline had gone off to her bath. Justine cleaned up the shards of glass from the floor. One of the edges had drawn a drop of blood from her thumb.

She now stood by the bedroom window, watching her husband's shape move away from the policemen. Headlights emerged from the gray mist and when they swept the three figures, Valentin stopped and kneeled down. James got out of the machine and crossed over and the men stared down at whatever Valentin had found.

Maybe the gunshot had been the spur-of-the-moment act of some sot wandering from Broad Street with a head full of bad booze and a loose pistol in his hand. Or maybe it was something else entirely. She would have come down on the side of an accident, except that it had happened on this particular Monday.

She now watched the two coppers move away and Valentin and James start for the house. Valentin glanced at the window, as if he had known all along that she was there.

The lieutenant had arrived and watched as Valentin crouched to the earth, a posture he knew well after being drawn into a half-dozen of his cases. They were so familiar that St. Cyr did not look up when James reached his side and did not offer any greeting other than to extend his hand and say, "See this?"

The lieutenant beheld the torn shred of a map. He peered more closely. "It's..."

"Jackson."

"And you found it here?"

Valentin pointed. "Hanging on the dead flower. Where he left it." He pondered for another few seconds, then stood up and tucked the fragment into a pocket. The lieutenant dismissed the coppers. Valentin waited until they had climbed into their sedan and started away to turn for the house. "Coffee's on the stove," he said.

Though he knew he might be on the streets through the day and the night, he would need a room, which meant a name to offer. He began with "John." He considered a dozen last names, including Saracena, from the Creole detective's family, but he thought it too prankish and not to his taste and so he settled on Blank, as bland an appellation as anyone could imagine. This would be his moniker for the next twenty-four hours, right to the moment he stepped back on the train that would carry him off into the Louisiana morning, his work done.

The desk clerk's name was Joseph. "I'll ring the bellboy," he offered.

"Not necessary," Mr. Blank said.

"Very well, sir."

The guest picked up his satchel and turned for the elevators. In his wake, Joseph allowed himself a shaky sigh. The man's eyes, pale blue and glassy with the lids low had unnerved him, as did the voice that was cool and without the slightest inflection. He didn't look up again until the doors had closed, then returned his gaze to the ledger and forced an uneasy laugh. *John Blank,* indeed.

Frank Mangetta stepped onto the banquette and hung the sign on the door that read: CLOSED and under it: *CHIUSO.* If any of his most loyal customers arrived, he would of course serve them. Other than that, Mangetta's Grocery and Saloon would not be open for business until at least Wednesday morning.

He heard his name called and turned to see Each strolling up the banquette. Of course, he was out early on this final day.

"Well, this is it," he said as he stepped up to give the saloonkeeper's hand a clumsy shake.

Frank said, "What have you seen?"

"More houses closing up," Each said. "The madams and the girls moving out. I figure maybe twenty will still be open tonight." He was quiet as he surveyed the street. Then: "Is it really finished?"

The older man waved a vague hand. "The people done everything they could. No use. Mr. Tom and Miss Lulu is both gone. So... *Si, e finito.*"

The sun was peeking its first rays between the buildings as they stood watching the almost empty banquettes. On any other day, dozens of drunkards and hopheads would be staggering along, blinking in the rising light as domestic workers hurried to one house or another.

Each snapped his fingers. "Did you hear about Mr. Valentin?"

"What?"

"You ain't going to believe it."

The Sicilian's brow stitched. "Bad?"

"Well, it ain't good," Each said.

On any other day of any other year of the past decade, the news that someone had fired a bullet through Valentin St. Cyr's Dumaine Street bedroom window would have made the startled Uptown rounds in a few hours. But on this second Monday of the month, minds were elsewhere; and for that at least, Valentin was grateful.

They sat at the table, nibbling from the plate of cheese and fruit that Justine had prepared and sipping coffee he had laced with brandy from the bottle in the cabinet. These were the first settled moments under that roof since the pistol had cracked and the Creole detective's eyes kept roaming to the scrap of the map of Jackson, State Road 68, and the surrounding land. A tiny **HOS** marked the hospital.

James reached out and said, "May I?"

Valentin handed over the scrap and sat back to consider that it had been eight years since he and James had first met. Though the officer's copper hair was showing strands of gray, his freckled face was still that of a young man's.

He passed the piece of map back and said, "Do you want to make a report?"

Valentin thought about it. "Have there been any other windows shot out in this part of town lately?"

"Only by accident."

"Then, no." He glanced at his wife, who was sitting with her arms crossed, directing her moody gaze to the swirls in her cup, and waited for her to speak.

She did, saying, "It was no accident. Someone was trying to shoot him. Or at him." She had addressed her words to James, ignoring her husband, even when he said, "I'm pretty sure he could have hit me if he wanted to."

The lieutenant waited out the next icy moments and then turned to Valentin. "So who would want to take a shot at you?"

The Creole detective said, "The question is not who would want to take a shot at me, it's—"

"It's who would want to take a shot at him *today*," Justine finished.

A knock on the back door came ten minutes later. Evangeline opened it for a bald Negro who was built like a steam engine but presented a placid face. His name was Eloi Marchand and he had been one of the Buffalo Soldiers on San Juan Hill, a member of the unit that had done the hardest fighting while Teddy Roosevelt's troops raced up the hill and took the lion's share of the glory. Soon after he and his wife and their four children moved onto Galvez Street, he made the rounds to offer his services as a carpenter, gardener, and general handyman. Valentin came to understand he could be useful for other tasks. He was pleased to see that on this morning, the former infantryman had employed the good sense to leave his Lee rifle and Colt 95 revolver on the back gallery. Though Justine would guess that the weapons were waiting there.

She greeted Eloi, then turned to her husband and hiked an eyebrow.

"He's going to stay around until this gets sorted out," Valentin said.

Evangeline saved him by saying. "Have you had anything to eat this morning, Eloi?"

"I have, Miss Evangeline." His voice rumbled. "Yes, ma'am. I had breakfast at home." He gestured toward the garden. "You got a bunch of them tallow tree vines out there," he said. "I'll go ahead and get at those."

Once he had closed the door behind him, Valentin said, "I need someone here."

Justine sipped her coffee but did not comment.

Valentin, Justine, and James carried their cups onto the back gallery and themselves out of Evangeline's earshot. For several minutes, they watched Eloi swing the scythe and listened to the early traffic on Dumaine Street.

The puzzling over who might want to take a shot at Valentin on this Monday hadn't gone farther than stops and starts. While he had a long history in the District, his work for the last twelve months had been humdrum, spent on a long and tedious case of embezzlement of profits from a riverboat gambling operation. Before August, he had been called to Storyville only twice, the first time when a novitiate priest had fallen into the clutches of sin and had to be convinced to leave the floozy who had lured him from the confessional, the second when a new police corporal had arrested and jailed Slow Pete, a simple-minded fixture of the District for the better part of twenty years, on a minor charge. Valentin had sorted out both with a minimum of fuss. And that was all.

"Maybe it has to do with one of your old cases," Justine said, holding the flat tone that was a signal that she was frightened, angry, or both. The men employed the good sense to let her continue by stating the most obvious name. "Picot."

The New Orleans police captain had done battle with Valentin since their paths first crossed. He had gone about trying to wreck the detective's career a dozen times with no success. Then he attempted a final desperate ploy that ended with him leaving the force and escaping New Orleans.

"The man I saw was not him," Valentin said.

Justine said, "But he could have sent someone."

"I suppose."

"I wouldn't put it past him," she said.

"How far back does the bad blood go?" the lieutenant said.

"All the way," Valentin said.

It was in the spring of 1907, in fact, a decade before almost to the day, and Picot had appeared at Anderson's Café in the wake of a shooting that left a well-known pimp named Littlejohn dead, the killer settling a grievance over a sister having fallen under Littlejohn's sway.

"That happened before I joined the force, but I heard all about it," James said. "The Black Rose Murders."

"Picot did not appreciate Mr. Tom hiring me in the first place," Valentin said. "When that case came along, he tried to undercut me every step of the way so that he could be the one to break it. He didn't. I did." He sipped his coffee. "He was reprimanded. Almost got demoted. That was my fault, of course. I was his enemy from then on."

Justine said, "And there was another one right after that involved him."

"About a year after," Valentin said. "That one had to do with his sister. And then it got worse. He started spending part of every waking day plotting my destruction. He never let it go."

He stopped, recalling the moment when his clashes with Picot had ended. Looking back, it was a long and involved drama, carried along on the captain's rage and bitterness. It still didn't amount to a conclusion.

"I'm not sold," he said. "It wasn't Picot, unless he lost forty pounds and gained six inches." He noticed the way his wife was studying him and said, "What?"

"This other business you've been chasing after. Is that what was this is about?" When he didn't respond, she said, "You've never done this before."

"Done what?"

"Kept something from me for so long." She said, "Lieutenant?"

James, who had decided that this was a good time to study the clouds, sighed and looked her way.

"How much do you know about it?"

"Probably not much more than you do."

"And *I* only know some," Valentin said. "I'll have the rest tomorrow, when a train pulls in with two men carrying a parcel of papers."

She wasn't having it. "Why does it have to be so secret?"

"Because it has to do with what's behind the closing of Storyville. In addition to the Navy base." He watched Eloi for a moment. "I think what happened this morning was meant to warn me."

"Warn you?"

"To drop what I've been doing. But I'm not going to do that."

She was only slightly mollified. "So why didn't that man just go ahead and shoot you dead when he had the chance?"

"Because if anything happens to me, James and Reynard Vernel will have everything in their hands on Tuesday. I'm guessing they know that."

"Who's they?"

"That I don't know. But I will come morning."

She shook her head. "That's some risk you're taking."

"It is the last time I'll be doing anything for Storyville."

Justine treated him to a sharp look. "I hope it's not the last time you'll be doing anything, period."

With that, she turned to the lieutenant, said, "You can take him with you," and disappeared into the house.

James said, "She isn't pleased."

"No, she's not." Valentin had been proclaiming to his wife as the date drew near that he'd spent far too much time on those scarlet streets over the years and had attended far too many funerals because of it. But how could he not witness the final moments of a strange monument? She had often said that the District was in his blood and maybe it was so.

"Where will you be?" he asked the lieutenant.

"I'm going back to the precinct. After that, Basin Street, Liberty, Franklin. I figure that's where the trouble will start."

Valentin understood. Most of the strumpets in the dirty back end of the District had already been swept away like so much refuse. The long-serving madams of the finer houses that remained would be the ones putting up a fight, stubborn in their refusal to accept that it was over and refusing to surrender. If nothing else, there would be a show worth seeing, but that was still most of the day and the rest of the night away.

Mr. Blank pulled a chair to the window and looked down on a Canal Street that was now crowded with black machines and derby hats that bobbed atop heads of busy men on the way to their labors. Among them were random ladies in gray dresses. The only other color was the green of the streetcars. In another hour, new hues would appear: the palette of long touring cars, women dressed for their morning shopping, carts of fruit vendors rolling away from the French Market to the Garden District, and white sorties of river birds rising from the banks of the river.

He could see the south end of Storyville and it appeared as a carcass on the way to being picked clean. By the next morning, it would be a ghost town with the ghost of one Mr. Valentin St. Cyr on the ledgers.

He returned his attention to the sheaf of a half-dozen pages in his lap. On them was the life of St. Cyr—or *Saracena*, the true family name that he had dropped years before in order to fade away and wreak vengeance on his father's killers.

That vengeance had not quite been wrought. Instead, St. Cyr embarked on a life of crime, followed by a short career as a police officer, followed by his true calling, keeping the red-light district secure for Mr. Tom Anderson. He had spent a decade in that role and then left it behind for a quieter life. Mr. Blank had not been told the reason, but it was his mission to see that he did not escape Storyville. Of course, the Creole detective had more than one way out. Mr. Blank knew that he wouldn't take any of them.

He laid the papers aside and picked up the list that had been printed in a precise hand on a white card. The first item had been concluded with a shot fired a foot from St. Cyr's head. He read over the instructions, one by one. It made no sense, but sometimes that's how it was. Once the work was finished, he would go away again. Exactly as it had been explained to him. As he reached the last of the items, letters trembled and danced on the card. It happened to him almost daily since his wounding at Malate.

The dizzy moment lingered and then departed. With the way the light was slanting into the window glass, he could just make out the faint shadow of the cleft that began at the hairline above his left brow and back and down to his ear, as if drawn with the help of a ruler, straight and sharp and white. He stared at the reflection until the telephone chattered. He had been expecting the call.

Neither Justine nor Evangeline wished to lurk about the house waiting for... for what? So they decided to treat it as any other Monday, which meant a trip to the market, housework before lunch, and laundry. There would be no preparations for dinner. Valentin wouldn't be on the premises and she had continued to make it clear that his wife wasn't happy about it.

"I can drive you," he offered in a meek way that almost made her laugh.

"You mean on your way to Storyville?" She spoke the words without rancor, a simple statement of fact.

"I'll go in later," he said.

"We're taking the streetcar," she said.

He understood that she did not want his company. "Then Eloi can at least ride in with you. I'll come collect you after."

"Fine," she said, though nothing about the way she spoke the word affirmed that.

———

Eloi waved as he stepped on the westbound car. The women crossed the tracks and descended the steps to the street and climbed the steps to the oaken doors of Blessed Trinity.

As they moved up the aisle, Evangeline whispered, "It's all right for you to fret, you know."

Justine stopped to see concern on that kind face. "A few inches to the left and..." She grabbed the back of a pew and Evangeline wondered for a startled moment if she was going to break down.

She let her get through the moment and then said, "But that was not the intention, was it?" She bent her head to whisper. "How about if we just light candles and then go to market?"

Justine smiled. "Yes, please," she said. "And light candles for who?"

"For all of us," Evangeline said.

They had finished their shopping and were having coffee and sweets at one of the little cafés. Justine noticed that now Evangeline was distracted, her gaze wandering. She barely had a word to say and spent minutes gazing into the distance.

It was time for Valentin to come collect them and as they finished their coffees and began gathering their things, Evangeline said, "Wait." She shifted slightly, holding Justine's eyes. "A man is watching us."

Justine kept still, another ploy that her husband had taught her. "Where is he?" she said.

"Moving about. In and out of the stalls. He bought coffee and drank it standing up." She turned her eyes away and then back. "He's not hiding. He's letting me see him."

Justine produced a small smile. "Perhaps he's interested in making your acquaintance." This was something else her husband had taught her. Unless there was immediate danger, keep the moment calm.

Evangeline didn't appreciate the stab at humor. "This gentleman does not have good intentions," she said. "He looks mean. And cold."

Justine said, "If he's not sneaking, I want to see his face. So we'll get up and walk over there. Maybe I'll talk to him."

Evangeline nodded, though her expression was concerned. After they had collected the parcels and got up from their chairs, Justine turned around.

There was no missing him. He was standing motionless while almost everyone else was moving about. His flesh was a deadly white against his gray coat—except for the streak of a white scar on the left side of his head. His eyes were as pale as marble and piercing. She didn't flinch, and instead returned his stare with a dark one of her own as she approached.

"Tell him to stop," the man said. "Or else."

He must have sensed even at that distance that she was about to move and in a quick second he turned and lost himself among the shoppers and the sellers at their stands. It was such a sudden movement that the two women stood, both now wondering if he had been there at all. They carried their bags toward the street. Justine's worry had been replaced by anger and her cheeks flushed.

Valentin was waiting outside the market. He looked between them and said, "What?"

He had loaded their bags and they were sitting in the Ford while he scanned Decatur Street. Evangeline had gotten longer looks at the man and described him. Justine added the details of the way he had held himself, stiffly with his shoulders squared. Valentin stared through the windshield as if he could shatter it with the heat of his eyes.

The women exchanged a glance and Justine said, "Valentin? We need to go now."

Mr. Blank had slipped through the market and stepped out further down Decatur Street, where the pedestrian bustle was even busier. Earlier, he had wished to linger on Dumaine Street and get a look at St. Cyr in the daylight, but he couldn't take the risk. The man had a reputation for sharp eyes and quick hands. Mr. Blank couldn't remember how many he had killed. Four or five, and all of them justified in the eyes of the law. Valentin St. Cyr did not commit murder, but he did get away with it. He, on the other hand, did commit murder and he got away with it, too.

He moved into the French Quarter, stopped to lean beneath a balcony, and turned his thoughts to the two women. The detective's woman was a lovely creature, but quadroons were often blessed that way. Even with a coat on, he detected a full figure, built for hard work in the bedroom. Mr. Blank knew from what had been written on the paper that she was not simply a wife, but had been involved in his cases. So she had wits about her, too. The last thing he considered was the way she had stared back at him, her eyes shooting dark fire. Mr. Blank had never been one to be taken by the charms of a woman, but this one had stirred something, if even for a brief moment.

Now he mulled the older woman. Like *Justine*, she was striking, a Creole of a different mix.

He had caught her eye first and she gazed back at him with absent curiosity. There was something regal about her and she was no more fazed by him than St. Cyr's wife. So any more attempts to shake them would likely be a waste of time. It had been a foolish notion from the start, but not his idea. And now the detective—his quarry—had another angle on him. He couldn't make any more such mistakes. With that thought, he tossed the butt of the Camel into the gutter and moved on.

Six

Tom Anderson kept much to his bed and the Morris chair with the heavy cushion that was placed before the fireplace that glowed in all but the hottest months. His needs were few. He no longer craved pleasures of the flesh, neither wine, nor fine food, nor the caresses of women. He had no lust for the power that he had once held in his hands as the man they called "The King of Storyville." He was so removed from that world that it was his housekeeper Lucy who reminded him that on this day, Storyville would be closed down forever.

She carried his coffee and a biscuit with butter and honey into the sitting room and placed them on the table next to his chair. The old man's eyes were barely open and she spent a moment considering how over the time she'd been in his service, the vigor had waned from his being so that he now slumped, his flesh pale and mottled and all but drooping from his bones.

When she called his name, the eyes that opened were dull blue and watery. "Mr. Tom?"

He cleared his throat and tilted his head forward, coming on the streets. "Yes? What is it?"

"Just your coffee and something to nibble on," she said as she bent to straighten his shawl, providing him with the sight of her breasts, round and heavy beneath her thin cotton day dress. He gave no sign of noticing and if that wasn't proof of his decline, she reflected, nothing was.

She straightened and stood back. "It's today, Mr. Tom."

He looked up, blinking. "What's today?"

"The District. Today and tonight, and that's all. Eight o'clock tomorrow morning, everyone has to be gone. After twenty years."

After a moment's pause, the old man said, "And a hundred before that." He reached for his cup and took a sip. "So that's the end, then."

"Is there anyone you're going to want to speak to?" Lucy said. "The mayor? That new chief? Mr. Valentin?" This was a gambit. It wasn't likely any of those men would have anything to say to him these days. She just hoped it would make him feel better to think he was still important.

"And what would we talk about?" he retorted. "The weather?" He shook his head. "I want no part of it anymore. I saw the error of my ways. Let it die. It's for the best."

He fell silent, staring at the burning log as Lucy moved off. She stopped at the door and looked back at him, imagining him as a true king who had lost his throne. Though it was true that he had chosen to give up his crown after a threat came too close to his door, turning instead to God to save him from the fires of hell. Or some such nonsense. But, oh, what glorious times he had seen...

"St. Cyr," he said, breaking into her musings.

She was puzzled. "I'm sorry, Mr. Tom? What about him?"

The old man's expression was grim. "That he gets out of there."

They returned to the house and while the women put up their purchases from the market, Valentin called Parish Precinct and found Lieutenant McKinney back in the detectives' section after his visit to Storyville. He reported the incident at the market.

James said, "And he didn't threaten them?"

"Other than staring and saying those six words, no. So now we know for sure what this is about. And that someone's after me." He paused. "Or us."

The lieutenant said, "What do you want to do?"

"What can I do? I'll wait for him to make another move. Eloi's here with the women, so they'll be safe. How are things in the District?"

"Fairly quiet, so far. I wish something would happen so we could start dealing with it."

"Soon enough," Valentin said.

The lieutenant waited to see if there was more before saying, "I'm going to go out and have another look around. Talk to some people. The Mayor wants to see us at eleven-thirty." He read the silence that followed and said, "I understand with what's happening, you might want to bow out. I can explain."

"No, I'll be there. I'm not going to let them keep me off the streets. And you need to stay alert, too. He probably knows we work together."

"I'd be delighted to make his acquaintance," the lieutenant said.

After the call ended, Valentin reached the operator and in a half-minute, heard the familiar voice. In a few quick seconds, he related what had transpired in the hours before.

Geary said, "Damn. Someone's been watching. Probably all along."

"It's too late to do anything about it," Valentin said. "So, are we ready?"

Geary explained what he had in hand. "I can go deeper," he said when he finished.

"No, leave it there for now. I need whatever you have by tomorrow."

They discussed the arrangements. Geary said, "The two men will be on the train. And I'll call you before daybreak. Where will you be?"

"At Mangetta's. You can leave a message if I'm not there. You know it?" Geary said he knew it well. Valentin said, "And I'll be sending a payment. I'm grateful, Patrick."

"What did you think I'd do?" Geary said. "I'd probably still be in jail if it wasn't for you."

"I only did that because I knew I'd need your help someday," Valentin said. Geary laughed and hung up. Valentin made a final call, this one to Each's rooming house. The landlady said that she hadn't seen him all morning.

He lingered in the foyer, pondering his next move. Once again, he had tried to keep those close to him out of danger and had failed. Though this time, he had fair warning, a small relief.

The smells and sounds from the kitchen were wafting through the house and he pulled himself out of his brood to join the women he had put in peril.

By the clock over the door, it was not yet eleven and he felt like he'd been up a whole day. Evangeline heaped a plate for him and she and Eloi went out to the back garden. Valentin was distracted for a brief moment by the rich scents of scrambled eggs and boudin. Evangeline had baked bread earlier and the loaf was still warm and fragrant. He wondered why life couldn't be this simple. But for as long as he could remember, there had been trouble waiting if he but turn his head. Still, he had managed to carry on, even be happy. It was a true—

"So, what now?"

Justine had returned with her cup of coffee and was standing across from him. He looked up to catch something in her eyes he'd seen before, a shadow that held a sweet light. It caught him so blindly that he could only say, "What now?"

"Yes, *what now*?" she said. "That's what I asked. What are you going to do? What are *we* going to do?"

He knew that this was a time to tread carefully. "I haven't decided yet."

"Are you going to wait for him to fire another bullet through another window? Or until he breaks down the front door?"

She was angry and he didn't blame her. She knew he had brought this on.

"I'll get away from the house," he said. "See if I can draw him out."

The back door opened and Evangeline stepped inside, brushing her palms.

Justine barely noticed. "What about leaving the city?" she said. "Packing some things and driving away?"

"I can't do that," he said.

"Can't do that why?" She looked at Evangeline and shook her head. The older woman demonstrated the wisdom of her years by not uttering a word.

"It's not that," Valentin said. He took a sip of coffee. "I've been hired to be there tonight. They're counting on me."

"And getting our window shot out and then having someone tailing us at market doesn't change that?"

"Well, I can't just hide," he said. "What good would that do?"

"Not much, other than keeping you alive."

The heat in the room was rising and now Evangeline did speak up. "We'll be fine for now. Eloi will take care that nothing happens. But please be careful."

"I will be. I promise."

Some calm returned. Still, Justine was not happy as she returned to the stove to pour more coffee from the enameled pot.

"I'll need to get going," he said.

"No," she said. "You finish eating first." It did not come out like a suggestion and Valentin bent his head over his plate.

Mr. Blank decided to enjoy a decent breakfast as a reward for the decent start on the day's work and left the hotel, turning north. He was not about to eat in Storyville proper, but chose something close, a tidy eatery across the tracks on North Rampart Street. A window table afforded him a view of the District when the trains weren't passing.

After he had ordered eggs, ham, grits, and white toast, and the girl had poured his coffee, he sat back to survey the scene across the way. He was tracing the progress of two tiny workers moving furniture out of a house and into a waiting hack when he heard a man at the table behind him say, "You know St. Cyr? That detective worked for Tom Anderson?"

Mr. Blank sat up, perking an ear.

The man's companion murmured something in response. "Someone took a shot at him this morning," the fellow said. He lowered his voice and Mr. Blank couldn't hear any more, but the snippet had been enough. The food was tasty and he enjoyed it all the more knowing that word of his exploit was already making the rounds. Mr. Smith would be impressed. That was the pleasant part.

He had finished his breakfast and as the girl was taking his plate away, he noticed a man in a long black coat standing with his back to him and pulling a slouch hat down low over his forehead. A few seconds passed and the man turned to stare at him with a cool he could feel at twenty paces. In the next abrupt instant, the man crossed to the door and made his exit, allowing a chilly shot of air in his wake.

Mr. Blank almost rose to follow, then thought better of it and sat back to finish his coffee, for the briefest instant shivering from a tiny, alien spark of fear.

Justine stood in the hallway and spent a few seconds studying the window with the one odd pane before stepping in to gather her things for her bath.

Even as she tried to fix her mind on the notion of a drunkard rambling the Mid-City streets with a gun, she knew as soon as Valentin pulled her off the bed that it was the start of something. The scrap of the map proved it. There was going to be trouble.

She closed the dresser drawer and sat down on the edge of the mattress, staring at her hands.

The bathroom door opened and she heard Evangeline's footsteps in the hall. The older woman stopped to peer in at her.

"Are you all right?" she asked.

"No, I'm not," Justine said. "What about you?"

"I'm worried, too." Evangeline watched Justine. A lovely daughter. "Are you angry at him?"

Justine came up with a thin smile. "If I did that every time something like this happened, I'd spend half my life that way. But I knew who he was and what he did when I first started with him."

"And then you went ahead and married the man."

Now Justine met Evangeline's sweet smile with a droll one of her own. "Yes, I did, didn't I? What was I thinking?" She stood up and returned to the dresser.

"Twenty more hours and it will be over," the older woman said before continuing down the hall.

"God, I hope so," Justine whispered.

James McKinney knew that there were more than a few of the brass and street coppers who resented him. He had made a fast rise from uniform to detective and rumors fluttered this way and that about the cases he worked with Valentin St. Cyr and the favor he had earned from Chief Reynolds.

Though Captain A.G. Warren had held official responsibility for the red-light district, he had no interest in soiling his hands with those sinful blocks and so his subordinate Lieutenant McKinney found himself responsible. Then the captain met a gruesome end of his own, an act of revenge. No one was assigned to take his place and without any official action, Storyville was left to the lieutenant, who suspected that he was there to take the blame for any disasters.

Now as he reached Basin Street for his second visit of the morning, he wondered what the day and night would bring and what would remain come Tuesday.

There were few early-risers and he strolled at his leisure until he reached Mahogany Hall, once the grandest mansion on the street. Lulu White had abandoned the address after fifteen years, unwilling to face the pressure that she for once could not withstand. A madam named Rose Allen, gambling that Storyville would survive, had taken it over. She had lost her bet and now stood on the gallery, watching as a crew of laborers hauled the heavy furniture out the door.

She spotted James and waved him inside.

The kitchen table and chairs had been removed, so they leaned against the counter, cracked cups in hand. After a minute listening to the workmen moving about in the front of the house, Miss Rose reached into the cabinet for a bottle of rye and two shot glasses. They toasted and drank.

"Are your girls all gone?" the lieutenant asked.

"Out of the house, yes," Miss Rose said. "Half of them left the city. Or they're about to. The rest will wait and see what houses open here and there." She poured again. "I swear, folk have it in their heads that once Storyville goes away, there won't be no more fucking."

James laughed. For years, he had been reading pleas in the newspapers from citizens claiming that sin would disappear right along with the District, as stupid a notion as he had ever heard. And yet enough voices had been raised to accomplish that very end.

He sipped his whiskey. A copy of the eviction notice that the houses had received was lying on the sideboard and he picked it up. The language was high-blown for such a tawdry action.

MAYORALTY OF NEW ORLEANS,
CITY HALL, *Oct. 29* 1917

14 DAYS NOTICE TO VACATE

State of Louisiana
Parish of New Orleans — City of New Orleans

To: M. *Rose Allen*
313 Basin Street

By order of the Office of the Mayor of the City of New Orleans, You and any residents are hereby ordered to remove therefrom the premises no later than midnight on the twelfth of November, by the order of the Mayor and according to City Ordinance 5891. There will be no exceptions made. Any residents found within these premises will be subject to immediate arrest, as per section 8 of Ordinance 5891. Failure to comply with the order will subject you to the penalties provided.

Martin H. Behrman
MAYOR

John P. Coleman
Secretary to the Mayor.

He replaced it. "Have you heard of anyone planning to make trouble? Fight it out? That sort of thing?"

"Not on Basin Street," the madam said. "At least, not yet. I heard there's some digging in farther back. There will be parties. At Miss Antonia's, for one. They got more in mind. Some are saying the coppers will have to carry them out." She shrugged. "I don't know what'll happen. It's just what some have said."

Because James had never taken more than the most minor graft, the madams trusted him, and would come to him for help with this and that. Alas, he could do nothing about the official machinery that was about to sweep away the fabled parcel of real estate. And yet he still felt it was important to maintain his status, so instead of asking for names, he changed the subject. "What about you, Miss Rose? Where will you be going?"

"I have family out by Eunice," she said. "I'll go stay with them for a few weeks."

"Until things settle?" James said.

The madam smiled. "Oh, I'll be back. All those sailor boys. What will they do for female company?"

James drained his glass. What she said was true. The trade would start up again, just not in Storyville. And *that's* what Tuesday would bring.

"And you, Lieutenant?" Miss Rose said. "What's next for you?"

"I haven't been told."

The madam was surprised. "Haven't been told?"

"That's right," he said. "Maybe they'll get rid of me, too."

After Valentin had finished breakfast to his wife's satisfaction, he climbed in the Ford and drove to Parish Precinct. Once inside, he found a spot in the corner of the lobby to wait for the lieutenant. He was not out of sight and he caught the glances that the uniformed officers and detectives in their suits cast his way. The New Orleans Police Department had never been taken with him, an interloper who sometimes broke cases when they had floundered. And now he was about to lose a large chunk of his turf. Or so they surmised. Storyville had been fading into his past for some time and was no longer his *turf* like in the glory days.

After ten minutes of looks and occasional whispers, James appeared, descending the marble steps. He crossed the lobby to shake Valentin's hand, a small show intended mostly for the benefit of the audience. The gesture was appreciated; at least one policeman was standing true. James said, "How are things on Dumaine Street?"

"She's not happy," Valentin said.

"Anything more to report?"

The Creole detective said, "I'm going to have something in hand by tomorrow morning. It won't change what's going to happen tonight."

"How bad?"

"I won't know until I see it," Valentin said. "But from what Geary said, bad enough for certain people to want it buried."

The lieutenant studied him for a moment before saying, "You still sure you want to be out walking around?"

From anyone else, the question would have been an insult. Valentin understood the concern and said, "I want to be on the streets. I can't stay indoors." He smiled in a sardonic way. "Anyhow, you'd be lost without me."

Mr. Blank felt that it was safe to be in the open again and found a seat on one of the benches that had been placed along the walkway atop the levee. It was still early and the Algiers Ferry was packed with automobiles. A leather-bound notebook was resting on his knee and he held a fountain pen in his right hand. He had drawn a grid representing Storyville's streets on the page before him, four tending east to west and five south to north. Now he scrawled the names of the streets. From south to north, it was Iberville, Bienville, Conti, and St. Louis, where the cemetery huddled, a silent pasture of stone.

East to west began with Basin, the main thoroughfare, and behind it Liberty, Franklin, Marais, Robertson, and Claiborne. He had done his study and knew that the skills and the hygiene of the women, the beauty of the houses, and the quality of the entertainment descended by steps over the first four before dropping into a gutter on the last two.

This was the territory that St. Cyr had patrolled in the employ of Tom Anderson. Together, they had managed the vice and the crime and those who played parts in both. And so it had been until Anderson's grip began to fail and the detective found other work to occupy him. Though it was true that St. Cyr had never truly shed Storyville. Something always drew him back. Good news for Mr. Blank.

A freighter horn blew loud and long and he gazed over the river. He knew the detective only by reputation and had seen him only as a silhouette in a window. As he watched the ship pass, he marveled at the instincts that alerted him to an intruder outside his home.

The plan had been to shoot out the pane as a first warning. Seeing the quarry standing there was a surprise. Mr. Blank raised the pistol and was surprised a second time to see St. Cyr dive away just as he pulled the trigger. He faded into the shadows and was about to steal away when he remembered the torn shred of the map. Bending down, he laid it on a wilted flower. Only then did he make his escape.

It was some peculiar business, but then no two jobs were the same. Here, he found himself unnerved at the thought of St. Cyr at the window, picking him out of the shadows, later the detective's quadroon wife meeting his eyes with something flinty and a little dangerous, and finally the strange fellow turning to glare at him in the diner.

He lowered his eyes to peruse his map. Before the earth turned again, he would tear the page out, lift it into the air, and let the wind carry it away, while Storyville, New Orleans went the same way. Valentin St. Cyr and a few other individuals whose lives it entwined would be gone, one way or another. And Mr. Blank, having collected his fee, would disappear in his own manner. For now, he had a new piece of business to attend to.

———

Valentin and the lieutenant rode the elevator to the third floor, where they were escorted into Major Sont's office. They were surprised to see that Acting Chief Cook had not taken the major's desk, but sat in one of the tall chairs as if he was a guest and a grudging one at that.

The major addressed Lieutenant McKinney. "What do you think we can we expect in the District tonight?"

James said, "Most of madams and their girls will go quietly."

"And what of the rest?"

"There will be some trouble. No doubt about it."

"What trouble?"

"A few will have to be dragged out. We'll have the paddy wagons waiting. And we'll be ready for any violence."

The acting chief said, "What violence?"

"Mostly fights," James said. "A good bit of public drunkenness. Maybe some furniture thrown around. Bottles flying. Bonfires. I hope nothing more serious."

"You *hope*?" Cook said.

"There's no way to predict."

Major Sont waited to make sure the acting chief had nothing more to say, then turned to Valentin. "What do you have to add?"

"I agree with the lieutenant. There's no way how to tell how it's going to go until it starts. That will be after sundown. Storyville has twenty years of history. I don't think the end can pass without a good bit of noise. But we'll be watching."

Sont had kept his gaze fixed on Valentin. "Speaking of trouble, the lieutenant told me about what happened at your home this morning."

The acting chief said, "What happened?" It was his first sign of life.

Valentin related the incident, then said, "I don't know that it's anything to worry about."

Cook cocked his head as if trying to decipher the detective's words, but did not speak further.

The major said, "Well, I hope that's the case." He glanced at the acting chief. "Anything else, sir?"

Cook pushed himself out of his chair. "The commissioner and the mayor will want regular reports through the day and night. So you'll tender those to Major Sont. And he'll report to us."

"Of course," James said. "Yes, sir."

Cook said, "That's all, then."

As they were exiting the room, Valentin noticed the glance that passed between the major and the junior officer. So instead of heading for the elevators, they moved to the stairwell and descended to the landing halfway to the second floor. Presently, they heard the voices of Sont and the acting chief rise and then fall.

"He wouldn't meet my eyes," James said.

"Who wouldn't?"

"Cook. He's *never* met my eyes."

"Well, he's a cold fish," Valentin said.

"And Sont and the mayor both think there's something going on with him."

"Such as?"

"No telling. But Sont wants to make sure he doesn't jump the gun on every little thing tonight and create more confusion. Everyone wants this to go quietly."

Valentin produced a bent smile and said, "I don't."

The lieutenant snickered. "I don't, either."

Valentin said, "I guess it really is time for it to be over, but I think it deserves a party before that happens."

One of Major Sont's aides appeared on the landing above and beckoned to James, who said, "More fun," and started back up the stairs.

Valentin said, "I'll wait for you outside."

Acting Chief Cook was gone, having been nimbly escorted out by Mr. Pettibone. The lieutenant joined Major Sont at the window and they cast their eyes on the slow bend in the river. A lonely figure was perched on one of the benches as a freighter made a slow pass. The lieutenant understood that Sont was waiting to make sure that the flustered chief did not think of something else and walked back in the door. After a minute passed, the major said, "What will St. Cyr have?"

"He'll have something tomorrow. Coming in on an early train."

The major pondered for a few moments before saying, "I'm sorry the weight of all this landed on you, Lieutenant, but that's the way it is."

"I understand."

"And Mr. Valentin's presence will not be welcome."

James said, "It will go easier with him over there."

"Oh, I know." Major Sont smiled. "But the officers see him getting away clean without his comeuppance. Without paying a price for stepping on our toes all those years." James sighed and nodded.

"What about that business at his house? It couldn't have been random?"

The lieutenant said, "No, sir." He explained about the women at market. "This fellow is stalking."

"Why?"

"Trying to warn him away."

The senior officer turned to stare at him. "Sounds like someone is scared."

"I'd say a number of someones."

"And the warnings won't work."

"They will not," James said. "It's too late. And Mr. Valentin isn't the sort to run."

The major was quiet for a few seconds. "All right," he said. "You have a busy day and night ahead. Report as often as possible. I'll be spending most of my time at City Hall." He took a weighted pause. "And I'll be dealing with the *acting* chief."

The lieutenant left him standing at the window, his gaze fixed on the now empty bench on the walkway by the river.

Valentin and James exited the building onto Poydras Street.

"So?" the Creole detective said.

"Cook will be kept out of the way."

"Which probably suits him just fine."

"I suspect so," the lieutenant said. "He'll be around to take the credit, though."

"As long as nothing terrible happens."

"Then it's our fault."

James clapped him on the shoulder and told him he was heading back inside to address some paperwork. Valentin would be going home for a couple hours in hopes of making peace. They were about to separate when a young patrolman stepped out the front door, looked around, and spotted them.

"Lieutenant?" he said. "We got a report of an incident. A fight in a saloon on Basin Street. Fellow got stabbed. They took him to Mercy. There's uniforms at the scene."

"Which saloon?" Valentin said.

The copper hesitated for just enough of a cool instant to make it noticeable. "Fewclothes."

"I'll go," Valentin told the lieutenant. "I'll call you later."

They walked off. James turned a frigid stare on the patrolman. "A word, officer."

Seven

Buddy had been gazing over the flat fields and studying a fragment of a melody going around his brain when he noticed the man with a camera, like the one that crippled-up what-was-his-name used to carry around making photographs of the sporting girls, catching their lost eyes and haunted smiles. It wasn't him; this fellow scurried. From the other side came one of the guards and the tall fellow who had appeared three months before, a bearish sort they called Big-something. Murdered a man, they said. And not just any man, somebody important. But Buddy couldn't bring a name to mind.

The three met in the middle and the man with the camera did quick work, telling them where to stand, fiddling with the box, holding up a finger, bobbing his head, and hurrying back the way he had come. The guard watched him go, then turned to eye the big man, who was now staring down at the earth the way so many in that place did. As if they had lost something that they could not and would not find, but kept searching all the same.

Now Buddy heard voices coming close. Two of the attendants had stepped to the next window to view the yard. One produced a paper packet and the other a lucifer. A flame was struck and they blew smoke that made fancy gray designs in the air.

He had been back at his music for a half-minute when he heard the word "Storyville." Then "Closing it down. Today. They sure as hell are. It's over."

———

Each arrived at his rooming house on Port Street to learn from the landlady that Mr. Valentin had called looking for him. So he picked up the phone in the foyer and dialed the number. Evangeline answered in the voice that always sounded like music to him. She beckoned Valentin and he came on the line.

"What happened this morning isn't all of it." He held his voice down low to explain, which Each understood to mean there was a row going on inside the house.

When Valentin finished telling him what had happened at the French Market, he said, "You got any idea who it is?" Each said.

"I've been around the District ten years," Valentin said, "All those cases I worked. I have enemies on both sides of the street."

Each knew that time and again, Mr. Valentin had crossed bloody paths with criminals and people in power. He could name a couple dozen citizens and coppers who might want revenge before Storyville closed.

"So what do you want me to do?" Each said.

"Go ahead and make some rounds. See if there's anything brewing. But listen. We don't know what this business is about. So be careful."

Each was miffed. "Ain't I always?" he said.

Valentin had an answer that he kept to himself. "Meet me at Frank's when you're done," he said and broke the connection.

Mayor Behrman leaned with his hands on the sill of his fifth-floor window and gazed at the streets below. So the final day had arrived. Now it was a matter of getting through to the next sunrise. From where he stood, he could see the roofline of the once-famous Anderson's Café along with the peaks of some of the grander mansions. The business they had done! Millions of dollars! And now the monied parties behind the scene were pretending that losing that revenue was of no concern. He hadn't heard much more than a squeak from a police department facing a huge drop in graft payments, meaning empty pockets, starting Tuesday morning. Meanwhile, the sin they claimed as the reason to close the District would now be spread all over New Orleans instead of contained. It didn't make sense. Perhaps St. Cyr could puzzle it out when he got—

He heard a tap on his door and Mr. Pettibone stepped inside on his gliding feet and murmured a few words.

"Yes, all right," the mayor said with a sigh. "Show him in."

The assistant held the door wide for Acting Chief Cook. Behrman waved him to one of the chairs for the next in a string of mainly pointless meetings.

"What are you hearing from the streets?" the mayor began.

Cook said, "No trouble so far."

"Because it's early. Wait until it gets dark and they begin to realize there will be no reprieve."

"Perhaps they'll go quietly," Cook said.

The mayor laughed and shook his head. "Those who would go quietly are gone. The rest will raise some kind of a ruckus. We just need to manage it." His voice fell. "Until it's over."

The acting chief knew that Behrman had fought tooth-and-nail to save Storyville. As the final day drew closer, the atmosphere around City Hall was like the countdown to an execution and still the mayor had argued like the famous Clarence Darrow to save the condemned quarter. It had done no good and he had surrendered at last.

He now came up with a crooked smile. "There are some hard women back there."

Cook had nothing to offer on that subject, either. After some more seconds went by, Behrman said, "Valentin St. Cyr."

He noticed the acting chief stiffening. "What about him?"

"Well, two things. You heard what happened at his house this morning. It came within a foot of his head."

Cook didn't respond, but the mayor saw the shadow of a smirk come and go.

"Strange that it happened today."

"Is it?"

Behrman noticed the acting chief's quick turn to disinterest. But that had been the man's general state of mind. And the look on his face, like he—

"What was the second thing?"

The mayor said, "Sorry, what?"

"You said there were two things about St. Cyr."

"Oh, yes. Are we clear that he'll be in Storyville tonight?"

After a pause, Cook said, "Yes. But I don't see the purpose. Unofficially or any other way."

Mayor Behrman was irritated. "The purpose is to help keep things calm. He knows the place better than anyone. Knows the people, all that." Cook appeared miffed and he said, "He'll work with Lieutenant McKinney to get us through the night. The commissioner agreed to it. So I know we can count on your cooperation."

Cook got the message and said, "Of, course," even as his jaw took on a set.

The meeting was at an end and yet he lingered, in no hurry to leave. The mayor understood; he was waiting in hopes of hearing that the word "Acting" had been removed from his title and he was now Chief of Police.

Instead of speaking the words his guest longed to hear, Mayor Behrman said, "Anything else?"

Along with the three saloons that stayed open twenty-four hours a day, every drinking establishment in the District still in business had unlocked their doors within a few minutes of nine o'clock. Even on this momentous date, there appeared at first to be the usual traffic: sots who had no homes to go to, didn't want to go if they did, or were not welcome there if they had homes and did want to go to them; the burned-down drunkards who ambled from wherever they'd been slumped to begin a new day of cadging or stealing or finding a way to earn a few dimes to slake their thirsts; and those creatures of the night who roamed the streets on various hustles. Among their number was Each, who appeared at Fewclothes to begin a day of farewell visits while keeping an eye out for trouble, as Mr. Valentin had instructed.

He was greeted by the voice of Prince Albert, a local character who had earned the moniker by his claims of royal birth and noble upbringing. It was all an act, though with his "I says" and "cheerios," the dusty, dented bowler on his round dome, and the week-old copy of the *London Times* protruding from his pocket, he put on a good show. This morning found him in the midst of a loud consideration of rumors that the District would not be closing after all.

"The mayor, that fine man, he has the goods on certain officials and he's threatened to use them. There are more foxes in the henhouse."

Each stepped up and raised a finger to Harry the barkeep. "And where do you get this from?" he asked Prince Albert.

The prince turned a baleful eye his way. "I have information," he said. "Confidential, that sort." He winked and the chortles rose.

Each said, "What information would that be?" Prince Albert sniffed with regal aplomb and leaned closer to whisper in his ear. When he finished, Each stared at him and said, "Who else knows this?"

"Only the wise," the prince said with a cryptic wink before turning back to his regular audience.

Harry arrived with a short glass of whiskey as Each was mulling what he had just heard. The barkeep pushed the dime on the bar back to him. "Free drinks for our good customers," he explained. "I got barrels with no place to go."

They listened to Prince Albert prattle for a few moments. Harry crossed his arms on the bar and said, "What's this I hear about Mr. Valentin?"

Each cocked his head slightly. "I don't know, what?"

"That somebody shot up his house."

Each gave an exasperated shake of his head and said, "That ain't what happened. It was a shot through one windowpane. That's all."

"Some drunk with a pistol?"

"Probably."

"On Dumaine Street?" The barkeep was dubious.

"Yes, on Dumaine Street." Each paused. "That's all you heard?"

"So far," Harry said. He clearly didn't like the hedging.

Each said, "It was just one of those things."

"It's just that it happened—"

"Today," Each said. "I know." He downed the rest of his whiskey.

Harry looked over his customer's shoulder and frowned. Each said, "What?"

"That fellow."

Each turned to the door. "Who?"

"He was just... standing there staring at you."

"I don't see anyone."

"He's gone now."

"What'd he look like?"

"Like he was made out of wax."

"Like wax. Oh, that's good, Harry." He placed his hat back on his head. "I'm going to have a look around."

Outside, he gazed up and down Basin Street, but saw no one who looked to be made from wax.

Lieutenant McKinney arrived back at Parish Precinct as the midday traffic was stirring the streets. While Storyville's twenty blocks would grow more chaotic as the day wore on and darkness fell, everywhere else it was just another Monday, if there could be such a thing in New Orleans.

At his desk, he jotted on his pad, noting the Dumaine Street location and the time of the incident, the spot where the shooter had likely stood, and the odd detail of the shred of map.

He finished, pocketed his pen and pad, and slouched back in his chair to cast an eye around the section. The other three detectives were bent over their desks, filling out forms with dull strokes of their pens. They looked bored and he pitied them. Because his career had been anything but.

He had been lucky to stumble into working with Mr. Valentin on a series of bizarre cases, following the twists, sharing the danger, and taking down serious felons, while advancing from street copper to detective for his efforts. The brass had expected him to spy; instead, he simply held back some of his reports.

That was ending, too, but the Creole detective had already been drifting off, pushed by a wife who wanted to get away from the life and his need to protect her and Evangeline, the baffling woman they had brought into their home two years before. And he still had not solved her mystery. No matter what would happen come Tuesday, his time would be finished.

The thought that the adventures were done cast a cloud over the lieutenant and he turned his attentions to the trouble at hand. That someone was out to get Valentin St. Cyr was not striking. The Creole detective had spent a decade on the scarlet streets and J. Picot was only one of the enemies he'd left in his wake. The incidents that had transpired since before dawn pointed to something else.

Word had gotten out that Valentin was closing in on damaging information with names attached to it. The kind very important people would go to great lengths to bury. One of them was panicked enough to send a felon to try and stop the man gathering it. Good luck with that. And all of it coming to a head, by the way, on one very specific date.

He didn't want to sit there and wait for whatever was next, so he pulled his coat back on and walked out of the section, down the stairs, and through the lobby. Once on the banquette, he stopped to take in the morning, drawing his collar against the chill. While it was calm on the street, he sensed a hint of something stirring underground.

He began walking in that direction of the District. City Hall had been wise to schedule Storyville's final hours on a Monday, when half of the houses were closed for business anyway, a New Orleans tradition of taking a day of rest before plunging forward. Of course, there was still money to be made from those gentlemen of means who had spent a hard week getting richer and then the weekend with family, church, and social responsibilities and longed for some sweet relief as the grind started all over again.

The choice of the late fall was all the shrewder. No one wanted the extra element of crazy heat at such a tense moment. By the time the church bells tolled, the temperature would be in the fifties. Not frigid, but not a Crescent City steam bath, either.

The moment he arrived on Canal Street, he was struck by the notion that he was being watched. St. Cyr had taught him that, too: be still, don't look or listen but just be there and stay alert as the panorama changed. It was how Mr. Valentin had known from the cozy quiet of his bedroom that there was someone stalking his home. Now Lieutenant James McKinney felt eyes on him that were not friendly.

Reynard Vernel sat at his Underwood, his gaze resting on the yellow sheet of newsprint. His mind had been wandering for days, to the point where Kassel asked was he ill and did he need some time off.

"Last chance to sample a Storyville girl," the editor had quipped. "At least in Storyville. Half of them will stay around. What did they expect?"

Reynard replied with a droll smile and pretended to busy himself with his notes. He had never chosen to sample the District's trollops. Or any woman, for that matter. His interests went in a different direction. There were places for men like him, but he had so far been too timid to visit any of them. Though he kept his secret, he had long suspected that the detective St. Cyr had sensed something about him but didn't care.

Kassel had assigned him the stories on the closing of the District, seeing that he had spent more time there—at least, more professional time—than any of the other *Times-Picayune* reporters. He had gotten to know powerful madams and crazy street characters. He had been privy to eccentric dramas, some of which had swirled around murders. Perhaps, he had mused now and again, I'll write a book about it. Though that would not be for some time; after a century of scarlet pleasures, much of the public would now be content with the disappearance of the red-light district.

He typed:

The Storyville Era Ends

Then:

Notorious Tenderloin Closing
After Twenty Years Under Legal Sanction

Finally:

By Reynard Vernel

His fingers were poised over the keys, ready to strike. But nothing came. He could compose a good story in his sleep, but he wasn't about to reel out the obvious. The whole of New Orleans had been told that the Department of the Navy had forced City Council to vacate the ordinance that had legalized vice in Storyville, and thus began the process of shuttering both the gilded fabled doors of the mansions of Basin Street and the filthy cribs that lined Robertson Street. So they said.

No, Reynard decided, if he was going to write anything, it would be a testament to a place that the world had never seen before and might not ever again. So it could not be just any string of verbiage. It would require a proper obituary.

That was no use at this moment. He glanced across the newsroom to see Kassel's door closed and took the opportunity to grab his jacket off the back of his chair and make an escape. He needed a drink and by now a dozen saloons would be open.

EIGHT

After wandering Basin, Franklin, and Liberty streets from one end to the other, Each arrived back at Fewclothes and spent some time talking to two characters who hadn't been there earlier, one he'd known since he was a little snot, the other a half-crazy character who went by Moses, and swung daily between drunken ranting and biblical sermons, though it was often hard to tell which was which. Prince Albert was no longer on the premises.

Neither fool believed the District would be shut down, no matter what the politicians and the police and the papers said. They expected to be standing on their exact spots come the next morning. And then Wednesday and Thursday and on and on.

Each retreated to the bar to finish his whiskey and have a word with Harry. A few minutes later, he pushed his empty glass across the bar and started for the door and so he didn't see Harry raise a finger and point or hear him say, "Hey, wait, that's the fellow who—"

He found his exit blocked by a man whose features he couldn't make out for the light behind him. He was just about to say "Excuse me, pal," and pass when the man said, "Something for St. Cyr."

In the next instant, he felt a blow and a searing shock of pain in his chest. He turned and his legs gave out as the room went black.

———

Valentin raced along the banquettes, slowing to a walk only when he crossed Basin Street. A crowd had gathered outside Fewclothes and he recognized a few faces, old-timers who had been around Storyville for longer than he had. This last day had not changed their routines and this morning found them at the saloon, just as they had been every day for years.

Except on this morning it was different and whispers went through the crowd at Valentin's appearance. Two uniformed officers looked at him and then looked away. The customers stood back to let him pass and a few murmured kind wishes for Each. Inside, he found Harry standing at the end of the bar and staring down at the gruesome patch of blood on the floor.

"What happened?" the detective said.

As Harry related it, the saloon had been only a bit rowdier than usual for a morning, but nothing like during the glory days, when even at daybreak the music was loud, the whole room drunk, and the sporting women raving.

Valentin made a rough gesture of impatience to bring the barkeep back to the business at hand.

"Sorry, Mr. Valentin," Harry said. "So Each was leaving out. I saw this odd fellow in the doorway again."

"Again?"

"He was there earlier. Each was at the bar and he come to the door. He just stood there staring in. I told Each, but by then he was gone."

"Did you recognize him?"

"I couldn't see him too good," Harry said. "The sun was behind him. I believe he was a tall man, though. Pale-faced. That's what I said to Each. It was like wax. He was wearing a dark coat. Dark gray. That I noticed for sure. But I don't believe he's anyone from around here."

Valentin knew without hearing another word that the same miscreant who had stalked Evangeline and his wife at the market had taken his game to a murderous level. "Tell me how it happened," he said.

The barkeep tilted his head. "He was standing there real still, I knowed there was something wrong. I called to Each, but he didn't hear me. He gets to the door and lets out a shout and turns around, that's when I saw." He placed both hands on his chest. "It was all over his front and it was bad." He stopped to take a breath. "He comes staggering back. I ran around the bar, but by the time I got to him, he was down." Now Harry nodded to the red stain. "I took off my apron and had one of the fellows hold it on him. And I went to call the coppers and an ambulance."

"They took him to Mercy?"

"Yes, sir."

Valentin knew that Harry had seen more than a few dying and dead bodies on the sawdust floor and he said, "How bad? Is he going to make it?"

The barkeep said, "I'd say if I was sure, Mr. Valentin. It didn't look good for him. But he's a hard case, ain't he?"

"That he is," Valentin said. "All right, then."

"You have any notion of who done it?" Harry said.

"I do," Valentin said and left it at that.

He stepped behind the bar to call Justine. There was no way to make it anything but brutal. "I'm at Fewclothes," he said. "It's Each. He was stabbed here a little while ago."

"Stabbed?" He heard her catch breath and her voice trembled. "He's not dead, is he?"

"Not yet," Valentin said.

"Not *yet*?"

"He left here alive. I'm going to Mercy now." At this, he heard his wife sob. She had been the closest to Each since he had entered their world ten years before as a kid called Beansoup.

"Hey, he's tough," he said.

"No, he's not." she blurted the words. "He's the same sweet boy he always was. Who did it? Was it him?" Before he could reply, she said, "It was. Oh, my God, Valentin…"

He stayed quiet for the moments it took for her to settle herself. "I'll tell Evangeline." Her voice was low.

"Call Eloi to the phone, please," he said.

As he was leaving, Harry waved a hand and said, "Mr. Valentin? What about..."

"Oh. Just get the blood cleaned up and then let them back in." He stepped back onto the banquette and passed through the quiet crowd.

Mr. Blank had walked away from the saloon, then all the way down Conti and into the filthy warren that was Robertson Street. Most of the crib whores had already been chased away and the block was empty. He slowed his steps and came to a stop, imagining the look on St. Cyr's face when he heard the news. Was the fellow called Each dead? Those weren't his instructions, but dead or alive, so be it.

He backed into the dirt passage between two lines of cribs, lit a Camel, and regarded the three ragged trollops who were standing on the opposite corner in their stained Mother Hubbards, looking in his direction in a vague way. Such tramps seemed to him always tottering on the edge of a deep hole as they stumbled through their days performing lewd acts for strangers for nickels and dimes, spending what they earned on anything that would blot out their minds, and then doing it all over again. To a woman, they were homely and riddled with diseases.

He tossed the half-smoked cigarette into the dirt and moved on, thinking that before morning, they and whichever of their filthy sisters were left would be swept from the streets like so much garbage. Indeed, they should have been gone long ago.

He went on his way, a man with more business to attend to. From this point on, neither Valentin St. Cyr nor those close to him would be easy targets, like the unlucky fellow lying at worst in a hospital bed and at best on a cooling board at the city morgue.

————

Valentin stepped through the doors of Mercy Hospital with a bitter taste on his tongue. After he spoke to the nurse at the front desk, he spent the time climbing the stairs thinking about how many people had ended up in that building because of him. Justine once. Now Each for the second time. There had been others. Why hadn't he seen something like this coming?

He turned a corner and moved along the hallway. And what of those who had landed there as a victim of a murderer he had tracked down, but alas, too late? There, or in a grave? Too many to count.

Mariette, a quadroon like his wife and the one-time sporting girl he had helped out of the life and into nursing, was waiting in the hall. "Mr. Valentin," she said. Her pretty smile was wan. She knew Each from the Storyville streets.

Valentin lived by having information and the sooner the better. This time, though, he stopped a few paces away and hesitated before saying, "What's his condition?"

"It's critical," Mariette said. "It was a large blade and the wound was deep. There was organ damage." She paused to let the information sink in. "It's a very serious situation, Mr. Valentin."

"Is he going to live or not?"

Mariette said, "I don't know, sir. Honestly. It's a wonder he didn't die on the spot or on the way here. It's that bad."

"Can I talk to the doctor?"

"He's with another patient. Man crossing the tracks got hit by a train. Trying to save him." She watched his face and saw something terrible there. "Do you want to go in?"

Valentin looked away from her. He felt weak and reached out a hand to the wall.

"Mr. Valentin?" Mariette took hold of his arm to steady him. "He's not conscious. He won't know if you're there or not. So you don't have to."

Valentin looked at her and said. "Yes, I do."

———

He stepped to the bed, feeling his heart drop. The damage was all below the neck, except for the bruises and scrapes from his fall to the saloon floor. He was very pale. His torso was swathed and a bottle hanging from a fixture attached to the bed frame dripped a solution into his arm.

Standing there, Valentin conjured a memory of two boys, one white and one black, Beansoup and Louis, both out of the waif's homes and spending much of their time roaming the streets, day and night. Louis had been so dazzled by Buddy Bolden that he took up the trumpet, went on to grand things, and now played music for the upper crust from coast to coast. Meanwhile, his childhood friend Beansoup—Emile Carter—had attached himself to Valentin St. Cyr; and because of that was now lying in a hospital bed, perhaps dying from a stab wound.

Valentin had not been religious since God had betrayed him when he was young, but he now whispered a small prayer: *Let him live.*

When that passed, he felt the bile that had lurked deep in his gut since the moment he had seen his father cut down from a tree rise and linger until the shade over his eyes cleared. He stepped away from the bed. "I'll come back. But if there's any change..."

"Yes, sir," Mariette said. "Where will you be?"

Valentin thought for a moment. "Mangetta's. Frank will want to know what happened anyway."

The nurse cleared her throat. "Yes, sir, I understand." She looked past him. "Wait," she said. "There's Doctor Laurent now."

The physician entered the room like a large bird swooping to a landing, his gray hair a mass of wild curls and the tail of his white coat flapping. Valentin was at once relieved and dismayed. Relieved because he knew the doctor was as skilled as he could have wished for and dismayed because—

"You haven't sent any business our way lately," he said, casting a hard eye on the detective.

Now he ignored the detective as he stepped to the bed to check on the patient and consult in a low voice with Mariette, who took the opportunity to remove his dirty glasses and clean them with some alcohol and a square bandage. Valentin turned his head to gaze out the window and ponder Dr. Laurent's quip. How many *had* landed in Mercy or some other hospital on his watch? And how many on a cooling board at the City Morgue? The numbers were something more than few. And now Each had joined them.

The doctor finished with Mariette and moved to the door. Before Valentin could ask the question, he said, "Forty percent chance he makes it." He walked out. Mariette followed him, stopping to lay a kind hand over Valentin's heart.

He was turning away when she said, "Who else is in danger, Mr. Valentin?"

She had always been a sharp woman. "I'm taking care of that," he said and walked out of the room and down the hall, considering that in another situation he might have sent Each to Dumaine Street to protect his wife and Evangeline.

James was arriving just as he reached the street door with a detective Valentin didn't know. He had come running as soon as the news reached the precinct which was just as well. Valentin had forgotten to call him. They moved inside and to a corner of the lobby.

The lieutenant gestured. "This is Detective Sergeant Cochran. Valentin St. Cyr."

Cochran said, "Sir. Sorry about all this. I hope he makes it. I'll be staying on the case."

"And reporting to me," James said. Valentin stared as if he hadn't heard. "What's his condition?"

"It doesn't look good. It was a large blade. Deep wound. He's hanging on, but that's just about all."

"Well, goddamn," the lieutenant said.

"I told him to be careful," Valentin said. He stared at the floor for a moment, then said, "What about the investigation?"

"It happened the way Harry described it," James told him. "The suspect caught him by surprise, did the stabbing, and then disappeared before anyone realized what was going on. Most of those characters were in their cups already. None of them saw anything we could use."

"Until he went down," Valentin said.

The lieutenant didn't ever remember placing a hand on the detective, but he did it now, laying a palm upon his shoulder and feeling him sag in a rare moment of weakness. "I'll go up and make sure they know where to reach me."

Valentin said, "Mariette is his nurse."

James moved his hand away. "That's good. She'll take care of him. And what a sight when he wakes up and sees that face." Valentin managed a smile. "What will you do now?"

"Me?" Valentin came out of his daze. "I'm going back to the house. To tell my wife that someone she loved, someone I should have protected, might die." He paused to collect himself. "I'm going to move her and Evangeline out of harm's way, so the same thing doesn't happen to them. Then I'll be back." His eyes hardened and he said, "You know I'm going to kill him."

Sergeant Cochran stared and the lieutenant drew back, startled. He had heard St. Cyr's tone of menace before, but never near as frigid as it sounded in that echoing hallway.

Frank Mangetta was standing in his doorway watching hacks filled with furniture moving by when he saw Valentin approaching from Iberville Street. He stepped out to greet him, his expression tragic. So he had heard, too.

"How is he?" he said, his face dark with worry. Valentin explained. "*Managgia*," Frank said. "Who did this?"

"Someone who's after me. But nobody is safe. *Capisce, Zio Franco? Nessuno.*"

The saloonkeeper was watching his godson's face. "*Va, Valentino,*" he said with a wave of his hand. "Have a *piccetta*. I think you need it."

Inside, they moved to a table and Frank called to Carmine, the nephew who worked mostly in the grocery and was shy except when there were comely young ladies on the premises. Then the Sicilian blood rose to the top. Now he hurried to place two glasses on the bar and poured from a brandy bottle.

Frank sipped and said, "So what about *Giustina* and...?"

"Evangeline. I have a man with them. He won't let anything happen."

"Why is this *cafone* after you? *Come se chiama?*"

"*Signore...*" He searched for the word. "Blank?"

"Blank. *Vuoto.*" Frank snorted. "*Signore Vuoto.*"

"It has to do with Storyville," Valentin said. "The closing. It's more than they're saying. And I know what that is. Or part of it."

"So they're trying to get at you? Your house, and then the ladies, and now this with Each?"

Valentin sighed and said, "Yes."

"So what will you do?"

"Find him," Valentin said. "And finish him. Before he finishes me."

Reynard Vernel left the Easy Five after a sot they called Frog recognized him as a writer for the paper and decided to take the opportunity to recount a history of the District going back sixty years, spewing verbiage and spittle his way, leaving no time for him to explain that he knew the story quite well.

"So right after the War, it was all wide open back-of-town," Frog proclaimed in his metal grate of a voice. "And them goddamn Yankees saw that and come in with their bags of money. Them and the madams got together and started building up Basin Street." He snickered. "And when New Orleans got better, got some money back, they run them bastards out. But that's when it really got going."

Reynard knew what would come next, but he was even deeper in a corner, because two other drunkards had for lack of anything to do wandered closer, bringing their foul clouds with them. Next there would be tales about America Williams, Bridget Fury, and Bricktop Jackson, the vicious harlots who had battled with chains and knives and broken bottles to rule the back alleys of the District. Followed by the story of the stylish madam Hattie Hamilton, who was found with a smoking pistol in her hand and her wealthy lover Senator Beares dead on the floor, only to have no charges brought against her.

He never got to that part, because a buzz of chatter rose near the bar that caused Frog to stop in mid-sentence. Reynard made an escape and found a rounder muttering to those gathered around.

"—know if he's dead or not, but from what I heard, he ain't doing too good. He got stabbed. And he might die." The rounder gave a wistful shake of his head. "Him, of all people, after all these years."

Reynard put on his reporter's hat and stepped up. "Who is *him*?" he said.

"That fellow goes by 'Each'," the rounder said.

Justine was sitting at the kitchen table, her coffee cold in her cup. Evangeline stood at the sink, washing the vegetables. They didn't speak and the only sounds were the gentle stream of the water and the quiet songs of the birds in the garden. They both had taken some time to gaze out the window where the last dry leaves of summer were clinging to bare branches.

At one point, Evangeline looked over her shoulder at the younger woman and saw on that pretty face the first cracks of a heartbreak. She had felt the same thing, like a cold wind, and remembered: there had been such times before.

A voice spoke to her. "Evangeline?"

The cloud moved away. Justine was at her side, reaching to close the tap. "The water," she said.

Evangeline saw that it was just below the top of the sink. How long had she been standing there like that? "Oh, I'm sorry. I'm so..."

"It's all right," Justine said. She was turning away when the sound of a Ford engine drew near the house and then went silent. "That's him," she said and leaned her back against the sideboard.

A long minute passed before they heard the key in the front door and another half-minute before he walked into the kitchen.

She said, "Is he gone?"

"He was alive when I left," Valentin said. "You can call Mariette and check on him." He opened a cabinet door and took down a bottle.

She drank from the glass he poured, wiped her eyes, and let out a shaky breath. "Can I go see him?"

"Not now," he said.

"Why not now?"

"Because it's too dangerous."

She placed her hands on her hips, a first sign of bad news. The sharp light in her eyes was the second. "Do you happen to recall someone shooting out a window pane this morning?" The rough edge on her voice was strike three. "You dug a bullet out of the wall."

Valentin decided this was a good time to stay where he was.

"He could have shot you dead so easily."

"But he didn't. I think he's saving me."

"For what?"

"For the end, I guess." He paused to see if she had anything to add before saying, "I can't stay holed-up here. I'm needed in the District. I agreed to do this. And I have a case with a lot hanging on it."

"He'll be waiting for you."

"Yes, I'm counting on it," he said.

They glared at each other and to escape the cold silence that followed, Evangeline got up, crossed to the door, and stepped into the garden, her thoughts roaming.

Over the last few years, she had wandered in strange places where she hadn't understood others, nor they her. She had lived as if behind a misted window. Because terrible things *had* happened to her. She didn't recall what they were, but after the last one it all went blank.

Sometimes she looked in the mirror and almost remembered. But she only got so far and then the murky pictures she couldn't quite see and the words she could not quite hear would fade again and she would be back in the house on Dumaine Street. Images and sounds would wind their way through her head, and sometimes the faces and the names of people she had laid to rest. And now a cloud hovered over them.

Like Justine, she worried every time Valentin walked out the door. And also like Justine, she kept it mostly to herself. This day had brought something different and she could see it in that young woman's face. It wasn't just little quivers of fear; she was angry, too.

She had walked into and out of danger to arrive beneath a roof with Valentin and Justine and their kind patience. She witnessed how they were together, how they did little things for each other, small acts of love. This brought a dim memory, too.

As if to punctuate the point, she heard the voices rise from inside. The time when she would have left them alone to battle it out was past and she crossed the garden, opened the kitchen door, and stopped there, gazing between them. They were like twins with their copper cheeks flushing red and their dark eyes all lit up. She almost smiled.

Justine said, "Tell her what you just told me."

"I want to move you," he said.

"To the lake," Justine said. "He wants to hide us up on the lake."

"It's for your safety," Valentin said.

"And what about your safety?" Evangeline said, gently, and almost adding, "son" for what must have been the thousandth time.

Justine was still fuming. "That's what I asked. Why won't you stay at the lake, too? Or would that be too wise? Or just too boring?"

He took a breath, slaking his ire. "He shot at our house. He stalked the two of you. He might have murdered Each. You know I can't turn my back on that." He caught a breath. "I made a promise to be in Storyville through the night. And there's this other matter to attend to." He addressed the older woman again in a slight plea. "I just need to get you away from whoever is doing this."

"And what if he follows us there?" Justine said. "Does she even have a telephone?"

"She does," the detective said. "I'll have James talk to the Spanish Fort precinct. To tell them to keep an eye out."

Evangeline said, "I suppose it's the best thing we can do right now."

Justine shot a glance her way, as if to argue the point, then turned back to stare at her husband for a long few seconds. "I'll need to pack," she said, and walked out of the room.

With a loud breath, Valentin sat down in one of the chairs.

"We can be ready in a half-hour," Evangeline said and left him alone with his thoughts.

NINE

Buddy went for a cool drink of water and returned to the window to watch some more and think.

They had taken him away from New Orleans and put him in the hospital because he wasn't safe. He was breaking into pieces and hurting people. One night, something bad happened and the men in the uniforms came to the door and carried him off. It wasn't three days before he was placed where he could do no one harm.

They thought he knew nothing, but this wasn't true. He saw and heard and understood much. There were rooms they kept locked and men in those rooms who wept or bellowed or sat so still and silent that they might have been dead. Men on the ward fell apart and were taken there and locked behind the wall. If they came out it was covered on a stretcher. When that happened, the corridors fell silent.

It wasn't like in New Orleans, where they hauled a man to his glory to the sounds of crazy brass and pounding drums. He had blown a horn, yes; but he forgot about it until a little band came to play for them and he saw the golden curve of a bell, heard a reedy clarinet, and felt the rhythm of a guitar. The band performed merry tunes, none of that low-down drag with a crying cornet to stir the guts, no steam-train barrage that made the bodies bounce. It was plain and there was nothing to get anyone excited, but still enough for him to remember what it was like before, back when they had called him "Kid."

Now the tall man, the killer, was walking below in a circle, his wide shoulders hunched against the cold, with the attendant standing by. Some time passed and he stopped and looked up at the window, at him. He waved and produced a fractured smile, as if greeting a friend from long ago.

Each of the women had packed a bag and they all climbed into the Ford without a word between them. Evangeline now gazed out the window at City Park and the deep, rolling green under a November sky that was dappled with clouds. Here and there, mothers and nannies pushed prams, a sight so at odds with the peril that had driven them away from Dumaine Street.

In the silence, thoughts that had been on her mind in the garden came back around. Presently, she said, "Valentin?"

He turned his head partway. "Yes, ma'am?"

"Tell me about that fighting over the docks."

Justine looked over at him for the first time since they had left the house. After a puzzled moment, she said, "Do you mean the Orange Wars?"

"Yes. The Orange Wars. People were fighting, isn't that right?"

They had reached the intersection of Fillmore Avenue, but instead of continuing on, Valentin turned the corner, pulled to the curb, and shut off the engine. The clattering of the cylinders died.

Justine was again staring through the windshield, her brow stitching. She guessed that her husband was just as vexed as she at the sudden raising of that history.

He turned around in his seat. "Yes," he said. "People were fighting. It was a bad time."

"And some died, didn't they?" Evangeline said. It wasn't really a question and Justine and Valentin waited. "Over what? Money?"

Valentin said, "Yes. A lot of money." He paused. "But not enough to make it worth anyone's life."

The words came out with a brittle edge and now she studied him, her gray eyes steady.

"When is it ever?" she said.

They were quiet for a few more moments. Then Justine said, "Why are you asking?"

Evangeline drew her attention from Valentin. "I'm sorry?"

"About the Orange Wars. Why are you asking?"

"I have these memories." she said. "The Italians were fighting over the docks." She produced an odd smile. "I mean the *Sicilians*."

Justine, who had heard the story in bits and pieces, said, "It was the..."

"Matrangas and Provenzanos," Valentin said. "The two families who ran the produce trade. The oranges and all the other fruit off the freighters. But they weren't fighting. Not until—"

"—someone got them going at each other," Evangeline said.

"That's right. So they could steal all the business from them."

Evangeline said, "Who did that?"

"A half-dozen different men," he said. "Henry Harris was the main one. He tried to get rich on the Sicilians battling each other."

What Justine saw in his fixed gaze brought something to mind. "Wait. He was involved in one of your cases. The one that started on Rampart Street." After a cool pause, she added, "What was the young lady's name?"

Valentin felt his face redden. "Anne Marie Benedict. She was the first victim's daughter." It was a ridiculous moment in the midst of a sad, strange narrative.

The older woman had been listening and trying to follow along. Valentin took the opportunity to escape. "Anyway, innocent men died."

A truck passed and the birds returned to their songs. The breeze was slight. Before Valentin realized the words were coming out, he said, "My father was one of them."

Justine looked away. He felt the heat of Evangeline's eyes on him.

"How did that happen?" she said.

Henry Harris, John Benedict, and their shipping company cohorts had failed to beat back the dominance of the hard-working Sicilians, so they hatched a plan to turn the two families' uneasy peace into war by way of rabid rumors and acts of violence committed by private coppers in the employ of Police Chief David Hennessy. Neither clan was fooled and no vendettas were issued. The day-to-day labor on the docks continued, employing hundreds of men, including Valentin's father Antonio Saracena.

One evening in the midst of all this, Hennessy said good-night to a friend and had just turned toward his house when a man ran from the shadows and fired a shotgun. The chief fell, mortally wounded, as the friend—one Albert Keaton—rushed to his side. By the time the police sedans and an ambulance came screaming up the street, Hennessey had lost consciousness and would linger in that state until the next day, when he gave up the ghost.

In the wake of the shooting, Keaton reported to anyone who would listen that when he had bent down to ask the chief who had fired from the brush, Hennessey had managed to gasp, "The dagos did it!"

Two-dozen members of the Matranga and Provenzano families were rounded-up without any evidence of involvement and held in Parish Prison. The cases against them were weak and a month later the jury in the first trial issued not guilty verdicts and the district attorney refused to pursue the charges on a second. All the prisoners were ordered released within forty-eight hours.

The news of the outcomes spread and the mob that formed on Canal Street was whipped into a frenzy by one speaker after another. All over New Orleans, Italians locked their doors and shuttered their windows, Valentin's mother and father among them.

A gang of thirty men split off from the main mob and raced to Parish Prison, where they broke inside, snatched up seventeen of the Sicilians, dragged them into the yard, and beat and then hanged them.

It would go down as the worst mass-lynching in American history and Valentin never forgot the images of his parents waiting and listening for the smallest sign of danger.

A week later, they were strolling along Bayou St. John when a pair of drunkards insulted his mother. Carmine beat both men bloody, even as she begged him to stop. Three days later, he was found hanging from a tree on the banks of the bayou.

In the pause that followed, Valentin was turning away, angered at letting the old tragedy claim him once again, when he noticed how Evangeline's cheeks had paled. "I know that story," she said.

He stared at her. "You do?"

Evangeline said, "Is it why you left?"

Valentin was confused. "You mean then or now?" But her gaze was clouded, as if she hadn't understood her own question.

Justine spoke up. "He had to leave. Before something bad happened to him, too."

"Something did happen," he said.

He met his wife's gaze for a moment before climbing out to crank the engine. Then he got back behind the wheel, pushed the shifter into gear, and pulled into the street.

Miss Lulu White hadn't slept well during the early morning journey. She had guessed that this might be so and she spent the hours staring out into the Illinois, Tennessee, and Mississippi nights, and then the Louisiana dawn. When the train chugged into Union Station, she questioned for the tenth time the wisdom of her making the trip. Stepping onto the platform, she peered across Basin Street and let out a groan of such dismay that passengers close to her turned to stare. She couldn't bring herself to leave the station. What she viewed was a shabby ghost of the boulevard that had once been beyond grand. Anderson's Café was shuttered, with half the balustrade posts leaning this way and that and the paint peeling away in tatters. She pushed her gaze past Mahogany Hall, where she had once reigned. Down the line, every other mansion was closed. Monday had always been a slow day. Now the street was all but deserted, the only activity a crowd gathered at the doors of Fewclothes Cabaret. An urge to get right back on the train assailed her.

As she mulled this, a Mick paperboy passed by, selling the morning *Times-Picayune* that blasted the headline "STORYVILLE CLOSING TODAY!" while handing out copies of *The Blue Book,* the guide that had once contained the names of almost two thousand strumpets and dozens of madams, now only a thin rag. And come Tuesday, a useless one. She didn't bother with either, instead stopping the boy to ask for the word on the street.

He gave her a quick rundown: the houses that remained open, the few madams who were digging in for a fight or a wake, the Creole detective St. Cyr, Lieutenant McKinney, and a dozen street coppers out to police it through the night.

"Oh, yeah, and a fellow got stabbed over to Fewclothes this morning. He might be dead already, I ain't heard." He pointed. "That's how come all them men is over there."

"What fellow?"

"Name of Each. Used to go by Beansoup. He ran with Mr. Val—"

"My Lord!" Miss Lulu took a startled step back. "I know him. Who did it?"

"Folks is saying the same one went after Mr. Valentin."

Miss Lulu was lost. "Went after him how?"

"Shot out a window at his house. It was before dawn."

"Shot out—" She stopped and put a hand to her forehead to settle her spinning brain. The paperboy waited a moment to see if she wanted anything else, then strolled away, leaving her to grapple with the news of Valentin's house being damaged and his long-time sidekick attacked, perhaps murdered, and both on the District's last day. In that moment, she decided to stay. Because Storyville might still need her.

———

Valentin had not visited Eulalie Echo in almost two years. He had telephoned ahead to ask the favor and received an immediate, "Yes, of course!" in response.

She was waiting on a gallery that spanned the front of a house that was festooned with flowers, hanging herbs, and a variety of charms and decorations, and offered a view of the green Pontchartrain waters. She stood, tall and broad-shouldered in a patterned Mother Hubbard, her bronze face smiling, full of light. She had always been partial to chignons, but on this day her hair was in a long Indian braid that reached halfway down her back. Her gray eyes, the wisest Valentin had ever seen, traced them as they approached the thirteen wooden steps.

She greeted the older woman first. "Miss Evangeline. It's a pleasure. Welcome to the lake."

"We thank you for your hospitality," Evangeline said.

Miss Echo turned to Justine to say, "And you. More lovely every time we meet."

"And you say that every time I see you," the younger woman said.

"But you look troubled. What happened?" Her gimlet gaze shifted to Valentin. "Did someone die?"

"He's alive. Just barely."

"Your doing?"

"Yes, ma'am," he said. "My doing."

A half-hour later, they had worked through the gunshot on Dumaine Street, what happened at market, the attack on Each, and the fast approach of the closing of the District. Miss Eulalie had met Each once when her godson Ferdinand Lemothe, who had by then taken the moniker Jelly Roll Morton, brought him and a colored boy named Louis for an afternoon by the cool waters. Now she asked after him.

"I don't know much," Valentin admitted. "Last I heard he was in New York, gaining fame."

"And now there won't be any Storyville for him to come back to."

Valentin chose not to tell her that Mr. Jelly Roll, having tasted fame, wouldn't be coming back to New Orleans, even if the mansion parlors where he got his start could somehow be spared. In the silence that ensued, the voodoo woman gazed from face to face, sensing something else amiss, but deciding not to probe any further.

"Well," he said. "I have business in the city."

He said his good-byes. Justine walked him to the Ford and stood back with her arms crossed until he had cranked the engine and was about to drive off before saying, "I don't think this is wise. The man has been sent here to kill you."

"Maybe," he said. "But I won't let that happen."

"How are you going to stop him?" Her face hardened at his foolishness.

"By being careful."

"Just like you're being careful now?" He didn't have an answer and raised his hands, palms upward. "Well, go, then." She walked away, then stopped. "But come back."

Valentin saw her shoulders heave as she reached the bottom step and was about to call to her. But then she straightened, climbed the steps, and disappeared inside the house without turning around. As he drove off, he didn't look up to see her watching from a window.

TEN

Buddy had scrawled the first line on the front of an old envelope. He had been there for two years and the kind Negro attendant Baptiste urged him to put words to paper. Then and later, they were just what came into his head. Sometimes at night it helped to take the pencil from the drawer in the stand next to his bed and add a few words. Sometimes he would go back and erase what he had put down. He had unfolded and folded it so often that the page had frayed. Baptiste offered to get him a new sheet. He didn't reply and the attendant left him alone.

Now he opened the page as if making a paper flower bloom and read the words.

> *I am the one who does not speak*
> *Left with breath and beating heart*
> *Minutes, hours, days and weeks*
> *I play alone a lonely part*
>
> *Silence rides an empty wind*
> *My bleeding mouth, my bleeding hands*
> *Another empty day will end*
> *Where the silence of the night begins*
>
> *I still see shades from long ago*
> *My brother and I, made of air*
> *Listening to the last bell toll*
> *When we said our prayers*

I stand on one side of a lost river
And you are on the other
I can see you clear
But I can't reach you, my–

"You still writin' on that?"

Baptiste was standing with another patient, a mulatto who looked too young to be in that place. Young and scared, a bird trapped in a net.

"Mr. Bolden, this is Mr. Robinette. A new guest on the ward." He waved one of his big hands. "Mr. Bolden here, he been working on that one piece for a good long time. Some kind of a poem, I believe. But I ain't never seen it. He won't let me look. And that's all right."

Buddy listened to these words with a certain wonder. Sometimes the way people spoke sounded like music.

"Or maybe they be words to a song," Baptiste went on. "Mr. Bolden was a musician. Horn player in New Orleans. Some say the best there ever was. Better than Keppard, better than King Oliver, better than that Louis Armstrong. Or if not the best, for sure the loudest."

Buddy leaned forward as if hearing a story, riveted as he waited for the ending. It did not arrive, because Baptiste led the young man away. In the next moment, he heard the sound of glass breaking, but he knew there were no cracks in any panes, no shards on the floor, and no bloody fingers. It was inside his head.

He crossed to stand at the window. Very far away, the outline of the river gleamed, a silver thread. From somewhere in the clouds a humming sound grew.

Wasn't it always that he heard it before he saw it? That sound. It lifted and fell, getting louder until.

And then the moment came when he began to look, turning his head to the horizon in every direction, to the clear places above the trees. And then it was there, a tiny cross traveling across the whole of the sky.

Though he had seen it so many times before, he could not get his mind to grasp that there was a man up there. A single man in a fragile box of wood, cloth, and tin, alone in a vast blue sea. If some small thing happened, the box would tumble like a dying leaf and the man inside would not be saved, any more than a sailor who had fallen overboard and no one knew until it was too late and he was a speck in a green ocean that would carry him away and finally under. It was as lonely as... as lonely as being shut away inside of a room that was inside a building that was surrounded by a wall. Though it was safe.

The humming of the engine faded as it moved south. Following the river to New Orleans and then to where it almost ended in the wide gulf where a body might float forever, never to be seen again. And where an airplane might stutter and fail and drift down to and into those same waters, to sink like a stone into a deep and dark pond.

The bell tolled three-thirty.

Those still in the houses were up and about, along with the few dozen crib girls and mattress whores who had found a place to lay down for the night. Anyone passing along the banquettes saw sleepy, puzzled faces in the windows and noticed that the women who worked the streets staggered even more crookedly, as if they were lost.

For all its sin, Storyville had never required extraordinary policing, with a dozen coppers patrolling even at the busiest times. Now there were twice that number and in full view rather than whiling away the hours holed-up in some saloon or eatery. All had been ordered to stay alert for signs of trouble.

No one was in a rush to pack and be on to wherever. There was still time to do some business, after all. So no one took too much notice to the random comings-and-goings, such as the arrival of Bella Fine to Antonia Gonzales' front door.

Miss Gonzales, a *Cubana* who had managed a house on Basin Street for the better part of fifteen years, welcomed Miss Bella, who had managed seven girls in the Jew Quarter, to have a seat at heavy oak kitchen table. They spoke of nothing until Miss Antonia's girl Molly had hung up their wraps, poured coffee, laid out a tray of sweets, and left the room.

Then Miss Antonia hunched forward. "Are we just going to go away like this?"

"What else can we do?" Miss Bella said. "Even the mayor has given up. There's hardly anyone left."

"There's still what, a hundred women? It's not nothing. We can't stop it. But we can stand up one more time."

Miss Bella laughed in a droll way. "And the girls can lay down. Let them see what they'll be missing."

"That's what I mean. A celebration. Right here. But only for certain ladies. And special gentlemen." She smiled and winked. "Of course, we'll need some help."

"What help?" Miss Bella said.

Miss Antonia offered only a sly shrug and they returned to minor matters until Molly announced from the foyer that there was another caller and then stood aside to allow Miss Lulu White to pass.

After the sound of the Ford's engine faded, Justine stepped back onto the gallery to ponder what was happening to them. Why couldn't he have stayed? Or gone in to close the house and then come back to carry them farther away? So what if he promised? With or without him, Storyville would be deserted at the break of the next day. Who knew what kind of mayhem would ensue over the afternoon and night? What if he walked into something and she never saw him alive again? He was not quite the razor-sharp detective he had been ten years ago. And his investigation would not change anything before morning.

She found herself trembling and it was only the gentle voices of Evangeline and Miss Eulalie from the kitchen that drew her mind off her dark path. Better to spend the time on prayers for Each to recover. If she could only see *him* alive again. So that she might ask his forgiveness for drawing him so close as a child and letting him stay in the way of danger. And what of Evangeline? The fellow who had shot out their window, appeared at the market, and then attacked their friend would not stop. What if he found them there? That thought brought a small smile, thinking that he would do well to stay away from the three women under that roof.

Valentin drove to Mercy and found Mariette. She spoke up before he could ask. "No change. He comes up, then goes down, then settles again. He's fighting."

The detective sighed. "Of course, he is."

Mariette said, "James McKinney has been calling after you. He's at the precinct."

"Could you call him back, please? Tell him I'm here? I want to..." He gestured toward the bed.

"I will. Oh, something else. The administration office said they got a call. Someone asked to cover all the expenses."

"Who was it?"

Mariette shook her head. "He didn't leave a name." She left the point of that unspoken.

When he stepped outside, he found a police sedan waiting with the same two officers who had been on Dumaine Street before dawn.

"Lieutenant McKinney says we're to carry you to City Hall," the driver said. "He'll meet you there."

Mayor Behrman realized that for the last week he had been spending too much time staring out his wide window. In truth, he was in a state of despair, feeling himself a failure at having decided too late to have St. Cyr dive into the corruption that he suspected. Now he once again waved off his lunch, pleading no appetite, and sent Pettibone to fetch the Creole detective and Lieutenant McKinney back.

———

Valentin arrived and was met in the lobby by James and Mr. Pettibone. They rode the elevator to the fifth floor and Pettibone ushered them into the grand office and then left. Though Behrman was a hard case, having survived the city's wild political wars for two decades, Valentin always found him a mournful man. As it turned out, he had all the more reason to be so now.

"It's a terrible goddamn state of affairs," he muttered by way of greeting.

"Yes, it is," Valentin said.

"I heard about the boy," Behrman said. "How is he?"

Valentin said, "Still alive, but..."

"Major Sont told me the one who stabbed him is the same one who shot out your window."

"Yes, sir," Valentin said.

"And today." Behrman shook his head, then said, "The information will be here in the morning?"

"It's on the way," Valentin said.

"Will it be worthwhile?"

"My man says definitely."

The mayor ruminated in silence for a few moody seconds before saying, "Do you know what I went through to try and keep the District in business?"

Valentin again heard a question that did not require an answer and again stayed silent. He did recall most of it.

"I knew it was better controlled in one place than spread all over the city. I was on Mayor Flowers' staff and I convinced him to work with City Council on an ordinance. Mr. Story was especially helpful. He did most of the work drafting the document. And so he was honored by having it named for him."

"I don't believe he took it that way," Valentin said.

"No, he surely didn't. He was appalled. But so it went. We were lucky." After a pause, he said, "Tom Anderson was exactly the right person to run it. The madams of the mansions, Lulu White and those others, gave it true class." He spent some more time gazing at the streets below. "Twenty years. Another sixty before the ordinance and now they're closing it down. Shutting off a fountain of money. All because young men, young sailors, might want the affections of a woman before they go off to die."

"So they said."

The mayor pointed a finger. "Yes. But it didn't matter. They had that to hide behind and I couldn't stop them. I did everything I could, but it isn't enough."

He turned around to face his two visitors. "I know better than to expect a funeral. I just don't want a damn riot. It's on you two to get us through the night without any serious incidents." He looked directly at Valentin. "And yes, this other situation. If you corner this sonofabitch, I'll leave it up to you to resolve it. Understood?"

Valentin said, "Understood, Mr. Mayor."

Behrman said, "Lieutenant?"

"Yes, sir. Understood."

They waited for an elevator, listening to the groans and whirrs of the cables and gears. "Not often you have the mayor of a major city grant permission to shoot someone dead," Valentin said.

The noise stopped and the gilded doors opened. "But much appreciated," James said as they stepped into the car.

The lieutenant had business in the building to attend to and they separated when they reached the lobby with a plan to meet later.

Mr. Blank hired a car to return him to Dumaine Street. He was disappointed but not surprised to discover St. Cyr and his wife and the other woman gone. The detective had wasted no time in moving them away. Maybe there was time to find out where and maybe not. Valentin St. Cyr had led a lifetime of secrecy and yet was leaving himself exposed. It was just a matter of knowing where to search and who to pay. It didn't matter one way or another; there were still a dozen ways he could send messages to the detective to stop what he was doing. Whatever it was.

Studying the house, he noticed that the broken window had already been replaced and stood out against the dustier ones inside the frame. He entertained an urge to shoot it out again. But he was not inclined to such foolish moves that might draw attention. Not until the right moment arrived.

The light shifted behind the new pane in an odd way and he peered closer. Maybe the detective hadn't left after all, but had sent the women off and was now lying in wait. As he was pondering this, he caught a slip of movement between two houses on Lopez Street.

Mr. Valentin had been one of Eloi Marchand's customers for six months, and like any wise handyman, he kept his ears closed and eyes averted from his customers' private matters. Still, he couldn't completely ignore some of the comings-and-goings inside the house on Dumaine Street. The two men had something in common: both had been police officers at one time and had engaged in illegal business at another. He had served time in Angola. St. Cyr had not, instead finding his way into Tom Anderson's employ. Eloi made the wise choice to learn a trade while in prison and the even wiser choice to pursue it rather than go back to his criminal ways.

The detective recognized his value beyond hammers and saws and when Eloi shared his history, he asked him if he might be willing to add keeping a sharp eye on the property and the two women living there to his duties. He agreed instantly; they were kind ladies and he needed the money.

But he was not prepared for what happened that morning. Mr. Valentin called to explain in a few terse words and when he arrived at the house, he saw the damage for himself. He was pleased that the detective did not ask if the possible danger bothered him. He spent the next hours inside or near the house. He had heard the weeping, then voices arguing from the kitchen. Mr. Valentin took him onto the back gallery to tell him about Each. Sometime later, he carried the ladies' packed bags to the Ford and they rolled away. Mr. Valentin told him where they would be and had him memorize the phone number.

He had just finished replacing Mr. Valentin's crude repair of the smashed windowpane with new glass when he spotted the figure across the street. His prison yard antenna told him who was lurking there. The man might have been able to make out St. Cyr's silhouette in the dark before dawn, but now the sunlight was on the window and Eloi guessed that he would have been a blur at best.

He backed out of the room, grabbed up the hooked linoleum knife that he had honed just that morning and stole out to the back door. His hope was to come around from behind and catch the fellow unawares. He cut down the alley to Lopez Street and arrived on the corner of Dumaine.

He felt the stare fixed on him as soon as he stepped out. As if he'd been expected. So he went straight down the banquette.

The man could have run. Eloi knew that with his size and the brutal strength he broadcasted, he could be a frightening presence. But this one stood his ground long enough to let him get a good look at a paper-white face and flat eyes, bringing him up short for an instant. Something like a smile touched the man's hard mouth and his gaze shifted.

In the next moment, Eloi was cursing himself. He had fallen for an old dodge, turning his head just long enough to let the fellow make a sudden start and swift jag across the street, walking through traffic as if he was made of air. Horns blared and tires squealed and by the time Eloi got to the other side, there was no sign of the dark coat and homburg hat.

Just to be sure, he rounded the block, considering what he would have done had he gotten hold of the murdering bastard. Likely choked the life out of him or flayed the meat from his bones, right there on the corner.

He returned to the house, thankful that the women and Mr. Valentin were gone. Though he suspected that by now the detective was back in the city and on the hunt.

Valentin thought he was seeing a ghost when he turned the corner onto Bienville Street and saw a familiar figure coming his way.

She had aged as much in the year she'd been gone than in the five before. Her flesh had a gray tinge and her gait was halting. She had always prided herself on her dress, but she now wore a plain shift and instead of one of the gaudy wigs she had donned day and night, her hair was frizzy gray under a shapeless hat.

And yet her eyes were bright and her smile wide as she approached him and for a moment he thought she might begin weeping. He felt his own emotions rise. They had been friends and partners of a sort for the entire time he had been there. She had reigned as erstwhile queen to Tom Anderson's king. As she wrapped her arms around him, he considered that she had been and was Storyville, once-proud royalty reduced to shambles.

Still, he was puzzled at her showing up like that. "You came back," he said.

She released him. "I wanted to be here at the end. When I did get in, I almost turned around and left." Her eyes widened. "Then I find out about all the trouble. Each. That poor boy. How is he faring?"

Valentin said, "Holding on."

"What about Justine? And Miss...?"

"Evangeline. I moved them out beyond Spanish Fort."

"To Eulalie Echo's?" Valentin gave a bemused shake of his head. She hadn't lost her wits.

"So what can I do?" she said.

Valentin thought for a moment before saying, "Just keep your eyes and ears open. People might talk to you. Whatever you can find out might help."

He saw her hesitate. What he was asking would open some old wounds and they both knew it. But she said, "All right, Valentin."

Something else occurred to him. "Each. Maybe you can visit him in the hospital. If you'll be staying for a little while. And if he doesn't…"

Now she smiled, though sadly. "I can do that. What else?"

"Nothing I can think of at the moment," he said.

They arranged to meet later in the afternoon and he turned away, then turned back. "Wait," he said. "Tell me where you'll be."

Mr. Blank stepped onto the streetcar, huffing his relief at escaping the mulatto by dancing through the traffic. The big man would be no one to play with, charging at him with that look in his eye that announced that his next victim would not be his first. It was another close call, but Mr. Blank had to admit that it added spice to the game, something to make up for the senseless ploy of drawing it out. He had hoped to find the women at the house and take one or both. They were gone, hidden away, no doubt, but it wasn't a total loss; the mulatto would find St. Cyr and let him know that his territory had been breached again.

He gazed out the window at the dimming sky, as much to look somewhere other than at the other passengers in that crammed box as to follow the end of the day. It was his habit to avoid public transportation at any cost—and the public, too, for that matter. And wasn't this the proof of the matter? A mob of tired and dirty bodies half displaying their annoyance and the other half so gay it made him sick, so that a red mist crept over his brain. He stood rigid until it passed, though if he had his way, he would have thrown open the door and started heaving them out one by one until the car was empty.

Instead, he took it as long as he could and stepped down at Claiborne Avenue. Turning south, he walked at a deliberate pace until he reached St. Louis Cemetery No. 2. He hoped that the young man named Each would be adding to the number inside those whitewashed walls, the result of staying too close to Valentin St. Cyr.

Mr. Blank crossed to Robertson Street and the northeast border of the red-light district. The cribs were all empty, their doors slapping open. Parts of broken beds had been tossed into the street to mingle with the garbage that was being perused by a small army of rats. The only creatures in sight were another two haggard street whores staggering along, their brains rotted away on rye whiskey or canned heat or whatever diseases were raging in their veins. He knew he could draw his pistol and relieve them of the misery to come with a couple quick clicks of the trigger. But what did he care if they had agonizing deaths? They deserved no better.

He moved on to Villere Street, his eyes alert for any sign of St. Cyr or the cop McKinney. There was more work to do.

ELEVEN

Justine left the two older women in the house and walked west along the shoreline. She heard the distant drone of an engine and looked up to see wings glinting in the sun and recognized the mail plane flying from beyond the lake to the field at Seabrook.

Gazing across the flat green water, she pushed her thoughts to a calm place. With no sound save the lapping of the bare waves, the sweep of all that had happened in a few short hours overtook her. Indeed, a year's worth of trouble in one morning.

Her family was under attack and all she knew about it was what little Valentin had been willing to share. To protect her and Evangeline, he had said. The pale man had been sent to stop him from whatever he was doing. But what if he had it all wrong? It had happened before. What if *she* was the target? What if it was Evangeline? Was that possible?

She closed her eyes and cast her thoughts back over the years since she had escaped the bayou, leaving the cruel drama of her childhood behind. Then came her years on the road as a dancer in a traveling show, learning that there were other ways to make money. She recounted the short time between when she had arrived in Storyville and had met Valentin, even as her nights were nights spent entertaining one rich fellow or another. She could imagine nothing from those two years, either. Though who knew if she had wounded some mad character's pride enough to bring a horrible revenge on her?

And what of Evangeline? They knew nothing of the history that had led her to the convent with the iron angel over the gate where Valentin had found her. Both had suspicions, mostly unspoken. She knew he had let himself mull the possibility that she was the mother he had lost so long ago. Without ever using his skills to dig deeper. Or coming out and asking her.

There was no telling who she might have crossed or betrayed enough to want to terrorize and perhaps destroy her adopted family. There was her odd mention of the Orange Wars and the tragedy that had been inflicted on Valentin's family. So say it did have something to do with Evangeline and not Justine or her husband. But then how did the attack on poor Each, someone she had known only slightly, fit into that design? It made no sense.

She began walking again. She knew Valentin would be puzzling in earnest over these same questions while trying to keep a lid on whatever might boil over in Storyville come evening and then the darkness. The place would not die in silence; that, she knew. The noise would rise in a last revel and he'd be in midst of it.

She wondered where he was now. Him and the pale man who was hunting them.

Just as Valentin crossed over from the Quarter, he caught a glimpse of the man who had shot out his window, stabbed Each, and approached his wife and Evangeline.

He had been making rounds through the District, making mental notes of which houses had been vacated, which were in that process, and which showed no such activity, a statement of defiance. From what he could tell, half of the dozen standing firm had been run by madams he knew well enough for it to be no surprise. They were mounting a stage for a last show of some sort.

Musing on this, he turned the corner from St. Louis onto Liberty and caught a flash of motion behind him that seemed out of place. Over the years, he had developed a sense of being stalked and it was always the same, a feeling of someone closing on him in a certain way with a change in the light to go with it. So when he reached Orleans, instead of going straight, he made another quick turn and ducked into a walkway between two houses. A car passed on Rampart Street and in the silence that it left in its wake he heard a patter of footsteps. The man following him realized he had been tricked just a second too late, because he was still turning around to head back the way he had come when the detective took a quick step onto the banquette.

For Valentin, it was a fleeting glimpse of a gray coat, gloved hands, and one side of a very pale face, and he was not surprised when he reached the corner to see that the stalker had turned the tables and disappeared in kind.

Mr. Blank was in a cold, angry sweat as he passed through the watchmaker's and into the courtyard behind. It was his luck that the front door had been open, even though the shop was not. The owner, who had just arrived, turned in astonishment and did not managed to get the words "Sorry, closed" out of his mouth when the specter was in the front and out the back. He hurried outside to find the courtyard empty.

Because Mr. Blank had found one of New Orleans' passageways between two buildings so narrow that he barely could fit. He arrived on Royal Street and peeked around the bricks before making a move. That St. Cyr was not in sight did not mean he was gone. Now he wished he had put a bullet through the detective's chest, even though that was not the plan he was being paid to follow.

He dropped a hand and patted the pocket where his pistol rested. St. Cyr would be armed with the Iver Johnson .32 he was known for, along with the stiletto he strapped to his ankle and the whalebone sap he tucked in his back pocket.

For the second time in as many hours, Mr. Blank cursed over finding himself on the edge of being cornered. He could finish it the next chance he got. And even more importantly, before St. Cyr did it to him. What if that game was already in motion? What if the stranger in the café that morning was after him? His instructions had been clear: threaten and torment St. Cyr until the end of the night. Stop him on way or another or there would be no more payment. Now he decided that whatever happened, he would not be the dead one come the dawn.

Tom Anderson still read his *Times-Picayune* every morning without fail and so he knew all the details of the closing of Storyville, the place he had all but created. He noted that the mayor had gone silent after months of using news stories and editorials to rally support for keeping the District alive. But he had not offered a word on the subject for the last three days and Mr. Tom understood this to be the death knell.

The same reporters—and the one named Vernel, in particular— had called to badger *him* for quotes.

He had refused. It was ending and there was nothing more to say. He had not traveled on Basin Street in over a year, but he heard the reports of how it was crumbling away, as if it had been made of nothing but sand and straw all along.

As the final day approached, he had considered leaving the city, perhaps to somewhere on the Gulf where he could rest his bones on a gallery for a week or so and look out on the shifting tides while he pondered his life and God's universe.

He chose to stay. He thought he might attend morning and evening mass at St. Ignatius in his ongoing quest to wash away his sins. Of course, his church and a dozen others around the city had made millions off the properties they owned, some of which operated as houses of sin. So who were they to offer forgiveness?

He decided to remain secluded in his house on Annunciation Street, not quite admitting to himself that he did want to witness the final moments. He did not count on the interruption from Lucy after she answered the phone and spoke in a whisper to the caller.

She appeared in the parlor doorway. "That was your fellow at the police department."

"What did he want?" Mr. Tom had never spoken the spy's name and she had never asked.

"Someone shot out a window at Mr. Valentin's house this morning." He stared at her. "Is everyone all right?"

"He didn't say otherwise, so I suspect so." She hesitated. "But..."

"But what?"

"He said there was an attack on Basin Street. At that saloon. Fewclothes. The fellow is fighting for his life at Mercy."

"Who was it?"

"The one they call Each. St. Cyr's man. He's been here at the house. The last time when they—"

"My God," Mr. Tom said. "What happened?"

"He was stabbed. Right out front. So the officer said."

The old man sank back in his chair, forcing his slowing mind into gear. It didn't require too much in the way of wits to understand that the two events were connected—and that there would be more to come. What a fool he and everyone else had been to think that the red-light district would simply go off to sleep! He had always imagined that there would be a final drama and this, he feared, was it.

The thought stirred his bones and quickened his blood and he roused himself. "Please call the precinct and ask someone to find Lieutenant McKinney." He paused. "And see if you can locate Mr. Valentin, too."

J. Picot stepped from the train to the platform and stood wondering why he had just taken a seven-hour ride on the basis of one strange phone call. The voice had said that he was needed. That there was an important job for him to do. There would a reward. It had been enough and there he stood.

Peering across the tracks at a mostly quiet Basin Street, he understood that he had let his excitement get the better of him. He also did not know what would be waiting. A cloud might still be over him. Or worse, a warrant that had been unserved when he escaped the city. And yet the dark voice on the phone was as alluring as some lewd harlot's.

Riders, railroad employees, and street arabs were passing this way and that. None took notice of J. Picot. Had they forgotten so soon that he had been a person to fear, a police captain who set his own rules and the "law" be damned? He had been able to inspire fear just by walking by. He had been *someone* then—someone who commanded notice. Now, as he stood in the midst of the milling bodies, he was just another heavyset fellow in an old brown coat and dusty tan bowler. A nobody, in other words.

He decided that this could be his cover. As far as anyone was concerned, he was gone forever. And on the off-chance that someone recognized him, he could just fade away before any trouble reached him. Finally, if he was being set up with the phone call business, well, he had some cunning of his own.

He left the station and crossed the tracks to stand before what had been Anderson's Café, taking grim pleasure in the clearest sign that the District was on its deathbed. So where was Mr. Tom now? Or Lulu White? And what of those bastards St. Cyr and McKinney? He did hope that he would cross their paths.

He began a slow stroll, wondering if he might yet extract his revenge from one or more of them before the next morning arrived.

The sun was going down when Valentin stepped into the hardware store on Canal Street where they knew him to use the telephone. He called Parish Precinct, left a message for James McKinney and then made a hurried walk to Mangetta's, casting an eye over his shoulder. Though it was unlikely that there would be trouble so soon after such a close call. The smart move would be to dive for cover and wait for another chance.

He arrived on Marais Street to find the grocery doing slow business. Frank waved a hand, jerked his head toward the saloon, and said, "Somebody waiting for you."

Reynard Vernel was seated at one of the round tables, his moody gaze directed at nothing. He looked up when Valentin approached.

"How did you know I'd be here?" the detective said.

"I didn't," the reporter said. "I just figured you would be sooner or later. And I didn't want to be hanging around the newsroom anyway." He waited as Valentin pulled out a chair and sat down. "Poor Each. How is he?"

"Alive, the last I heard," Valentin said. A quiet moment passed. "Are you going to write a story about this?"

"I am. I've already been to Fewclothes. I got nothing. No surprise. But so you know, nothing will run until the evening paper tomorrow."

"You're waiting to see if he's going to make it or not."

"Yes," the reporter said. "And whatever happens, I don't want the story lost in all the print about the District closing. He deserves better." He paused. "Will Lieutenant McKinney be coming by?"

"In a little while." Valentin saw Reynard hesitate and said, "Go ahead. It's all right."

A pad and pen appeared. "How long have you known him?" he asked.

Valentin smiled and said, "Since he was quite young,"

The questions about the attack were general. Still, Valentin was relieved when they ended. Carmine appeared with a plate of sliced meats, cheeses, and a crusty loaf of Italian bread. After he left, the proprietor stepped back into the saloon and moved behind the bar for a bottle and three short glasses.

"I'll need to call in my notes," the reporter said after nibbling an olive and the heel of the loaf. He stood up and walked into the hallway, carrying his glass with him. He was back in five minutes and James appeared a few minutes after that. Frank poured him a glass and he sat down to answer the reporter's perfunctory questions. No one wanted to dwell on Each.

When they finished and Reynard was closing his notebook, he caught the flick of a glance that passed between Mr. Valentin and the policeman.

"Do I need to leave?" he said.

Valentin said, "Not as long as you keep anything we say out of the paper."

"Not a word."

The detective proceeded to tell them about the close call with the same fellow sent to wreak havoc on his life. James asked for a description.

"That would be what he *didn't* look like," Valentin said. "Tall. Pale. Thin. His face was like a plaster mask. He wore a grey paddock coat and a black homburg. The same as what Justine saw."

"Sounds like a spook of some sort," Vernel said.

"That's a good way to describe him," Valentin said. "He'd scare a child."

He didn't have any more to offer and James said, "It's something."

They sipped in silence. Frank got up and stepped out to check on the grocery. The reporter said, "How will you two be spending the rest of the night?"

The lieutenant spoke up. "I'll be moving around the District and placing patrolmen where they'll do the most good. And hoping we get through the night without any major trouble."

"Mr. Valentin?"

"I'll be with the lieutenant and I'll have a few of my people out." He felt a rueful twinge at the thought that it would be the first time in as long as he could recall that Each would not be with them. "Other than that, I'll be working hard not to be the next victim."

A few minutes later, Frank poked his head into the doorway to tell the lieutenant that he had a phone call from the precinct. The officer got up and then reappeared wearing a crooked smile.

"Somebody just spotted that sonofabitch Picot."

"I guess we should have known," Valentin said. "Where was he?"

———

J. Picot had lasted all of ten minutes before two low-down rounders passed him on Franklin Street and in their wake he heard one of them say, "Did you see who that was? Fucking Captain...what was his name? You know..."

They stopped. He kept on, his head down and shoulders hunched, breathing angry curses. *Well, so be it.* Nothing he could do now. Still, there was no point in taking chances. Maybe someone would be out to get him or maybe it was all forgotten, at least for this day. He made his way to Canal Street and the telegraph office with the phone booths.

The clerk answered and he asked for Sergeant Maris, giving the false name that had always been their private signal. "Tell him it's Willard Ross."

When Maris came on the line, Picot could hear the surprise in his voice. "Jesus Christ Almighty. Is it really you?"

"It's me, Jack."

"How long has it been?"

"A while. Over two years."

"Where are you?"

"Less than a half-mile away." The captain read the stunned silence. "Yes. I came back. Can we meet?"

The sergeant said, "What? All right. Same place?"

"Same place. A half-hour?"

"Yes, all right." Picot replaced the handset.

Back on the banquette, he wondered if he should be worrying about Maris running to some officer to announce that J. Picot was in New Orleans and ready to be snatched up for certain prior crimes. Let them try. He figured he still knew enough to sink half the officers of the New Orleans Police Department.

Frank had taught Carmine to cook and though he had decided to close for the night, the stove and oven in back were pressed into service.

"You maybe be out all night, eh? Eat now and you don't have to worry about it no more."

Valentin and the lieutenant didn't bother to argue. The Sicilian was already calling instructions to Carmine. Reynard went out to file the rest of his story. Ten minutes after he stepped back into the saloon, plates of pasta with a red sauce were placed under their noses.

The reporter let out a little groan. James breathed it in, closed his eyes, and sighed. "What do you dagos say? *Che...*"

"*Che bella.*" Valentin lifted his fork. It was a moment of simple pleasure amidst all the mayhem. Who knew when one would come again?

The clouds rolled across the twilight sky, carried by a gray wind and the clock on the wall told Buddy that it was his time to be out on the grounds. So he pulled his old coat over his robe, wrapped a scarf around his neck, and waited with the others until Baptiste arrived to turn the key in the lock.

Six of the thirteen men moved off in two groups of three. The rest fanned out on their own lonely paths, getting as far from each other as they could while still staying in sight of the attendant. If they wandered too far, he would call gently. "Mr. Kelly? Mr. Bolden? Come back this way, please."

The chill on this evening kept them close to the building, where the breezes were gentler. Still, the legs of their pajamas rippled. Buddy didn't feel the cold; his eyes and his brain were focused on the fellow they called "Big Kenny," who was watching him from a hundred paces across the grass. The attendant walking with the large man noticed the stare and pointed it out to Baptiste by gesture.

Baptiste walked over to Buddy and said, "You doing all right, sir?" The patient of course didn't answer so Baptiste said, "Do you know that gentleman? He's looking this way like he recognizes you."

Someone observing this would question why Baptiste spoke to the patient at all, since there was no visible response. But time and patience had brought minute reactions, as if they were talking together by way of notes that were just barely above silent. Like at this moment, when the patient moved a half-inch one way and then the other. *No, sir, do not know the man.*

The attendant looked at his watch. "All right, then, let's get everyone out of the cold." As he herded his wards inside, he glanced over his shoulder to see Big Kenny now staring at Mr. Bolden's retreating figure.

Justine arrived back at the house a few minutes shy of five. The miles she had walked up and down the shoreline had not dispelled her tense mood. Evangeline and Miss Eulalie saw only the flush from a brisk pace on her cheeks.

"We thought you had decided to float down Bayou St. John," the voodoo woman said.

"Why would I do that?" Justine said.

Evangeline treated her to wise eyes. "I can't imagine."

Miss Echo said, "We'll be starting on dinner. I believe Miss Evangeline has some skills in the kitchen."

"Yes, she does," Justine said.

"It will be ready in an hour or so," Miss Eulalie said.

"Then I'm going to lay down for a bit."

They began talking about favorite recipes and did not hear Justine opening one of the kitchen drawers. She stepped into the bedroom and closed the door behind her. An hour would give her all the time she needed.

They had finished their meal and were planning out the details of the night when Carmine beckoned to Valentin and mimed raising a telephone to his ear. The detective left to take the call and was back in a few minutes. "That was Eloi," he said.

Frank said, "*Qui?*"

"He does work around the house and watches the place." Valentin looked over at the lieutenant. "Our friend paid a visit. Eloi tried to corner him, but he got away."

Reynard said, "And he was there why?"

"To let me know that he could do it," Valentin said. "Another warning."

A few minutes after six o'clock, Patrick Geary walked into Union Station in Washington, DC with two men in tight-fitting coats and bowlers, one short, the other tall, but both solidly-built and stony-eyed. Geary, though the smallest of the three, broadcast the same no-nonsense posture to any trifling fool or loose-lipped drummer who might try to engage him.

He handed a thin satchel to the shorter of his two companions and stood by while they climbed aboard the Seaboard Express headed southbound. He saw no sign of anyone tracking them. The whistle blew and the engine chugged and the cars began to move. Once it had left the station, Geary walked to the Western Union office, stepped into a booth, and dialed the number for Mangetta's Grocery and Saloon in New Orleans.

Darkness had fallen and it was time to move. By the still-quiet street outside, the District remained in a state of calm.

Valentin, James, and Reynard stood on the banquette outside the saloon. Valentin peered south and then north and then smiled.

The lieutenant noticed and said, "What?"

"I think it's going to be starting soon," Valentin said.

"How do you know?" Reynard said.

"Just a feeling, is all." He didn't want to explain again that after ten years, Storyville was part of him, all the way down to his bones. As it had been for Tom Anderson. The difference was that Anderson was gone and he was still there and sensing the shift in the air that told him trouble was brewing somewhere in that twenty-block square.

Reynard waited to see to see if there was more. He looked to the lieutenant, who produced a smile of his own and a slight shake of his head.

"I'm going back to the newsroom," the reporter said. "Then I'll come find you." He glanced between the two other men. "If it's all right, I mean."

Valentin said, "We'll be pleased to have your company."

"Well, then..." Reynard waved and walked away.

"You have something you want to tell me?" James said.

"He's in the District," Valentin said. "And he's waiting."

TWELVE

Justine had found paper and a pen in the side table drawer and wrote a quick note. *Gone to the city to help Valentin. Sorry to miss dinner. I will call later.*

She waited until the two older women were deep into preparing the meal, talking and laughing and banging pans. The window sash rose with only a minor squeak and she crawled out onto the back gallery. She crept down the steps to Miss Eulalie's garden and then made a quick trot into the falling shadows, hoisting the hem of her day dress.

She was wearing her brogans and had been prepared to walk the four miles to the end of the Carrolton line. But after ten minutes, she reached the fourth house down from Miss Eulalie's and came upon a dapper young man who had just closed the gleaming hood of a blue roadster and was wiping his hands on a rag. He caught sight of her with surprise that turned into an enchanted stare.

"Well, hello!" he said, once he found his voice.

"Hello." She came up with a pretty pant that lifted her bosom. "My, that's a beautiful machine." He didn't answer, instead producing a dizzy smile. She had seen that look before. "What is it?" she breathed.

"What?" He came to his senses. "It's a Mitchell. Baby Four."

She now delivered her best vexed frown. "I'm sorry to bother you. But I was wondering..."

The young fellow swallowed. "Yes?"

"My ride back to the city didn't come for me. Would it be possible for you to—"

"Carry you someplace?" He became animated. "Well, of course. Yes, ma'am. I'd be pleased."

"Are you sure?" She took an inviting step closer. "Only to the streetcar stop."

She could tell that he couldn't believe his luck. "Anywhere!" he almost shouted. "Anywhere you need to go."

"Oh, you are too kind," she said and extended her hand. "My name is Charlotte."

Baptiste showed another kindness to Buddy by allowing him to take his meals at a table in the corner of the veranda when the weather was pleasant and in his room when it was poor, instead of in the raucous Colored dining room, where madmen babbled and shouted, and sometimes ran amok. This was only possible because his superior loved New Orleans and knew of Buddy Bolden—or the man he had once been.

He followed Buddy outside and got him settled. "Gets dark earlier every day," he said.

Buddy hiked an eyebrow at the inane comment, then turned his head to survey the grounds with his calm black gaze. Baptiste caught something, a sense that he wanted to speak. It had happened a dozen times before and now as then, the words didn't sound.

The attendant studied his charge for a moment before saying, "I'll be back to collect you, so don't you be wandering off nowhere," and stepping inside.

Silence returned. Buddy had heard the words. He heard everything, and often times what no one else did: blue notes, rolling percussion, drumbeats, strings played with bows. It made him smile.

He ate without tasting much, but he knew that if he didn't clean his plate, he'd hear about it from Mr. Baptiste. The chicken was dry and bland. The rice middling. The sweet potatoes were nice.

He caught movement and turned to see the big man edging along beneath the oaks that had lost most of their leaves, an attendant following behind. It was shackles that made him walk like that. Shackles for a dangerous man. For a killer.

As Buddy watched, the big man man turned to look back at him. He was too far away to read the eyes, but he could feel them. Sometimes the things he felt were wisps. But not now. The stare was sending him a message.

The fellow who drove her—he introduced himself as Howard—chatted merrily all the way to Paris Avenue and then along Galvez with repeated slides of what he must have thought were flirtatious eyes. He either didn't notice her wedding ring or didn't care. She noticed the band of white on his left hand which told her that at some point he had made his own ring disappear.

She gave it no more thought. They were deceiving each other. She ignored him. As they rode along, she began to feel shame washing over her at the way she had been avoiding thoughts of Each. Why wasn't she more worried about him? He had been a silly boy who had ambled into her heart as he ambled everywhere, with clumsy motions and always looking to please. She had feared for him when he got older and began doing riskier tasks for Valentin. He had the nerve but not the hard cool for rough business. She had raised these fears to her husband. He shrugged and said it was up to Each and he would be crushed if sent away. She was at least mollified that Valentin would be looking out for him.

It wasn't enough and now he was lying too close to death in Mercy Hospital. Maybe he would be the next person close to her to go away. And that was why she hadn't been pacing through the hours. It wasn't—

"You all right, Charlotte?"

She came out of her daze. "Yes. I'm fine. Fine."

"Because you look troubled."

She shook her head. He shifted in his seat and shot another glance her way. She understood; they were getting close and he hadn't yet made any headway with her. So she wasn't surprised when they reached

Esplanade and she asked him to stop, he cleared his throat and said, "Say, then, I can wait here for you to finish your business. Carry you to wherever you like after."

She saw the hungry eyes and knew that the next words out of his mouth would be an invitation to dine. Before he could deliver his line, she opened her door, said, "Thank you, but I'm meeting my husband," and stepped down and walked away.

He wasn't ready to give up, putting the machine in gear and creeping along to match her pace. "You know it's not safe around here."

"I'm sure I'll be all right," she said. "And your family must be wondering where you are."

She walked on. The Mitchell stopped. Ten seconds later, it went whizzing by and on down Derbigny Street and she crossed over into Storyville.

Hard as she tried, Lucy found that there was no talking Mr. Tom out of going to the District. It was even more vexing because he was unclear about where he was heading and what he would do once he got there. She could boss him in certain ways but it was clear as the afternoon wore on that this was not one of them. Her protests grew weaker.

At six-thirty, with the last of the cold sunlight having dropped behind the trees, he told her he was ready to go.

"I need to know where you'll be," she said.

"I told you I don't know quite yet," he said. "I will know when I get there. Call Louis."

"I'm calling George, too. We gonna need some help getting you into that machine. He can go along."

"Who? George?" The old man snorted. "I don't need him down there. Louis and I will do quite well without him, thank you."

She opened her mouth with a retort, but he glared at her with those gimlet eyes. Still, she wasn't pleased and stood with her fists on her hips and her mighty bosom heaving for a long second before turning away to find George and Louis the driver to get ready for a fool's errand.

From the day that Buddy Bolden had gone away, Valentin made sure that the hospital outside Jackson knew how to reach him at home or by leaving a message at Mangetta's or with James McKinney. Every now and then, he reflected on the moment when the call would come that Buddy had either sunk down so deep he was beyond reach or had died.

And so when Carmine came running with a message from Mr. Frank about a call from Jackson, he made his way back to Marais Street, dreading every step. It was more than likely bad news. Probably dire, or why else call at seven o'clock in the evening? Could his luck be so poor as to pile another tragedy on this of all nights?

When he reached the saloon, Frank handed him the number for the evening supervisor, Mr. Keeton.

Five minutes passed before the supervisor came on the line. "Mr. St. Cyr?" He spoke the name the American way, *saint-sear.*

Valentin said, "Is he gone?"

"Gone?" Mr. Keeton said. "Do you mean dead? Oh, no, sir. He's alive. But he's had a bad time, I'm afraid."

"Why is that?"

"There was an incident, sir. Our man Baptiste said you would want to know about it."

Frank was waiting and Valentin leaned on the bar to relate what the supervisor had told him.

Buddy had been doing what he did after dinner—and after breakfast and lunch, for that matter—pacing the hallways in his white hospital robe and slippers, touch some fixture or surface before moving on to the next, occasionally stopping to gaze out a window.

Baptiste was working an extra shift to cover another staff member. This was fortunate, as it was Baptiste who noticed that he was missing from his rounds up and down the corridor.

He walked all the way to the stairwell and was startled to find the door had been unlocked, so that any patient could have pushed it open and descended the steps to the first floor.

He stepped onto the landing and was about to call out, "Mr. Bolden, sir?" when he heard the sounds of a scuffle. He looked over the railing to see an attendant named Marles lying half-conscious and groaning on the landing below. From the next landing down came a rude shout.

Baptiste didn't stop to check on Marles, instead flying down the two sets of stairs to find Big Kenny, the man who had murdered the former New Orleans chief of police, holding Bolden against the wall and trying to choke him by pulling the chain of the handcuffs that were still on his wrists across his windpipe as Buddy struggled to fight him off.

Baptiste was half a head shorter than the murderer but carried the same weight, and he grabbed the chain that was around the big man's waist and spun him with a rough jerk. With the shackles on his ankles, Mullens couldn't keep his balance and tumbled backward down the first five steps. He was trying to rise when the attendant reached him with the sap that he carried at all times. With one sharp snap to the base of his skull, Big Kenny's eyes rolled up and he was still.

By this time, more had heard the commotion and two other attendants came down the stairs and converged on the supine body. Baptiste straightened and climbed back to the landing above.

"Mr. Bolden, sir. Are you all right?"

Buddy smiled a small smile and nodded his head.

"Wait," Frank said. "He *smiled*? Didn't they say he nev—"

"That's what the man told me," Valentin said. "I'm shocked, too."

The Sicilian was confounded. "This was the same fellow killed the Chief."

"Yes, him."

"But how did he get free to go after Buddy?" Frank said.

"How? Someone helped him, that's how."

"And why the hell did he want to hurt him, of all people?" The saloonkeeper had known Buddy for years and his little band had been a Saturday night feature at one time.

"The same reason Each was attacked. And our window was shot out. To warn me off."

Frank scratched his chin in puzzlement. "And tonight, this happens."

"It's their last chance." He paused to regard his godfather's kind face. "You need to be careful, *zio*. You see what's happening."

They pondered in silence. Then Frank said, "A sap, eh?"

"I'm not the only person who carries one," Valentin said.

Mr. Blank had instructions to call the man he knew only as Mr. Smith— oh, how clever!—at intervals throughout the day and night until dawn arrived. He reached the lobby of the hotel by way of the side door, and after a quick scan, stopped to whisper the number to the clerk at the desk, then stepped into one of the phone booths. It required all of twenty seconds.

As before, there was next to nothing from the other end, mostly because Mr. Smith seemed to be one step ahead, a sign that he might have eyes on him, even as he stalked St. Cyr. He recalled the man at the diner with the glaring eyes, wondering if he was Smith's way of telling him he best not fail.

"The first one is in the hospital and not at the morgue, is that correct?"

"That's what I know at this time, he could be—"

"Because murder was not in your instructions." He paused to let that sink in. "Now what about the others?"

"I've paid them visits."

"Is the house still standing?"

"It is, yes."

"Is there any sign he's in retreat?"

"I don't know." Mr. Blank decided he needed to turn the tables just a bit. "What about Jackson?"

Mr. Smith said, "He did as he was told. Someone came along and took him out of the picture."

"Dead?"

"Oh, no. But he's locked down."

"Do you think that St. Cyr has heard about it yet?"

"If not, he will soon enough," Mr. Smith said in his usual empty tone. "So you'll be going on to the next steps. And we'll be expecting results."

"Yes, sir," Mr. Blank said. "I'm about to make—"

The line went dead. Mr. Blank placed the handset on the hook, understanding that eyes would be on him from this point forward.

Evangeline went to fetch Justine for dinner and came back holding the slip of paper. Miss Echo studied her face for a few seconds. "She's gone."

Evangeline handed her the note and the voodoo woman spent a moment reading the carefully-printed words.

"What should we do now?" Evangeline said.

"Now? Now we sit down and eat dinner."

"What about after?"

Lulu White had accepted Miss Antonia's gracious offer of a room for the night. It wouldn't be her suite in Mahogany Hall—there would never again be a suite in Mahogany Hall—but it would serve. Once she was settled, she joined the madam in her parlor.

"You expecting any visitors?"

Miss Antonia poured brandy. "I am, yes. We had a half-dozen in this afternoon. There will be more looking for one last go." She regarded Miss Lulu over her glass. "What are your plans for the evening?"

"My plans?" Miss Lulu's expression was impish. "My plans are to play queen again."

Thirteen

With the night, J. Picot felt it was safe for him to venture from the back gallery of Jack Maris' house and onto Jena Street. The sergeant had not offered him a key, so he sat in a chair, listening to the evening birds and the sad horns of the freighters plying downriver. It did not escape him that he had once managed chunks of the seamier operations of the city, and now he was skulking about like some petty thief and even a former subordinate did not trust him on the premises. His glory days had ended, all because of that dago nigger sonofabitch St. Cyr.

He looked at his watch a dozen times until the hands reached seven-thirty and then started walking north, crossing St. Charles and covering more blocks to the corner of Liberty Street and the saloon where he and Maris had agreed no one would know him. He wasn't so sure; the name of the narrow thoroughfare niggled at the back of his mind from something long ago.

The sergeant was waiting in a corner booth with a glass of Raleigh Rye before him and one on the other side. Picot caught the look of surprise on Maris' face when the door closed and he crossed the room. Never a tidy or fit man, he had allowed his hygiene and health to suffer further, waddling to the table, sweating in spite of the cool weather, his mud-colored eyes almost lost in the folds of added fat. He thought about waving a hand, turning back, and forgetting about the whole business. The notion passed and he slid into the booth with a wheeze of relief.

He hated sitting with his back to a door, but this was an exception. As to the liquor, he had never been much of drinker, and barely sipped while they talked.

"So, Captain," the policeman began. "Where have you been hiding?"

"I haven't been *hiding*," Picot said, though of course that was exactly what he'd been doing.

Maris shrugged. "Well, then, where have you been staying?"

"Here and there," Picot said. There was no reason he could think of to keep the information from the sergeant, but he hadn't shaken his habit of not sharing anything with anyone. Though he did consider having someone know about the phone call and the invitation to return would be insurance.

Before he could finish the thought, the sergeant said, "So you decided to come back. Today."

This brought a bland wave of a hand. "I wanted to be here to witness the end of it all."

"Is that so?" Maris said. "Well, I don't know that there will be much to witness."

Picot smirked. "Oh, I think there will be. Yes, I do."

Maris thought that the captain looked quite sure of himself and was about to probe him further when Picot said, "So what's the news, Jack? What do you know about the goings-on that I don't?"

The sergeant said, "Well, you remember that fellow they called Each? St. Cyr's man in the District?"

"He used to go by Beansoup."

"That's right."

Picot's eyes narrowed. "What about him?"

Valentin left the District to make the rounds of the hotels on Canal Street and the Quarter. He was known at all of them and by most of the clerks. Because he had a reputation for allowing private matters to stay that way and because he paid well for information that turned out to be valuable.

The Crescent on Decatur was his seventh stop and he crossed the lobby to speak to a Creole bellboy who went by "Do'" for doughboy. He had travelled to France with the AEF, served a year, and came back wounded, though not enough to keep him from resuming his old job. If there was dope to be had, Do' had it. His green eyes narrowed and his mouth twisted in a smile when Valentin asked who was on duty at the desk and if he might get a look at the register.

"Who you lookin' for, Mr. Valentin?"

"I don't know. I might if I saw a name."

The bellboy grimaced. "This have anything to do with what happened to Each?"

"It does, yes."

"Well, then..." He jerked his head. Valentin followed him to the front desk where he asked one of the clerks for the register, handing him one of the two Liberty halfs that the detective had slipped him.

It required all of thirty seconds for Valentin to plant his index finger on an entry. Do' peered at the signature. "Mr. Blank," he said. "Now, that ain't suspect at all. Not one bit."

Valentin asked who had been on duty that morning. "That would have been Mr. Joseph," Do' said.

"I need to speak to him." Valentin looked his watch. "You know Mangetta's?"

The bellboy rolled his eyes. "Who don't know Mangetta's?"

"I'll be there by eight. He can come around that time."

"I'll make sure he does that," Do said. Then: "Mr. Valentin? Each gonna be okay? Is there anything I can do for him?"

"I'll let you know," Valentin said. "Now I need to have a look at Mr. Blank's room."

"You know just because ain't nobody seen him don't mean he ain't up there," Do' said.

"I hope to hell he is." Valentin saw that Do' was nervous. "It'll be fine," he said.

The bellboy did not appear convinced, but he said, "I'll get a key."

J. Picot had listened without saying a word until the sergeant finished relating what had happened at Fewclothes.

"So he's in the hospital. Still alive, last I heard. He might die, though. And whoever did it ain't been caught."

The notion to tell Maris his suspicions about the incident crossed Picot's mind, then went away. He said, "So St. Cyr is on the streets tonight?"

"With Lieutenant McKinney and a dozen or so patrolmen. There's more on call in case something gets out of hand."

"Are you one of them?"

"I'm on a shift at the precinct. Eight to eight. I'll go over if they need me."

Picot took a small sip of his whiskey and sat back, falling into the pose of cunning command that he had employed throughout his years on the force. When cunning didn't work, he would use threats of force or the real thing. He no longer had that authority at his disposal, but no matter; Maris would gobble the right bait.

Eyeing him, he said, "How would you like to come out of this evening a hero?"

Maris blinked. "How's that, Captain?"

For the briefest instant, Picot wondered if he was being played right back with the mention of his former rank. But the sergeant didn't have the wiles. He decided at that moment, that he needed someone to back him. He said, "By helping me."

Sergeant Maris smiled and leaned closer.

Justine was lucky that she saw the man in the gray coat before he spotted her. She had made her way through the District and was moving along Conti Street, keeping close to storefronts and bordellos and out of the growing foot traffic. Though she kept her head bent, she still managed to peek from beneath the brim of her hat. And so as she approached

Franklin, she caught sight of the figure she had seen that morning, a stark profile she couldn't mistake.

She had learned from Valentin to glide to a stop rather than draw attention by pulling up in sudden motion and did that now, slipping into the shadows of the gallery of a closed and shuttered house.

Watching him, he reminded her as nothing so much as one of the hawks she remembered from back on the bayou, the kites and harriers and ospreys perched as still as a rock except for the small movements of their heads and the piercing eyes that she could feel rather than see, even when they weren't fixed on her.

Moving at this point would only alert him and he would recognize her. It would not be difficult for him to commit an assault away from the dim streetlights and with so many people milling about, all of them caught up in their revelry. So she stood still as she let her hand drift into her bag and clutch the knife she had taken from the kitchen drawer when the two older women weren't paying attention. For the next three minutes, she stayed that way, still and silent and waiting.

Mr. Blank had been lingering on the corner, casting his furtive glances about when the feeling of being watched came upon him. It was not some fancy; he had learned to be on alert at all times and believed he could tune in to sights and sounds and sensations as if there was a radio antenna lodged in his brain. But now darkness had fallen casting shade in an already-shadowy place. And no one was standing still enough to hold a stare on him. So he shifted his eyes this way and that, trying to locate who it was stalking the stalker. The thought that it was St. Cyr brought a slight tremble. The detective could finish him before he could react. Had the lieutenant he traveled with found him and already given a signal that would bring coppers to surround him? Or was it just one of the odd characters who populated the District gazing at the one person who wasn't moving?

It was now a game to find out who would make the first motion.

———

Justine knew she couldn't just hide there. The man was a statue, and for all she knew, he could stay that way for hours. A few edgy minutes had passed as she cast about for an escape when she heard a ruckus from down the street. A hack loaded with furniture from one of the houses was approaching, the nag's hooves clopping on the cobblestones and the driver and his helper talking back and forth in loud, drunken voices.

The hack drew closer and when it rounded the corner, she saw her chance, moving out of the shadow and walking alongside the horse, careful to keep herself aligned with the animal's forequarters before making a quick shift to a few feet in front of it. The two men in the wagon stopped their chatter for a second, then resumed just as loud as before.

At the corner of Iberville, she made a quick jag to the middle of the avenue, keeping close to the other pedestrians until she reached Basin Street. She stopped to catch her breath and peer back the way she had come. A stark figure stood in the middle of the intersection, staring her way with a gaze so hard she could feel it. She reached the banquette and disappeared from his sight, feeling the thrill of the escape tingling her nerves.

Mr. Blank turned at the clatter of hooves and wheels, thinking that the sudden racket might flush out whoever had eyes on him. But when the wagon passed, he saw nothing else moving; or so he thought until he gazed at the retreating hack and noticed feet in front of the horse. He knew instantly who it was and hurried to follow, only to see her make a sharp turn at the next intersection. By the time he reached the end of the block, she was on Basin Street. After a long gaze cast his way, she disappeared. Feeling his stomach churn, he stalked after her.

———

Lulu White was standing at one of the tall windows that faced Basin Street, watching as the hacks and carts and automobiles crept this way and that, all laden with chests and odd items of furniture. A Model T passed with the neck of a bass fiddle sticking out one of the rear windows and the sight cast her back to a time when the driver wouldn't be leaving, but heading out for one of the dancehalls to play rowdy music—once *jass*, now *jazz*—the whole night through and into a bleary dawn. The wild bands like Bolden's weren't to her taste, but they had been an added attraction. Now that was all gone, too, like the last feeble notes from the bell of a horn.

So lost was she in this reverie that it took her a moment to notice that she had been watching the woman who was approaching along the banquette. No, not just a woman, a women she knew. It wasn't until the familiar figure started up the steps to the gallery that she spoke the name: "Justine."

Mr. Blank arrived on Basin Street just in time to see her climb the steps to one of the mansions. A swath of light silhouetted her as the door opened. The door closed and the gallery went dark. He pondered breaking in and doing damage to her and whoever else was inside. His instructions had not included ravishing St. Cyr's woman, but there was also nothing said about using her for his pleasure and letting *that* be a warning.

He thought about it for a half-minute before moving away. Any attack on her would not be easy. She was no blushing violet, a country girl from deep in the bayou, from what Mr. Smith had said, the type who would not go down without a fight. And he had no idea who else was inside the house and how they might be prepared. He walked back the way he had come. There would be better chances. And he promised himself that the next time, his victim would not escape the pain.

———

Valentin watched Do' lock the door to No. 505 back again and then wipe off the knob. They had given the room the same treatment after they found it as neat as a pin with not a speck of dust or even a fingerprint left behind, as if the maids had just come through.

"Ain't none of our maids get a room *this* clean," Do' said. "Why'd he do like that?"

"Because he wants to hide his tracks," Valentin said. "That, and he's sick."

Valentin left Do' with instructions and walked outside to find James waiting. He described Mr. Blank's room. The lieutenant had just taken a turn to report on his round of the District when Reynard Vernel called from across Canal Street. The reporter dodged the automobiles and streetcars to join them.

"So, gentlemen," he began. "What do you expect tonight?"

"Listen, Reynard," Valentin said. "Things are likely to be more dangerous that we thought."

"How's that?" the reporter said.

Valentin glanced at James, who said, "You might as well tell him. He knows what to write and what to leave out." He gave Vernel a hard stare. "Don't you?"

"Indeed, I do. So what is it?"

"The man who shot out our window this morning showed up at the French Market when Justine and Evangeline were there. They saw him. He wanted them to. He's the one who stabbed Each. I almost ran him to ground and lost him. He showed up at our house again, probably to try and burn it down."

The reporter was astonished. "Why?"

Valentin took a moment before speaking. "Because tomorrow I'm going to be in the possession of information that will cause important people all kinds of grief. Having to do with criminal acts they've been committing in the dark. They sent this fellow—he calls himself 'Mr. Blank'—to stop me."

Reynard said, "But wait. Why not just—"

"What, put a gun to my head and say, 'Don't do it'? Because they'll assume I have a plan for the information in the event of my demise." Valentin came up with a cold smile. "And of course, I do." He tilted his head toward James. "Standing right here."

"So fellow is..."

"Close by. In Storyville. Lurking. Watching."

To his credit, the reporter didn't start casting his eyes about, instead simply nodding in a casual way.

The lieutenant spoke up. "The point is, sir, that we can't guarantee your safety. Not until we take this character out of action."

Reynard considered before saying, "I think it's worth getting a good story."

James shrugged. "Your decision, then."

"So what now?"

Valentin said, "The lieutenant was just telling me what's been going on around the streets."

James had barely resumed his report when Black Jimmy, one of Each's street rats and white as milk in spite his moniker, came running along the banquette in a breathless rush.

"What is it?" Valentin said.

"Mr. Frank says for you to come by as soon as you can. He says it's important."

"It is about Each?"

"No, sir. I don't believe so."

Valentin said, "I can go. The hotel clerk who was on this morning is going to be showing up there anyway."

"I'll come with you," James said. "I'll need something to drink."

They started off with Reynard joining them. Valentin stopped and turned to Black Jimmy. "How did you find us?"

Jimmy came up with a smile that was missing multiple teeth. "There's people around that know everything that's going on anytime day or night." The smile waned. "Each taught me that."

Valentin patted the bony shoulder. "You know where to find us if anything comes up." Black Jimmy scurried off.

Important or not, they took a slow way around, covering Franklin Street and arriving back at Mangetta's just after seven-thirty. Frank had been peeking out from behind the blinds and he hurried to unlock the door for them.

"What's wrong? Valentin asked as they stepped inside.

"Mr. Tom," Frank said.

"What about him? Did something happen?"

"No, non penso."

Valentin could see that he was excited. "What, then?"

"He's coming. Here."

The lieutenant said, "Coming here when?"

Before the saloonkeeper could answer, an engine rattled to a stop on the street outside.

"*Adesso*," Frank said. *Now.*

The saloonkeeper opened the doors wide and then stepped to the banquette to help the man once known as the King of Storyville down from the machine. Valentin and James watched, mystified. What was the old man doing there and on this of all nights?

Mr. Tom reached the ground and stood catching his breath and eyeing the policeman and the private detective. "Mr. Valentin," he murmured. "Lieutenant."

Sensing a moment for decorum, Anderson's driver Louis stood back and allowed Valentin and Frank to take his passenger's arms and guide him inside. Carmine was standing behind the bar with a look of awe on his young face. He had heard all the tales about this great man, though seemed less than that, gray-faced and deflated as he settled with a groan into one of the chairs.

Frank made a gesture and Carmine broke his stare and hurried to fetch a brandy bottle and glasses. The saloonkeeper poured and the four men sipped. Valentin was studying Anderson, noting how his once-proud self was mostly gone, leaving behind the husk of a man, though still hanging on to some part of his once-formidable self.

"So, Mr. Tom," he said. "This is quite the surprise."

"I know it is," Anderson said. His eyes clouded. "I heard about your troubles. Do you have any idea why this is happening?"

Valentin weighed repeating what he had told Reynard and decided to wait. It would only release a barrage of suspicious questions and there wasn't time. So he said, "Someone is bringing a grudge against me. And maybe intending to kill me."

The old man stared, sensing something amiss. "I see," he said. "What are you going to do to forestall that?"

"Kill him first."

Now the King of Storyville produced a small smile.

"Tell him about Buddy," Frank said.

"Buddy...?"

"Bolden," Valentin said.

"Him? I thought he was long gone."

"So did we," Valentin said. "Until tonight."

FOURTEEN

Though the chicken and rice and beans made for a savory meal, neither Evangeline nor Miss Eulalie had much of an appetite and after their dinner, they moved to the gallery to watch the stars come out and talk about this and that, quickly arriving at what Justine hoped to accomplish running back to the city and into the danger lurking there.

"She could have told us," Evangeline said.

Miss Echo said, "She knew we'd try to talk her out of it."

"And that's what I would have done."

"But she wouldn't have listened."

"Then I would have tied her up."

Miss Eulalie laughed and waved a hand. "I guess it's just as well she didn't know about my machine."

Evangeline said, "Your..."

"My automobile. It's in the shed in back. A Model T. I got it fixed with the box on the back the way they do them now. For going to market and toting my plants and such. It's what they call a 'pick-up.'"

They changed the subject to their histories. Eulalie talked about her family maintaining proper upper-class Creole stature, except for the boy who had become a piano player in bordello parlors, changing his name so as not to shame the family, and the daughter who had found her way to the practice of voodoo and to the house in the wilds by the lake.

"So you do *voudun*," Evangeline said.

Miss Echo was pleased. "You know it?"

"Faintly. From somewhere." She sighed at another memory escaping. "So how does it work exactly?"

"It's just moving spirits and energies and such around. We use plants in various ways. To help people. There ain't nothing evil about it. Others do that."

"But you can't save Justine and Valentin."

"It's not like that. I'm not a witch."

"I know, I'm sorry," Evangeline said. "I'm just worried, is all."

Miss Eulalie studied her guest. "Justine told me that you don't recall much of anything from your past."

"Very little. I have some photographs I keep here." She touched a finger to her temple. "And now and then I hear a word or a name and I think I remember." She swallowed and her eyes moistened. "Something happened that made me this way. My mind broke. They took me in at the convent. Our Lady of Sorrows. That's where Valentin found me. He and Justine asked me to come stay with them. They made me part of their family."

Miss Eulalie patted her hand. "They wanted to take care of you."

Evangeline said, "And I want to take care of *them*." She sighed and dabbed her face with her sleeve. "But now they're both down in the city with that madman running loose."

"It's Valentin's work," Miss Echo said.

"Yes, but what about her?"

The voodoo woman didn't have an answer and they sat in silence as a half-moon rose higher over the waters of the lake. The word *mezza-luna* crossed Evangeline's mind and then went away again. More minutes passed and she turned to face Miss Echo.

"Your machine. Does it run?"

Miss Echo hiked an eyebrow. "Well, yes, I–" She stopped, seeing the look on Evangeline's face. "What is it?"

Evangeline said, "Just wondering," and poured another cup of tea.

———

The men in the room fell silent at the rapid tapping on the front door. The lieutenant put a finger to his lips with one hand, drew his Navy .45 from its holster with the other, stepped to the window, and pulled the blind back a bare inch.

"I think it's that clerk from the Crescent," he said and turned the lock.

The prim young man stepped inside, at first tense and then startled when he saw the venerable Tom Anderson himself seated in one of the chairs.

"Mr. Tom," he stuttered. "You won't remember me, I'm—"

"John, isn't it?" the King of Storyville said.

"Not, John, sir. Joseph." His face flushed at the close miss.

Valentin hid a smile. Anderson either didn't know or didn't remember the clerk, but had thrown out the most common man's name and still had almost been correct. He had seen him use the trick many times before.

"Joseph, yes," Anderson murmured.

Valentin spoke up before he could start asking about the family, but first sending a quick signal to Frank, who grabbed the bottle and a glass. "You were on the desk this morning?"

"I was, yes, sir." Joseph whispered, "Thank you," when the Sicilian placed the drink in his hand.

"Tell us about this 'Mr. Blank.'"

Joseph said, "That's what he was, sir. Blank. Bland. Very pale skin. He was in a dark coat. He carried a small satchel. He took that to his room himself." He licked his lips. "But it was his eyes. They looked dead. We had a gentleman pass away in one of our rooms last year. I was sent up to look and make sure. His eyes were the same as this fellow Blank's. Flat. No sign of life. Like I said. Dead."

"Did you see him again?"

"I didn't, no, sir. You might ask Do' if any of the other bellboys..."

"We did that." Valentin waved a hand. "Thank you for your assistance. Please, enjoy your drink." The clerk got the message, downed the rest of the brandy, handed the glass to Frank with another whispered thanks, and made his exit.

"So?" Mr. Tom said when the door closed. "Now will you tell me?"

Valentin gave him a report without hesitating to consider that Anderson had left Storyville behind over three years before. It was an old habit.

Not that there was much to tell. Mr. Blank had checked in at the Crescent an hour or so after he shot out Valentin's window. The best guess was that he arrived on an early train, but dozens were rolling in and out during those hours and it would be impossible to find out which one he rode. It wouldn't help, anyway.

"I'd guess that he spent a little time in his room and then went out to have a look around. He found out that Each worked for me and went to Fewclothes. He came back later when there were more drunkards about so he could strike and get lost in the confusion."

Anderson said, "And what's the boy's condition?"

"Hanging by a thread." Valentin did not add, *Or he's already gone.* Though he wasn't a superstitious man, he knew better than to mouth the words. "Justine and Evangeline saw Blank after they made market. Later on, I caught sight of him in the Quarter, but he got away from me."

"And where are they?" the King of Storyville inquired.

"I moved them out of town," Valentin said. "They're staying with someone I can trust."

The old man's lips lifted a small amount. "Eulalie Echo."

The detective heard James mutter in amusement. The old man still had some wits. "That's correct."

"So she's letting you go through this night without her help."

Valentin cocked his head. The old eyes held a certain sly light. Before he could respond, Anderson turned in his chair to address Frank.

"*Signore Mangetta,*" he said. "I'd like to impose on your hospitality for a few hours, if that would be all right."

Frank bowed a slight bit and said, "*Si, certo. Un onore.*"

Valentin drew his gaze from the old man. "Lieutenant," he said. "I believe we're needed on the streets."

Justine was so startled and happy to see Lulu White standing in the doorway that she almost burst into tears, barely noticing how worn the former madam—indeed, once the Queen of Storyville—appeared with her mottled flesh, ragged wig, and fraying shift.

Miss Lulu held her close and then stood back to say, "Did someone tell you I was here?"

"What?" Justine said. "Oh, no. I just came to the house. Because—"

"You were with Miss Antonia. Way back... how long ago?"

"Ten years."

"Ten years." Miss Lulu shook her head. "And you and Valentin are still married." She caught the younger woman's curious look and said, "I still have ways of keeping up. "Where is he?"

The answer came from the parlor doorway. "Out there trying to keep the whole place from going up in flames." Miss Antonia stepped into the foyer to gaze at Justine, showing no surprise. "So a little bird flies back to the nest."

"It was the first place I thought of."

"Of course." Miss Antonia waved the two women into the parlor. They settled in the same chairs where some of the richest and most important men in the city had perched while selecting which of the young doves would be theirs for the night.

The madam called out, "Molly? Some refreshment for our guests, please?"

A few odd moments passed while they waited for their drinks, with both of the older women thinking the same thing. After an exchange of glances, it was Miss Lulu who spoke up. "I'm sorry, dear," she said. "What are you doing here tonight? I mean in the District, with all this trouble."

Justine said, "Maybe saving my husband's life."

Miss Antonia was about to comment when Molly appeared with a tray holding a bottle and three glasses. As they sipped, Justine told the story of the day, from the bullet through the window to the incident at the market to the attack on Each to their escape to the lake.

Miss Antonia knew Evangeline and they both knew Eulalie Echo. "So you were all safe and they let you come back here," she said.

When she hesitated, Lulu White said, "Or did you just sneak away?" Justine blushed. "And so Valentin does *not* know you're here."

"No, ma'am." Again, she hesitated. "There's something I need to tell you. The man we saw at market?"

"What about him?" Miss Lulu said.

Justine drew a breath and then said, "He followed me here."

The lights on the ward had just gone dark. Baptiste walked by the cubicle where Mr. Bolden's bed and one other were arranged, giving the two patients some degree of privacy, but keeping them always in sight. He continued to the end of the floor and the two private rooms located there, usually where patients in various kinds of rages were strapped down and then locked in.

The attendant placed a key in the slot of the door on the right, turned it, and pushed inside. After the attack, he had arranged for Buddy to be placed there for the night and found him sitting on the edge of the bed, gazing out between the window bars at the half-moon to the east.

Baptiste stood for a moment studying his profile, as still as a painting on a wall. He had been a crazed horn player who had all but burned the city's saloons and dancehalls to the ground with his wild brass. And when he wasn't doing that, he was even more of a lunatic, drinking and kicking the gong and lying down with any woman who would lift her skirts for him, which was not a few. But then one afternoon something snapped and, convinced that his mother-in-law was trying to poison him, he bashed her head with a pitcher. They took him away, judged him insane, and brought him to this place.

He had heard all this from the New Orleans private detective St. Cyr, Buddy's friend from the time they were boys. The one who visited now and again, watching the man on the bed wander the corridors, lost forever.

As if he had read these thoughts, the patient shifted a slight bit and Baptiste said, "Buddy? You all right in here?"

Buddy turned from the moon, met Baptiste's eyes for a few seconds, then looked away again.

"You'll be safe," Baptiste said. "Don't fret. Ain't nobody going to harm you. I'm going to make sure of that."

As he had already done too many times to count, Buddy produced something just shy of a smile, as if attending to a private joke. Baptiste entertained a feeling that his patient understood and would be calmed. Then he laughed; who in this man's world was calmer than Mr. Buddy Bolden? And why would anyone want to injure such a peaceful man?

FIFTEEN

Valentin and the lieutenant were prowling Liberty Street with Reynard close bahind as the noise from the banquettes and crowds around some of the houses began to swell. "80s" made bright flashes and fearsome bangs as they came flying out windows and to the streets below. The serious carousing had begun.

Meanwhile, strumpets lounged in doorways, braving the cold in their thin cotton chippies, hoping for last chances to collect some cash before they headed off to land who knew where doing who knew what. Lucky for them there was no shortage of takers. The girls would linger on display until some besotted fellow with a few coins in his pocket would present himself like a proper suitor. Then the couple to disappear into one of the alleyways.

The three men had just turned the corner of Liberty Street when the lieutenant stopped and peered ahead. "Goddamn," he said. Valentin and Reynard looked. "That's no firecracker," he said and made for the call box on the lamppost.

Miss Eulalie and Miss Evangeline hadn't been able to keep their conversation going. They would start and then stop in the same way they had been pacing and then sitting since they had come inside from the gallery.

Eulalie stopped pouring nd put the kettle down. "What time is it?" she asked.

Evangeline looked at the clock on the mantle. "It's eight-thirty, Miss Eulalie." She smiled. "Back home, I'd be getting ready for bed."

The voodoo woman left the cups unfilled and stepped into the living room where their gazes met. "Is that what you want to do?" she said.

"No, ma'am, it is not."

"Well, then?"

"I'm ready."

Miss Eulalie said, "We'll need our coats."

The house on the banks of the lake beyond Spanish Fort wasn't the only place where the worry was stirring. Lulu White and Antonia Gonzales had been watching Justine circle the parlor, stopping every few rounds to peer between the curtains before moving again.

Just after the clock struck eight-thirty, they heard the bang of an 80. Justine gave a start and said, "I can't stand this. I have to get out there."

Miss Lulu sat up in her chair, alarmed. "You can't. The fellow could still be lurking. Or he could spot—"

"I'm not going to just stand here not knowing anything and not doing anything," Justine said. "What if he..."

She didn't finish but the madams understood. Miss Antonia said, "I'm going to send someone out there first." She called to Molly, who appeared in the doorway. "I need you to get out on the streets."

The maid did not look pleased with the prospect. "Ma'am?" she said.

"You're going to be our spy," Miss Lulu said.

At that, Molly began to smile.

Mr. Blank had told Mr. Smith that the chaos was a powerful weapon, because with a sly plan and the will to put it in motion, one man could create the mayhem of five. The fireworks were already starting when he walked away from the Basin Street bordello where the detective's wife had taken refuge and now stood on the corner of Bienville Street. He had been watching the sparkles and shoots for only a few moments when the idea came to him.

It was a simple enough affair. He found a hardware store on Canal Street and broke in the back door to help himself to two steel cans of kerosene. He crossed back to Conti Street, found an abandoned house, poured out half of one of the cans at the bottom of the gallery steps, and struck a lucifer. In seconds, the blaze was creeping up the steps to the gallery. He circled the block and returned with the small mob that was hurrying to view the fire. Among them he spied the police lieutenant McKinney, a short, thin fellow in a cheap suit, and Valentin St. Cyr.

The copper turned and moved away. Mr. Blank knew he couldn't take St. Cyr, but the man with him might do for the infliction of an injury. So he began to move to the other side of the street. When he came to the opposite curb, he looked down to check his footing and when he looked up again, both the Creole detective and the other fellow were gone.

Valentin scanned the windows as the flames licked the gallery steps to the front of the house. No movement didn't mean there was no one inside.

"Tell the lieutenant I went to check the house." He trotted into the dark walkway between the building and the next one over, which was made of brick.

The reporter waited for a few seconds before darting to a lit storefront two doors down. The lights were on, but there was no one in the store and the door was locked. He turned to see Lieutenant McKinney heading toward the burning house and chased behind him.

"Lieutenant!" James stopped. "Mr. Valentin went around back to see if there's anyone inside."

The officer muttered something and started for the walkway.

Reynard cast a glance at the flames that had now reached the gallery and were working their way up to the front door. He heaved a nervous breath and followed the lieutenant.

Valentin climbed the back gallery steps and peered in through the window. The kitchen was empty. He pounded on the door and got neither a reply nor heard the sound of footsteps. Smoke was beginning to drift his way. As he moved to the window to the left, he heard the faint wail of a siren.

The second window provided a view all the way to the front parlor and he saw what might have been legs sticking out on the dining room floor. The siren was joined by another, both drawing closer. But not yet close enough.

Covering his mouth and nose with his sleeve, he kicked the door open. The smell of charred wood and the sting of smoke were stronger. When he turned into the pantry, he found that the legs were attached to the body of a man dressed in ragged clothes.

When he bent down, he recognized a local sot they called "Half-Pint" or "Pint" for his small stature, known for his mediocre talents as a pickpocket and much greater skill at locating free drinks. The half-empty bottle that was lying parked next to his left side would have turned him into a torch. He reeked with sweat and filthy clothes and Valentin couldn't tell if he was dead or alive.

He shook the thin shoulder. "Pint?" He shook harder. "Pint!"

Half-Pint groaned, opened his eyes, and blinked. "Mr. Valentin? What brings you?" He sniffed. "Hey, somethin's burning!"

"Jesus and Mary..." Valentin grabbed his lapels, hoisted him to his feet, and half-carried his reeking bones through the rooms to the back gallery. By this time the sirens were at the next corner and he could see the flash of lights and hear shouts and the rattle of truck engines.

James and Reynard appeared from the front of the house to find Valentin and Half-Pint bent down and coughing. Two firemen ran from the passageway, both carrying axes.

"I didn't see anyone else," Valentin told them. "But I only got to the first floor."

The firemen bolted for the back door.

They reached the street, where Half-Pint was sent on his shaky way. Water was being pumped from a hydrant and the streams from the hoses had tamped the flames. The fire had blackened the front of the house to the top of the door and windows. As they watched, the window glass was shattered by one of the firemen's axes. The lieutenant spotted Fire Captain O'Reilly and asked about any other people in the house.

"That drunk was the only one," the captain said.

"You have any idea how it started?"

"Kerosene and a Lucifer," the captain said. He studied the damage for a moment. "I don't guess this will be the worst of it. It's still early, ain't it?" He walked away.

Valentin was gazing at the house and trying to remember the name of the madam who had managed it when he caught a motion out of the corner of his eye and saw Reynard about to topple over, after being slammed by someone passing behind him. A man in a dark coat moving into the dense crowd.

"James!" he said and pointed to the retreating figure. "It's..."

The lieutenant moved quickly for a big man. In three long strides, he had entered the mass of bodies. He scanned the heads from side to side, then grabbed up and handful of a coat collar. The wearer gave a startled jerk and when he reeled around, Valentin saw sandy hair and red cheeks.

He shook his head. James spoke a few words to the man, patted his shoulder, and turned him loose. As he rejoined Valentin and Reynard, his eyes narrowed. Valentin wheeled around to see Mr. Blank thirty paces along the banquette, regarding them with a lazy, sugary smile. They had just started to move when the crowd shifted again. The bodies dispersed and Mr. Blank evaporated.

"Well, goddamn," the lieutenant said.

Reynard said, "Who was... was that *him*?"

The two other men peered around the bodies, knowing it was pointless.

The half-dozen street coppers the lieutenant had summoned from other locations gathered around while he warned them to be on the lookout for the suspect, describing Mr. Blank with as much detail as he could manage. He got all puzzled stares in return. How were they to locate a felon who looked like nothing?

He was going through a patient repeat of the description when he saw them stiffen in unison. Valentin cleared his throat and he turned, prepared to face Major Sont or some other senior officer, but was startled to see Acting Chief Cook and Mayor Behrman standing with him.

"Mr. Mayor," he said. "Chief Cook."

Sont spoke first. "Do I have this right, Lieutenant? The miscreant who shot out Mr. St. Cyr's window and stabbed that boy—Mr. Blank, is it?—he started the fire, too?"

"I believe so, sir." James chose not to mention that that same person had just been standing not thirty paces away.

The major was about to continue when he glanced over at the assembled patrolmen. "Jesus Christ, officers. Stand down." The coppers relaxed. He next addressed Valentin. "You pulled a drunkard out of the house?"

"I did, yes."

"What the hell was he doing in there?" the mayor said.

"Holed-up with a bottle. You find an empty house in the District, there's going to be sots using it. Or hopheads. Or street whores serving–"

"All right, I get the point."

"And no sign of the perpetrator." Since it wasn't a question, neither Valentin nor James nor Reynard spoke up. The mayor was standing by with his arms crossed and lips pursed and appeared about to say something else when Fire Captain O'Reilly returned.

"Mr. Mayor." He hid his surprise and nodded to the two senior officers. "Two other fires were set. One on St. Louis and one behind Anderson's Café. Crews have them under control." He heaved a breath. "But the one on St. Louis... there was a citizen inside. Another drunkard. This one's a fatality."

Major Sont said, "That makes it a homicide. And the game has changed." His gaze shifted to Valentin. "So what do you think? More fires? More bodies?"

"More fires, yes, sir," Valentin said. "They could already be going." The mayor looked alarmed. "Look at what he's done with just the one. It's working. As to the bodies, no telling."

Sont turned to O'Reilly. "Captain?"

"I agree, sir. But we're ready."

The mayor muttered something and he, Major Sont, and Cook, who hadn't spoken a word, turned away and crossed the street to climb into the new Lincoln Model L that had been idling at the curb. Captain O'Reilly gave a wry salute and returned to his duties.

The lieutenant said, "A random murder, now. Just what we need."

Vernel's head had been bent over his notebook. He said, "Do you think any of them realized I was here?" he said.

Valentin looked at the lieutenant. They both had forgotten the reporter had been standing by, listening and recording every word. It didn't matter; by the time anything was printed, it would all be over.

James whispered, "Damn."

Valentin looked around to see Mayor Behrman and Major Sont heading back their way. The acting chief remained by the sedan. The mayor addressed Valentin. "All this is to get to you."

"Yes, sir."

"To stop you."

"It's too late. But they don't know that. So he'll kept at it."

The mayor lifted a hand. "You realize he could be perched in one of those empty windows right now with a rifle barrel pointed at your head." He glanced at Major Sont. "We could just turn him over, you know. A sacrifice." It was a joke, but he wasn't smiling.

"Sorry to say it wouldn't change anything, Mr. Mayor."

"Oh, and why is that?"

"Because he's saving me until the end."

"The end of what?"

"The end of Storyville."

Sixteen

Tom Anderson was annoyed when nine o'clock rolled around and Black Jimmy hadn't appeared with his report from the streets. When the clock struck the half-hour and there was still no sign of him, he got riled.

"If it was Each, he would have been here twice." He looked over at Frank, who was minding his own business behind the bar. "Do you know this fellow?"

"Black Jimmy?"

"Yes, him. And why do they call him that, anyway? He's whiter than rice."

"I seen him around. I tease him. Call him *Giacomo Nero*. But I don't know why they give him that name, no."

Anderson jerked his head. "Is your help still back there?"

"He is, Mr. Tom."

"Can you send him out? To find Jimmy or get a report on his own?"

The Sicilian said, "*Sì. Certo.*" Carmine was doing as little as possible, as usual.

Frank called him into the saloon and let Mr. Tom give the instructions. In the presence of the King of Storyville, Carmine gave his full attention. When the old man finished, he grabbed his coat and scooted out the door.

Anderson said, "And if Jimmy shows up, I want him out there, too." He crossed his arms. "A man can never have enough spies."

———

Black Jimmy's name was Jimmy Black and he had long ago tired of explaining this to people. When the first and last had gotten switched was lost somewhere in his childhood. After a while, he came to like it. Everyone in Storyville needed a moniker. Like poor Each, lying up at Mercy after being cut open like that.

Jimmy now followed the path that he believed Each would have taken, keeping to the edges of the stumbling crowds and diving into one saloon after another, on the lookout for suspicious people or talk. Especially about a stranger that fit a certain type.

He was standing where Villere Street crossed Iberville when he spotted just such a character wearing a long gray coat and a homburg and walking with his head down and body leaning forward. Black Jimmy decided that he needed watching and followed him in the direction of St. Louis Street.

It was quieter down that way, though a couple dozen men and half that many women were ambling about. The man in the coat reached the alley that cut through to Marais, came to a halt, and turned around.

"You," he said, pointing a finger. "You work for Mr. Valentin, ain't that right?"

Jimmy stepped closer. "That's right," he said with a touch of cool pride. "Do I know you?" The fellow turned away, as if about to escape down the alley. Jimmy said, "Wait a minute, now. What's your name, anyway?"

The man walked a few steps backward into the alley, hunching as if in fear. "My name?"

"You heard me," Black Jimmy said, following him.

In an impossible second, the man reached out, snatched him by the throat, pointed a pistol at his forehead and said, "Blank, that's my name," before pulling the trigger.

Reynard Vernel left Valentin and the lieutenant to find a shop with a telephone he could use to call in his story.

A cub reporter named Timothy Brown picked up the newsroom phone and as soon as he recognized the voice on the line he started babbling questions about Storyville's last night. Reynard cut him off. "Go through what I dictate and you'll know everything that I do."

Brown's voice did a dive. "All right, yes, sir."

Reynard thought to tell him that he didn't need to be addressed as *sir*, but let it go. There was no time for anything save the matter at hand. Composing from his notes, he described the fires, the mounting chaos on the street, and the prowling presences of police Lieutenant James McKinney and private detective Valentin St. Cyr. When he finished, he had Timothy Brown read it back to him.

"All right, then," he said. "I believe that will do for now." He decided not to mention being assaulted.

"I think it's a fine story, sir."

"Then we'll leave it there." It was a warning that no cub reporter's grubby pen was to touch it. "I'll call back in an hour or so," he said and clicked off.

He stepped onto the banquette and was about to go in search of his night's companions when he noticed the makings of a commotion.

For a woman who exhibited such calm, Eulalie Echo was a madwoman behind the wheel. Evangeline had enjoyed more than a few heart-stopping moments riding with Valentin and Justine as they raced through town in the Model T. Miss Eulalie was their match. They had just screeched around the turn to leave the lake behind when her hat went flying.

"I'm so sorry!" Eulalie shouted.

Evangeline shouted back something that was lost in the wind right along with the hat.

The voodoo woman slowed the machine to a more sedate pace when they reached City Park and the road and engine noises quieted. "Are we going to..."

"To Storyville? Yes."

"I've never been there. I mean, I don't think I have. But I wouldn't know, would I?" Evangeline looked over. "Have you?"

"I have. Oh, yes. Many times." She saw Evangeline's eyes widen and laughed. "Not in any sinful way. I would do some work, helping the girls with my *voudun*. And there were a few instances when I went to drag my godson out of a bordello."

"The piano player?"

"Ferdinand LeMothe. Now known as Jelly Roll Morton." She turned onto St. Ann. "He started playing in those houses when he wasn't much more than a boy. His mother wasn't about to go collect him, so I went. Not that it did much good." They could now make out some dim shapes of the downtown buildings. "That's how I come to know Valentin. And Justine. And now you."

Evangeline was peering through the windshield, for a few moments lost in thought. "Do you think she's in danger?"

"Justine? Well, the District won't be safe tonight. And with this business with Valentin..." She shook her head.

"How will we find her?"

Miss Echo turned to her with bright eyes. "I have some ideas." She pressed the accelerator handle and the machine jumped.

Ernest, the attendant on graveyard shift arrived and after sixteen long hours, Baptiste felt his bones sag with relief. It was time to get into his Chevrolet roadster and drive home to his wife and three children, though they'd all be long asleep.

He walked down the steps and through the gate to the gravel lot. The automobile, called the "Series H," sat at the far end, away from the dust kicked up by other machines. He considered that the extra shift would help with his next payment and that would push him past halfway to the end of the fourteen-hundred-dollar loan.

When he reached the roadster, he stretched to advance the ignition and then cranked the six cylinders to life. He climbed up behind the wheel with a weary groan and spent a moment waiting for the engine to warm and enjoying the tufted upholstery, the polished wood of the dashboard, and the sleek green and black bonnet before him.

His thoughts drifted to what had been a very strange day and with Buddy Bolden at the center of the drama. And Big Kenny Mullens, the murderer of the New Orleans Chief of Police, was now strapped down and locked alone in a cell. Baptiste felt a small shudder thinking about what would have happened had he not come upon that lunatic and Bolden in the stairwell.

He lifted his gaze to the third floor of Building C, counted across seven windows, and caught a breath. A familiar figure was posed there. In the next instant, the dark shape was gone. Baptiste tried telling himself it was nothing, likely that the patient had come awake and was now back in his bed. He adjusted the idle control to a steady churn and pushed the shifter into low gear. His right hand was resting on the throttle lever but he did not move it. He couldn't shake the feeling that something wasn't right in room 314.

Ernest was surprised to see him. "You ain't had enough of this place?"

"I need your keys," Baptiste said.

Ernest, never the curious sort, handed over the ring. Baptist climbed the three flights of steps and made his way along the quiet corridor. For all the silence and distance, he respected Mr. Bolden, and so instead of using the key and barging inside, he called in a soft voice and tapped. The door swung open.

Ernest jumped when he heard Baptiste's footsteps pounding on the stairs. He pulled his own feet from atop the desk and stood up.

Baptiste reached the landing. "Did he come by here?"

"Did who come by here?"

"Mr. Bolden."

Ernest said, "No, why?"

Baptiste hurried past him. "Because he's gone."

———

Mr. Blank had used a short time racing about to set the fires, ending with the one on St. Louis that had claimed the life of the poor sot whose bad luck it was to be holed up there. His attempt to burn the occupied house on Liberty Street had been too rushed and did only minor damage. He walked back around to study his work. When he spotted a piece of skinny white trash eyeing him from the next gallery, he stalked off toward Villere Street.

He had only minor pleasure in what havoc he had wreaked and was growing rankled by the plan that had been forced on him. So Mr. Smith and the people he represented did not want a murder on their hands—only that the fear of God be visited on St. Cyr to keep him from exposing them. For what, he didn't know and didn't care, because it had already gone too far for delicacy. He had seen to that when he plunged the knife rather than making a simple but ugly slice. With the other rat, he had no reason to shoot him dead but did it anyway, another urge he didn't control. Now one and perhaps two people connected to St. Cyr were dead and gone there was no point in playing the games anymore and—

He stopped walking. The point was to get paid the rest of the one thousand dollars he was owed and his only chance to claim the money was to follow orders. And yet the Creole detective would be a true prize, even if he never got paid at all.

When Valentin and James reached the scene, the madam of the house and the two hussies who remained there were standing on the gallery while the firemen did their jobs, drawing shawls around their shoulders to ward off the chill. Miss Mamie Lee was looking down at him with her hands on her heavy hips.

"Mr. Valentin. They going to try and burn us out or what? They just can't wait for us to leave?"

Valentin said, "Some felon did it, Miss Mamie."

The madam glared at him. "It wasn't just some *felon*," she said. "I heard there was three or four more. And that some poor man died in one of them."

"Three more," James said.

"What's that, Lieutenant?" So she knew him, too.

"There were only three more."

"Oh, only *three* more." Miss Mamie looked to her girls. "Then that makes it all right."

Valentin was about to respond when she said, "We ain't scared and we ain't running. We're staying to the end and maybe then some."

James said, "Ma'am, that's not such a good idea."

"Oh?" the madam said. "You think it's a better idea to let them run us off like lowdown trash?"

They were saved from answering when a street arab who was not Black Jimmy came running from the corner.

"Lieutenant. Mr. Valentin. I been sent to get you. There was a shooting down off Villere Street."

Valentin and James turned to follow him, but they didn't miss the finger that Miss Mamie Lee was wagging their direction.

When they arrived at the alley, two uniformed coppers, a corporal and a private who was holding a lamp were standing over the body while a second private held a dozen random onlookers far enough back so that they couldn't see anything but a shape. Reynard Vernel was standing by, looking unnerved.

"What do you have?" the lieutenant said.

The corporal said, "One shot to the chest. Close range."

Valentin took the lamp from the private and bent down. The hole close to the victim's heart was surrounded by a powder burn. Which meant that his assailant had been standing no more than four feet away. He tilted the light. "Good God. It's Black Jimmy."

"What's his true name?"

Valentin looked up at the lieutenant. "His name? I'm...I don't know. I only knew him by his moniker."

"We'll find out," James said. "We can ask around tomorrow."

Valentin said, "I wonder if he even saw it coming. I hope not."

The lieutenant told the corporal to call for a wagon to carry the body to the morgue. Reynard stayed behind when he and Valentin walked to the next corner, where they both took Omars from McKinney's pack. Valentin struck a lucifer and held it out.

"I'm guessing that Jimmy spotted him and put on a tail. It ended back there. Because of me."

The lieutenant looked about. There were more bodies moving in the dark, more noise and laughter, and more sounds of random breakage. "Going to be harder to find him in the middle of all this."

"I know," Valentin said. "Everyone else needs to be extra careful. He's out to injure or kill you and anyone else close to me."

The lieutenant said, "I know you'd like to be the one to trap him, but if the opportunity comes along..."

"Oh, by all means," Valentin said. "Shoot him down."

Mr. Blank's orders were also to avoid close calls. To do the work, slip away, and look for the next chance. He had wandered from that. But it was too delicious to creep close to St. Cyr and his women and his friends. He guessed that the detective with his fine antenna could sense something was skewed on the periphery of his vision. The close brushes with St. Cyr told him to have a place to slide away to at every turn.

After setting the third fire, he realized he could burn most of the red-light district to ashes. Half the buildings were of wood and old wood at that, slowing rotting away in the New Orleans damp. He imagined a hellish conflagration with the detective and his wife and police partner and all the madams and harlots trapped. It would be one for the ages. Alas, it could not be; he had to play a part in a game that might see him removed along with the others when it was all done.

A hack arrived to carry Black Jimmy's body to the morgue. Reynard left for Mangetta's with instructions to tell Tom Anderson and Frank what had happened and that Valentin and the lieutenant would be along presently. After he had walked off, Valentin said, "Didn't Mr. Tom Anderson give up the District three years ago?"

James said, "Something like that. Why?"

"I'm trying to figure out why I said we'd be reporting to him."

The lieutenant produced a smile. "Like he was still the King of Storyville?"

"Yes," Valentin said with a sigh. "Just like that."

The Ford slowed to a creeping pace as Miss Echo steered along Claiborne Street. It was a ghost town, with the cribs once used by hundreds of cheap whores completely empty, with no sign of life in sight.

"There was so much pain here," Evangeline said. "I can feel it."

Eulalie turned to stare at her. "You can?"

"I feel like I can hear them crying out."

After a few vexed seconds, Eulalie pulled her gaze away from that troubled face. "You sure *you* ain't a voodoo woman?" she said.

Evangeline's brow stitched as if she was considering the question in a serious way. "I don't know. I just..." She settled back, her thoughts shifting again. "How do we find Justine and Valentin?"

"I got some thoughts on that," Miss Eulalie said. She pushed the accelerator.

Baptiste and all the other attendants who could be spared searched the wards, the common rooms, the toilets, and the grounds, and came upon no sign of Buddy Bolden. As if he had evaporated. Baptiste knew that there were secret passages here and there and someone like him, who had said nothing for years yet had watched everything, was the type to learn of them. Had his silence been a ruse all along? Had he been waiting a decade of days to slip away? How did he unlock the door? And, finally, what did it have to do with the attack on him?

Baptiste had no answers, so he made another round of the grounds, coming to a stop where the gate faced State Highway 10, the road into town.

Walking at a slow pace, he told himself that it was not possible; that Mr. Bolden, of all the patients, could not have just found his way outside and then wandered off. Tired as he was, he decided to wind his way back to the buildings and check the dozen or so shadowy places where a man might hide. First, though, he asked the guard to open the iron gate and stepped out onto the gravel driveway to gaze along the empty road in both directions.

Miss Eulalie made the prudent choice to drive to Canal Street and then swing around to Basin, where she stopped the Ford.

"'Down-the-line' they used to call it and it was something to see," she said. "Every door was lit up. The saloons spilling onto the street. Music coming out the windows. The sporting gals on display. Men strolling from one end to the other. And look at it now. It's a—" She sat forward, staring.

"What is it?" Evangeline said.

"I think I know where she is."

"Justine?"

Eulalie put the machine into gear and pulled ahead.

Two blocks away, Tom Anderson was waiting grim-faced when Valentin and James entered from the alley in back of the saloon.

"One dead and another close to it."

The lieutenant said, "Two dead, Mr. Tom," and explained about the man dying in the burning house.

"And who knows how many more they'll find come morning?" the King of Storyville said.

Valentin decided he didn't care for the tone from the man who had abandoned the District and he stepped into the hallway to call the hospital. Mariette was still there and had in fact decided to stay through the night. He replaced the handset and stood staring at the telephone.

"So?" James said when he reappeared in the saloon.

"He's the same," Valentin said. As he moved behind the bar to pour a half-cup of Frank's coffee, he felt Anderson's gimlet stare on him and turned around and said, "Sir?"

"There's something you're not telling me," the old man said. He held Valentin's gaze for a hard moment. "And you're not going to tell me what it is, are you?"

"If I did keep anything from you, it would be for your own protection," Valentin said, knowing how weak it sounded even as he spoke the words.

"So I need *protection*," Mr. Tom said.

"Honestly, there's nothing solid. Maybe later. After the sun comes up. But not now."

Anderson was not too old to follow a twisting thread. "All this trouble. Because of this information you might or might not get?"

"That would be correct, yes."

"So that will have to wait."

"Yes, and I'll—"

"Lulu White."

"What about her?"

"Maybe she can help you. Since I can't."

Valentin wondered why he was surprised. "How did you know she was here?"

"I didn't," Mr. Tom said. "I guessed that she would come back if there was any way she could manage it. And you just told me that she did. I'm also guessing that she is at this moment no more that a few blocks away. At one of the mansions. Maybe Antonia Gonzales."

Valentin recovered enough to say, "I suppose that could be true."

He was about to continue when the phone rang again. Carmine answered it, listened for a few seconds, then put the handset against his chest and whispered in Italian to Frank, who in turned called out to the lieutenant.

"It's for you. Someone from the mayor's office."

———

As soon as Martin Behrman's touring car pulled up to City Hall, he decided that the last thing he wanted to do was to sit around with that sneaky dullard John Cook, which would match the enjoyment level of a wake. He asked the acting chief if he wouldn't mind waiting behind for any important news while he made a quick tour of the city. He was relieved but not surprised when Cook agreed with only a moment's hesitation. Too quick a moment, the mayor noted, and was glad that he had told Mr. Pettibone to keep track of anything untoward, like Cook making phone calls.

After the chief disappeared back into the building, he sent his driver to find Major Sont. Five minutes later, the major climbed into the Lincoln Model L and they rolled off toward Canal Street. Though the lights were bright, it was late-night calm.

"Any more fires?" he asked the major.

"Only those they're setting in the middle of the streets, Mr. Mayor. We expected that."

"What streets?"

"Mostly on Liberty. Some on Franklin and Villere."

"And this young man who was killed?"

"He was shot while he was out making rounds for St. Cyr."

The mayor stared out the window, shaking his head in dismay. "Two dead and the one in Mercy," he said. "And it's only what time?"

"Coming up on ten. Ten more hours to go." He waited to see if Behrman had anything to add, then said, "Do you want to go back in there?"

"To Storyville? I don't think so." The mayor took a few seconds to reconsider. "On second thought, let's have a look at Basin Street."

Major Sont leaned forward to tap on the glass partition.

J. Picot prevailed on Sergeant Maris to drive him to the District. He sensed that the officer was not pleased about it. Too bad. Picot had goods on him, as he did for dozens of others on the force: thieveries, beatings, rapes, and even killings for which no price was ever paid. The former captain had been skilled at gathering damning evidence, holding it secret, and then when the situation warranted, making it clear that it didn't have to stay that way. This information remained potent. So Maris would do what he was asked.

As they rode along in the Dodge, the sergeant told him about the body found in Storyville. "Street rat went by Black Jimmy."

"Doesn't ring a bell. He was killed how?"

"Shot in an alley."

"So?"

"So he was working for St. Cyr. Because after that other one— Each?—got sent to Mercy."

Picot feigned surprise. In truth, he had been expecting this, striking at St. Cyr from angles to convince him to stand down. The tally was a stabbing that was meant to be a murder, fires set in Storyville houses causing one fatality, and now the killing of another fellow in the Creole detective's employ.

Maris interrupted his musings. "I heard they have his name."

"What's that?"

"They have the name of the one who's causing all this trouble."

"What is it?"

"Blank. Mr. Blank."

J. Picot chortled. "Oh, that's perfect." They had arrived at Canal Street and he reached for the door handle. "I'm going to walk."

"You don't want me with you?" the sergeant said, hoping the answer was "no."

"No, I don't," Picot said.

"But you want me to wait."

"I do. Right here."

"What are you going to do?"

"I'm going to find *Mr. Blank* and introduce myself." With that, he climbed down and walked away, lumbering on his heavy legs.

Mayor Behrman pressed his face to the glass after they crossed the tracks and saw that the street was beginning to hum, now with several dozen men wandering this way and that. "Who's staying open?" he asked.

"Lizzie Taylor, I believe. Ellie Queen down the end of the line." Major Sont smiled. "And I heard Antonia Gonzales is throwing a party, starting at midnight. The *official* closing time."

The mayor laughed. "All right, then." The mayor directed the driver to take another slow tour up and down Canal Street and then carry them back to City Hall.

As soon as they climbed out, a corporal ran up to Sont and handed him a note. The major waved him away and unfolded the paper.

"Major?" Behrman said. "Anything wrong?"

"That depends on your point of view, Mr. Mayor." He handed over the note. "Tom Anderson is back in the District."

Buddy came to be standing by the side of the highway. It was now dark, the moon revealing a sliver of silver when it wasn't hiding in the clouds. The hour was late and it was also quiet save for the sounds of the insects, the night birds, and the occasional dry rustle of naked branches. Only one machine passed, a Ford with a stake back, and as soon as he noticed the lights, he stepped in the shadows and was lost from sight.

He didn't know why he was there, but the question *Why?* hadn't crossed his mind for a very long time. His past was a jumble of pictures and noises. He could mostly detect no future beyond what was right before him. He moved from one minute to the next with only a faint wind urging him on.

He looked back the way he had come.

They said that God would save my soul. That Jesus would lift me up but that I say the word—if I put down Satan's trumpet and pick up the Lord's.

The night swirled. *I've heard notes that crawled across the deserts of time. Notes that were too long to sing. Notes that if played aloud would echo like mirrors reflecting mirrors.*

Now it was the sound of some machine passing. *I heard a horn call out to me and the horn is on a ship and the ship is on the river that cuts through the heart of the nation, the waters flowing from the flat and empty lands far to the north and then passing in a slow drift by Iowa on one side and Illinois on the other. St. Louis and Memphis and Vicksburg and Natchez and the heat rising the closer it gets. Yes. The heat rising, the thunder rolling in, and the sun sparkling on the crests of the little waves like brass gems.*

This brought a smile. *In New Orleans, there are horns calling all over the river. I know, because that's where it came from. That's where I learned to play. That's where I became me.*

He stood still for what could have been a few seconds or an hour and felt it again. Like a gentle hand nudging him. Some more time passed and this time when he saw lights and heard the grinding of gears, he stepped close to the road and raised a hand.

Seventeen

As they were readying to leave the saloon, the lieutenant received another telephone call from Major Sont at City Hall. After he took it, he asked Reynard Vernel to give Valentin and him a moment and they stepped out onto the Marais Street banquette.

"Someone spotted Mr. Tom and it got back to the mayor," he said. "And he's hot about it. He wants him chased out. He's saying he wasn't here when he was needed."

Valentin said, "And he wants us to get rid of him?"

The lieutenant gave him a doleful look that meant *yes* and said, "Can this get any more difficult?"

Valentin said, "I don't want to go in there and tell him."

"Neither do I," James said. "I doubt if it would do any good. I say we let it be."

"And we still have a killer to catch."

The saloon door opened and Reynard poked his head out. "All right?"

"Yes, all right," Valentin said and waved for him to join them as they started north.

Justine knew who it was at the door without looking. She stood up as Miss Antonia stepped into the foyer. She heard a round of greetings, Miss Eulalie and the madam laughing, and Evangeline's gentle voice. They appeared in the parlor doorway.

"So you found me," she said.

"Miss Eulalie found you," Evangeline said.

"It wasn't hard," the voodoo woman said.

"What are you doing in Storyville?" Evangeline said in a scolding tone.

"I could ask you the same. Why didn't you stay at the lake?"

"You know Valentin doesn't want you here."

Justine's eyes were downcast, but not shamed. "I knew you wouldn't let me go," she said. "Or you'd make me bring you along."

"Leaving like that was not respectful," Evangeline said.

Miss Lulu cleared her throat and said, "Miss Antonia? Might we trouble you for some refreshments?"

The women settled at the dining room table. Miss Antonia fetched a bottle and five small glasses from the cabinet. After a silence that seemed to stretch for a full minute but in fact lasted less than ten seconds, Miss Eulalie said, "Where is Valentin?"

"We don't know," Miss Antonia said. "I've had my girl going out and reporting back."

"Does she know him?"

"I don't think she does. But she might know if..."

"Something happened to him?" Justine said.

Miss Lulu said, "Here's what we know. Three houses were set on fire and a drunkard died in one of them. Another young rounder was attacked. He was shot and killed."

Justine gave a start. "Who was it?"

"He went by Black Jimmy."

Justine closed her eyes. She remembered him. Skinny. Dirty. White. Part of Each's crew. She opened her eyes, but avoided Miss Evangeline until the older woman spoke her name.

She murmured, "Yes, ma'am?"

"Coming here really was was foolish."

"I know. I couldn't stand being away. I was scared for him. I am."

None of the older women had anything to say to that. Evangeline broke the silence. "So now what?"

Miss Antonia glanced at the clock over the doorway. "I told Molly to be here by eleven."

Miss Echo said, "So how do we spend the next half-hour?"

"Drinking," Miss Antonia began to rise from her chair. "I have more bottles in the pantry."

"I'll get it." Justine stood up and left the room.

It was past eleven o'clock, the sky was clear so that the moon cast some light, and there had yet to be a sign of Buddy Bolden, as if he had simply vanished. Baptiste, on yet another search of the wards and the grounds, wondered how that could be so. People still talked about the voodoo he made with his horn. Had he at long last summoned enough of that power to lift him over the wall? Baptiste's mother, who had heard Kid Bolden at a saloon when she was young, would say yes. He recalled her words: "He had some kind of juju that I ain't ever seen on another man." Baptiste thought something other than long-hidden magic powers to be at work.

He had reported to his supervisor Mr. Carney, rousing that gentleman from his bed. "Him again? Does this have something to do—"

"No, sir," Baptiste said. "He's never been any trouble at all."

The supervisor yawned. "Well, then, let's not worry too much. If he hasn't shown up by morning, we can report to Dr. Amis."

After he clicked off, Baptiste whispered, "No, *you* can report to him."

He now arrived at the doors of the reception building. The search had yielded nothing and the other attendants had gone back to their posts. He knew he could leave now, but he wasn't tired anymore. So when he drove out the gates, instead of heading for his home in Jackson, he steered onto the next dirt road.

Justine was back with two more bottles. She had found the wooden boxes stacked in the kitchen: drinks that would never be enjoyed in that house.

She placed the tray on the table and glanced in a shy way at Evangeline and Miss Echo before turning to the two madams. "Is there any news of Each?"

"The last anyone heard, he was alive," Miss Antonia said. "That's what I know."

"I'll call," Justine said and stepped into the parlor.

They were approaching the corner of Bienville Street when a short woman in a thin coat and loose hair rushed by, colliding with the lieutenant's arm. "Sorry, sir!" she shouted as she raced away. It happened so fast that Valentin didn't catch a good look at her face, but he turned to watch her run down to the next block and climb to Antonia Gonzales' gallery and disappear inside.

James said, "What?"

"Nothing, I guess." They walked on, rounding the corner. He began to say, "She looked—" when a blast of sound caught him up short. He stared for a second before saying, "Well, the party's started."

Justine spoke Each's name and asked for the nurse on duty. When the woman at the switchboard said, "You'll want to speak to Mariette," she all but sobbed with relief. The familiar voice came on the line, as always low and steady and she said, "It's Justine, Mariette."

She could hear the surprise come through the little speaker. "Where are you?"

"I'm here. In Storyville. At Miss Antonia's."

"I thought Mr. Valentin carried you off somewhere."

"He did. But I escaped." Her laugh was shaky. She said, "What about Each?"

"He's hanging on," Mariette said. Justine felt her bones quiver. "The doctors are surprised. Not one of them thought he would make it." She paused. "But he's not out of danger yet. He could take a turn and..."

"I understand," Justine said.

"He's getting good care," the nurse said.

Justine said, "Have you been with him the whole time?"

"Since they brought him in. And I'm staying. I owe it to Mr. Valentin. For helping me back when." Justine whispered something she couldn't catch, but she understood and said, "We'll talk before morning, then." The line went dead.

Justine wiped her eyes before stepping into the parlor. She had just finished reporting on Each when the front door opened and Molly hurried inside, her face bright.

Before the girl could open her mouth, she said, "Mr. Valentin."

Molly drew up short. "Ma'am?"

"Do you know him?"

"Do I...?" She looked at Miss Antonia, who said, "She doesn't, no."

Molly turned to the ladies in the parlor and said, "It is getting *wild* out there!"

Liberty Street was living up to its name with a milling, dancing, and staggering mob of every shade of brown right over to white. A brass band with a trumpet, trombone, tuba and bass and snare drums had settled on a set of steps in the middle of the block. The noises and the swirls of color were electric and it seemed every other citizen had a bottle in hand. Some had two. Fireworks sizzled and popped all over the cobblestones. Here and there, a fellow had a woman against a building or in a doorway with her skirts hiked.

The lieutenant crossed his arms and watched. Reynard stared, his pen frozen over his notepad. Valentin studied the spectacle, a reminder of his crazier nights that lasted until he came back to the present, cupped his hand, and leaned toward James to say, "This would be some scene for an attack."

"I was thinking that, too," the lieutenant said. "A stick of dynamite would turn it into a fucking stampede."

They both knew that what they were viewing was the kickoff to the last night of Storyville, and midnight deadline or not, the celebrating would rise and fall through to morning light with a hundred opportunities for Mr. Blank to commit more mayhem.

Valentin turned to Reynard. "I suggest you call and see if you can get someone out to take photographs. This might be one for the history books."

The lieutenant had spent most of the evening walking right next to Mr. Valentin, wary that any strange would bring a gunshot or knife attack on the Creole detective—or on him, for that matter. He had long been awed by the man's strange sense for knowing things unseen and he understood that if a true threat was close by, Valentin would alert him. Not a few of New Orleans' denizens would call it voodoo, though he himself would scoff.

"I just keep my eyes and ears open," he had snapped the one time James had marveled at the strange talent, but the odd note behind the words told the lieutenant that maybe it wasn't quite so simple.

James noted that Reynard Vernel had displayed the wisdom to stay just behind and between them as they moved from place to place. The shouts and shrieks and laughter keep rising and provided some cover for all three of them.

They continued walking and watching. After they had once again turned the corner onto Basin Street, Valentin nudged the lieutenant and said, "Back there at the saloon? I didn't just call to check on Each."

"No?" James said.

"I called Eulalie Echo's house, too."

"And?"

"And there was no answer."

"Do you think he got to them?"

"No, not that."

"What then?"

"Justine's in the District, that's what." They were passing Antonia Gonzales' mansion and he looked up at the light in the window. "Hell, for all I know, all three of them are here now."

————

The two detectives did not see Mr. Blank lurking on the other end of the block, surveying the same crowd that they were watching and he didn't see them. He was looking for someone else.

He had been correct that St. Cyr's wife, who along with her exotic face and curvaceous figure, possessed a country girl's cunning and strength and had worked with him on dangerous cases, would be willing to hide somewhere while he walked the perilous streets. He had just missed catching her. He wouldn't let it happen again.

He walked a few steps this way and that at the edge of the eddying bodies. As he mulled his next step, the mob shifted and he caught sight of St. Cyr and the New Orleans copper. Standing between them was a slight fellow scribbling on a pad—a reporter. *Good,* Mr. Blank mused, *make a story out of this.* He knew where they were and he knew where St. Cyr's wife had gone. Both were out of the way for now. He backed away and into the shadows, heading around the block and in the direction of Marais Street.

Frank opened the door enough to witness the parade moving past in a rowdy assembly toward the next blocks south.

"What's happening out there?" Tom Anderson said from behind him.

"Same as before, Mr. Tom. But more now."

He returned his attention to the street. Among the gentlemen in cheap suits came a scattering of the rascals he had seen too many times, rough characters in poor-fitting, ragged clothes with driving caps or dusty bowlers on their heads. Some had work, some stayed alive wearing this hustle or that. What they did best was make trouble. None were Sicilians and far too stupid to be real *criminales* like *La Mani Neri.*

He now watched a half-dozen of these types stalk by, their dirty laughter trailing behind them. They ambled down the street, toward the noise and music, and when they were gone, he noticed a man in a dark coat and homburg across the way, standing very still with hard eyes.

Franco Mangetta was a man who had known violence in his past and realized in that sudden instant exactly who it was staring back at him. He saw the brick in the man's right hand and the long piece of wood in the other. He yelled "*Managgia!*" and was ducking away when the glass shattered.

Tom Anderson came alert, his eyes blinking wide. The man took a long stride and planted a foot on the window frame and stepped through with a three-foot round of oak grasped tight in his hand. Frank had almost reached the bar when the first strike caught him between the shoulder blades. He went face-down on the dirty floor, taking a stool with him, and rolled over in time to see the next blow coming at his head. A bolt of pain shot up the arm that he threw out to block it. He tried to rise up but his body wouldn't obey. The round of oak was about to come down on his head when he heard a sharp *bang*! The man stumbled back, dropped the bat, and clutched his shoulder.

Frank turned his head to see Tom Anderson sitting upright with a Derringer in his hand, the single barrel smoking.

The bullet had struck the man—*Mr. Blank*—on his left collarbone, shredding the fabric of his coat. He grinned like a death's head and was bending to pick up the board again when the unmistakable click of hammers being cocked echoed in the room. Carmine stood in the door from the hallway, Frank's *lupara* in his shaking hands. Mr. Blank let out a raw hiss, then wheeled around and bolted back through the window, onto the banquette, and down Marais Street.

Anderson took over, yelling to Carmine, "*Bravo!* Fetch some brandy. Call Mercy. Tell them Tom Anderson said get a doctor here now." Carmine was still shaking and Mr. Tom raised his voice. "Boy! Put the shotgun down and do what I say!" Carmine snapped out of his daze and scrambled away. The old man reached down to take Frank's hand in his. "God damn," he said. "You dagos do have some steel to you."

Frank offered a smile that was more a gritting of his teeth and held on tighter.

Molly was excited as she described the scenes on the back streets. "If they thought it was going to go quiet and close up a midnight, they gettin' a surprise," she said.

The women asked for details and she described music, dancing, drinking, carousing. "And fucking, too!" she said, bringing a round of laughter. Evangeline gasped and her face went pink.

Justine did not share in the frivolity and once it died down, she said, "I'm going out and find him."

Evangeline said, "Oh, no..."

"Well, I can't just sit here." She moved around the table to fetch her coat.

"Justine..."

Miss Lulu held up a hand. "Wait. Please."

Miss Antonia saw the look on the younger woman's face and stood up. "We've got coats here and scarves that gentlemen left behind. Put on as much as you can."

Ten minutes later, she was bundled and ready to go out the door. She noticed Evangeline about to weep from worry and stepped close, bent down, and kissed her forehead. "I'll be back," she said. "With Valentin."

She had just reached the banquette when a man came hurtling her way with such fervor that she thought he was going to attack her. She was more startled when he rushed by and she saw that it was Mr. Blank.

He found an alley where a woman was about to go down on her knees before some lucky fellow and ran them off. After they had tottered away, he leaned against the bricks, pulled his coat and then his shirt from one arm.

The wound was slight, the bullet having just caught the skin atop his shoulder. There was little blood and the bone ached but was not broken. Had it hit an inch lower, he barely would have been able to continue. A few more down or right and he'd be dead. He drew the shirt and coat back on. Treatment would have to wait. He now took a few moments to run back over what had occurred.

The window had broken into a hundred shards, as he had expected and he threw his foot on the sill and charged inside. He was surprised to see the fat old man at the table but it did not slow him. He brought the round of oak down on the Sicilian's backbone and was going for the front of his head when the dago put his arm up, cracking the bone but not reaching his target. He was about to do that and finish the job with a blow to the skull when the pistol cracked and he felt the bullet snap at his shoulder and whistle near his ear.

After another minute, he felt ready to move. Before he did, though, he caught something out of the corner of his eye, a thick shape standing in silhouette at the end of the alley. He let his hand drop to his coat pocket and the Browning .32 that rested there.

"You won't need it," a voice called. The shape moved, taking slow steps, the arms and empty hands held wide as the figure took on features, a heavy body and a round, oily face under a derby hat. The fellow stopped at ten paces. "Mr. Blank? My name is J. Picot."

Baptiste had driven every backroad he came upon, winding deep into the woods, the headlights of his Chevrolet throwing ghostly beams into the branches and across the still waters when he crossed Thompson Creek and along the ponds that he rounded. Glittering eyes struck out from the shadows and he prayed his old machine would not break down and leave him at the mercy of whatever creatures were lurking. He breathed a sigh of relief when he arrived back at Highway 68, one of the six arteries into Jackson.

He found a pay telephone outside a closed gas station and spent a nickel to call the hospital. The attendant on the desk told him that no, Mr. Bolden had not reappeared, and yes, the city, East Feliciana Parish, and State Police had all been notified to be on the lookout. It would not be hard to spot a tall man in white pajamas, a hospital bathrobe, and a rough coat.

Baptiste went back to his roadster and sat behind the wheel. He looked at his watch: almost midnight. There was nothing for him to do but go home, get some sleep, and hope to wake up to the news that Buddy had been found and was safely back on the ward. Sitting in the shrouded darkness, a feeling came upon him that it wouldn't happen that way, that Mr. Bolden was still out there and it was Baptiste Marchand who would find him, alive or dead.

From somewhere from the bayou behind the station a loon was calling like a sad horn, and he sat forward, listening as he entertained a crazy notion. The road was pulling him, even as he knew that it was preposterous to think that Buddy would try to travel the two hundred miles to New Orleans on his own. He mulled it some more, glanced at his watch one more time, put the shifter into low gear, and pulled out.

EIGHTEEN

Justine was bundled so thickly that she looked like one of the creaky, crazy, whiskey-headed or dope-fiend women who couldn't get warm no matter how brutal the heat. She had allowed the older women to fuss as they wrapped her, the doting aunties she'd never known growing up. The temperature on the street was only fifty degrees and she was baking and her jangling nerves were heating her even more.

She turned off the busy boulevard and stopped short at the sight of a bonfire blazing atop the cobblestones a block down to the sounds of shouts, raucous laughter, and happy curses. The horn player on a gallery just above the fire weaved on his feet, but the notes from the bell of his trumpet were loud and steady.

To keep up her charade of another woeful piece of street trash, she moved along at a shuffling pace. All the while, her eyes were shifting as she watched for her husband, James—or Mr. Blank. She had made her way to the next intersection and was rounding the fire when a sport in his cups grabbed the sleeve of her coat and tried to drag her close. Her hand came up to clutch his lapel and fixed him with eyes so hard that he jerked back. She moved on, leaving him startled.

Fires were roaring at the intersections ahead and to her left and right, all of them attended by animated shapes milling against the flames, and the tableau reminded her of a painting of Hell that Valentin had once shown her in a book.

She considered that he was likely less than half-mile of where she stood. By this time, he would have called the house on the lake to find that she and the two older women were gone and would guess that she had escaped, that Evangeline and Eulalie had followed her, and that they were now somewhere in Storyville. She also understood that there would be hell to pay when they found each other.

Even as Justine, Valentin, James, Reynard, and Mr. Blank wandered the District, word had been going from mouths to ears and women began drifting to Miss Antonia's door ahead of the midnight hour. The foyer grew noisy with shouts and laughter as one after another of Miss Lulu's girls arrived. By 11:30, fifteen women crowded into the downstairs rooms to sample rye whiskey from the bottles Molly fetched from the kitchen. Some of them had been among the elite at Mahogany Hall. The others knew Miss Lulu from her reputation as the Grand Dame of the District. At one point, that lady was so overcome that she slipped into the washroom to collect herself. Then she went back out to join the reunion.

The first of the men arrived just before midnight and Miss Antonia stood by the door making sure that there was no riff-raff among them. Most had been guests of the house at one time or another. There were no professors anymore, nor a piano, so she had her girls take turns winding up the Victrola and they squealed at the strains of "Livery Stable Blues."

That was downstairs. Doors were opening and closing on the second floor, as women who chose to do some business pleasured one gentleman after another. Molly scurried behind, changing as many of the linens as she could manage.

Evangeline sat in the midst of the bedlam, first puzzled, then amused, then wearied. Miss Antonia noticed and stepped close to whisper in her ear. The madam escorted her upstairs and to the master bedroom at the end of the hall that had been hers for the last twelve years.

"You can rest now," she said. "I'm sorry about the noise."

Evangeline said, "No, it's all right. I won't be able to sleep with them out there anyway."

Miss Antonia pulled a wingback chair that had come all the way from France to one of the windows facing Basin Street.

Evangeline treated her to a droll glance and said, "Watch what?"

The madam promised to have Molly check on her every so often and left her to gaze out at the street. Just as she settled in, she noticed a thin young man running along the banquette, stopping every few steps to speak to someone before hurrying on. After following his movements for half the block, the notion crossed her mind that he could be looking for Valentin.

Along with the *lupara*, Frank kept a Colt Bisley behind the bar and after he had turned down the lights, he dug out a box of the same .38-caliber cartridges that Mr. Tom used in his pearl-handled Derringer.

The saloonkeeper came around the bar to find the old man gazing in an absent way out the broken window at Marais Street and the steady stream of bodies passing by. He said "*Con permesso*," lifted the little pistol from the table, pushed a bullet into the chamber, and set it back down again.

"Right in front of me and I missed him," Anderson said. "I really am getting old."

Frank touched his shoulder. "You got him a little." He waved a hand at the window. "You want that I put something up? A blanket, maybe?"

"Leave it," Anderson said. "I'm going to be here until the end and I want to see."

"That's fine." Frank turned to his assistant and said, "*Un fuoco*, Carmine." He and Mr. Tom watched as the younger man put some newspaper and a shovelful of coal in the stove and set it ablaze.

———

Mr. Pettibone stepped into the mayor's office, pointed to the telephone that had begun chirping, and said, "It's Lieutenant McKinney, sir."

Behrman waited for him to leave before picking up the handset and listened, replying with only single words, "What?" and "No!" and "Where?" A smile crept across his face. Finally, he said, "All right, thank you," and hung up.

"Good Lord!" He turned to Acting Chief Cook, who had been sitting all but motionless on the couch, and let out a laugh. "Listen to this. That Mr. Blank tried to force his way into Mangetta's Saloon. Tom Anderson pulled his Derringer and shot him in the shoulder."

The acting chief sat forward. "Is he dead?"

"Dead? I'm sorry to say no." The mayor laughed some more. "But McKinney said if he had lowered the barrel an inch, our troubles would be over." He waved a hand. "At least, those troubles." He shook his head in delight. "I take back what I said about that old man. Shot him with a Derringer. Ha!"

"So the fellow got away?" Cook asked.

"With a wound," the mayor said. He spent a moment puzzling over the odd look on the acting chief's face. "Yes, he's still out there."

Buddy felt like he was being carried along on a calm river. Save for the weak yellow beams that broke through to light the road ahead, all was darkness. He was sitting high up. To his left was a big wheel and behind that big wheel was a big man. A big black man. Like Willie. That was not the name of the man behind the wheel. He had said it, but Buddy had forgotten already, as it went lost in the wind and wafted into the night. But *Willie* stayed.

Now he heard *thump-thump-thump* from underneath the truck, the way Willie went *thump-thump-thump* on that big box with the heavy strings. He mused on that as the trees whipped past like men with no flesh on their bones running by. That was long ago and far down a tunnel of racing skeletons of trees like the one that arched over him now. And what he wished for was waiting at the other end.

———

Even with an eye that had been honed sharp over his twenty years on the force, J. Picot could not keep his gaze fixed on the man in the alley. One glance told him that he would not remember that face a minute after they parted. There was simply nothing striking that he could detect in the dark of this November night. And the voice: a flat drone, as if the speaker was reading the words off a sheet of paper.

Mr. Blank had led him to the narrow passage called Eclipse Alley. The name struck a chord, but he couldn't remember why. Little groups and lone citizens were moving down Franklin Street on one end and Liberty on the other. Picot paid no attention. He was bewildered by a foul something that was coming off Mr. Blank, a kind of rot that he knew from certain sick felons he had encountered in his years on the force, as if gruesome worms were devouring them from inside.

Still, J. Picot was glad to be on his side. "Have we met before?" he said.

Mr. Blank watched him without speaking until at length he said, "No. We have not."

"Do you know how I was found?"

"What I know is that someone passed your name along," Mr. Blank said. "And you were called."

Hearing it delivered in that toneless voice, Picot felt a niggle of fear. "I know you're out to stop St. Cyr," he blurted. When Mr. Blank continued to stare, he said, "I guess they figured I could help." A horse-drawn hack carrying a load of drunkards who were shouting and singing passed the mouth of the alley. After their voices and the creak of the wheels had faded, he said, "I can. And I will."

"That's appreciated, Mr. Picot."

"Captain."

"What?"

"Captain Picot."

Mr. Blank produced a smile that caused the sweat to prickle under Picot's scalp. The eyes kept staring, deathly hollows, and in a sudden instant the name "Eclipse Alley" dawned on him. He had read in the New Orleans paper that he bought every morning about a murder case that had begun and ended in that same dark throughway—one of *St. Cyr's* murder cases. He was so startled recalling this that he couldn't get his mind to decide if it was a coincidence or a trick someone was playing.

Mr. Blank was silent for another ten tortuous seconds and Picot realized that of course it wasn't any coincidence and that he—

"I have some work for you."

Picot all but gasped his relief. "Well, yes. What is you need?"

Mr. Blank explained with a dozen quiet words. Picot didn't quite believe what he was being told to do, but he was not about to refuse. So he swallowed, gave a quick nod, and said, "You can count on me."

"All right, then," Mr. Blank said. "You do this and meet me back here in two hours. Understood?"

"Yes, sir."

Mr. Blank started to turn away, then stopped. "I have a question. Why didn't you kill St. Cyr when you had the chance? Before you had to run off, I mean."

So he knows about that, too. "I wish I had," Picot said. "Maybe I still will."

"No." Mr. Blank's tone was sharp stone. "That's for me to finish."

Justine spotted a familiar face hurrying along the banquette. She couldn't fix on his name, but he worked for Frank at the grocery and saloon. She watched as he moved in a skittish way, stopping to bend his head and whisper to some passing someone. Whatever he asked brought either a shake of a head or a finger pointing. She understood. He was looking for someone. Her husband.

She followed him for two blocks as he looped around Conti and Bienville, then wandered to Villere, stopping a half-dozen more times along the way. He arrived at the corner of Bienville and when she saw him wave and call out, she ducked back into a doorway. Across the intersection, Valentin turned around.

She held herself still for a moment, seeing the same profile he had cut when she first met him. Like an alley cat. Why was she thinking about that now? Why not? Nothing else made sense on this night. He knew he was being hunted and yet he stood in open view, daring Mr. Blank, as hundreds of strangers passed this way and that, This, as she huddled a few short paces away in a ragged woman's clothes, with one person they knew dead and a second fighting for his life. And all the while, Evangeline, Miss Eulalie, and the two madams were keeping a vigil in a Basin Street bordello, waiting through the night for the last act. It was all so insane that she—

The boy from Mangetta's—*Carmine* was his name—now made a sudden jag to the other side of the street to whisper excitedly to Valentin and then to James McKinney, who had appeared from down the banquette. The trio started back in the direction of Marais Street.

So she had found him. Now, she decided, she would follow him through the next seven hours, an extra pair of eyes and hands, if the need arose. To make sure he would be alive come morning.

By twelve-thirty, Baptiste was beyond exhausted, his body and mind no longer aching for sleep. He had stopped a second time to call the hospital, only to learn that as he expected, Mr. Bolden had not been located. New alerts had gone around the parish. Baptiste knew they would do no good, either, because Buddy Bolden was gone.

But not *gone* as in dead, he reflected as he sat parked under a willow tree on the side of Route 68. And yet it was a preposterous notion that a man who could barely find his way to the sun room on his own would travel two hundred miles down dark roads in the dead of a November night to the Crescent City.

The authorities were already on the lookout for a strange character, and the wisest thing Baptiste could do would be to go home, go to bed, and hope for good news. That would be prudent.

After thinking about this for a few more minutes, he got out to crank the engine, then climbed back into the seat and drummed his fingers on the steering wheel. There was a filling station outside Amite City that stayed open all night and had a pay telephone so he could call his wife. She wouldn't be pleased, but he was a good husband and father, and she knew he wouldn't be getting into mischief. Finally, he wanted to be there if Buddy somehow managed to reach the place where he had once ruled as King Bolden.

The official midnight closing had been completely ignored. Valentin, the lieutenant, and Carmine arrived back at Mangetta's to find Frank sweeping up shards of glass and pieces of the window frame while a fire glowed in the iron stove. Tom Anderson had retired to last booth, now half-hidden in shadows. Valentin and the lieutenant crossed the room and sat down facing him. The Derringer lay on the table next to a half-glass of brandy.

For all the peril on the streets, Valentin felt like doing nothing so much as laughing out loud.

Instead, he allowed himself a small smile, said, "Well, now. Tell me how it happened. Tell me how Mr. Blank almost met his end here."

The King of Storyville made an imperial gesture and Frank stopped sweeping and spoke up in his stead. "I look out through the curtain and I see him across the street. Just standing there, like this..." He mimed a glaring stare. "I knew who it was. He had something in his hand and I turned around to tell Carmine to grab the *lupara* when he threw it. A brick. The whole thing just..." He flung his arms wide to describe the breakage. "Then he come running this way." The saloon-keeper took an operatic step backward. "He jumped right over the... the..." He mimed again. "*Come se dice? Davanzale?*"

"Windowsill," Carmine said.

Frank went on. "And that's when...*bang!* His coat went..." He flicked fingers at his shoulder, then turned to Mr. Tom, who had been listening, bemused. "The *signore* was holding that *piccolo pistola*." He shook his head in wonder. "Carmine, he come around with the *lupara* and your *Signore Vuoto*, he ran back out and then down the street. That's what happened."

"I used to be a good shot with it," Mr. Tom said.

"That's still not too bad," Valentin said.

"Well, he got away." The old man leaned back. "So now what, gentlemen?"

Justine had followed them as they made their way to Marais Street. Valentin looked back three or four times and she as if he sensed someone on this trail. She made sly moves out of sight and when they reached Mangetta's, stopped as they did to gawk at the damage to the saloon's façade. The men talked for a few moments, then stepped inside. She stayed where she was, bundled in her layers.

One side of her mind told her to give up the ruse, follow them, and take her punishment. The other told her to stay put, keep following Valentin, and do what she could to ward of the danger from Mr. Blank. She chose the second, fading into the dark enclosure of the doorway behind her to watch and wait.

As the dark minutes moved by, Buddy was lulled into a sleep that brought one of the dreams that came to him often, a steam engine pulling endless empty cars in a chain that stretched to the horizon. The first time, the vision had frightened him and the words *hellbound train* had come to mind, but then the sky changed as a golden sun rose and he heard the sound of a horn blowing a sweet run of notes that brought him such joy that he almost couldn't bear it. He would wake feeling tears on his cheeks.

Something jostled and he tried to snatch it back, but the reverie faded. There were no more little clouds of dust rising and now he no longer felt the thumping but a steady hum. He lifted his head and saw a splay of stars that he had seen before, the glittering roof of the world.

NINETEEN

The men spent a half-hour sitting around the stove. Reynard arrived, surveyed the damage, and listened in astonishment as this time Tom Anderson described what had transpired, and then hurried to call it in. He was on his way back when the telephone bell clattered. From the saloon, they heard him say, "One moment, please." He called out, "Mister Valentin? It's for you. The hospital."

Mr. Tom said, "Oh, Christ."

Valentin stepped into the hallway and took a long breath before placing the handset to his ear.

"Mariette?"

"Yes, Mr. Valentin. Something happened here."

"To Each?"

"Oh, no, sir. His condition is the same." Valentin sighed with relief. "I mean it's not him exactly."

"What, then?"

"There was a call to the nurses' station. Someone wanting to know what room he was in. She wouldn't give him the number and he hung up."

"Can you ask her if she heard anything in the background?"

"I already did that," Mariette said, causing Valentin to smile. "She said it was quiet."

Valentin said, "Are the coppers still there?"

Mariette said, "There's one at his door and another one down by the elevators. They've been switching back and forth."

"All right, then."

"I just thought you'd want to know about the call."

"Wait," he said. "I know it's late. How are you holding up?"

She said, "I'm fine. I pulled long hours before." She laughed. "You remember."

He thanked her and hung up the phone.

J. Picot set his plan in motion when he walked to Frenchmen Street and found a telephone in an apothecary that was staying open all night. The druggist took his coin and announced without being asked he was seeing injuries requiring his wares and expected more before the night was out. Not to mention the extra demand for paregoric and cocaine. He winked and said, "And I got the medicine."

Picot treated him to a cold look. Had he still been on the force, he would have shaken him down for the elixirs he had bragged on and some of the cash in the drawer, too. But things weren't like that anymore. So he walked to the end of the counter, made his call to Mercy, and left without a word.

Outside, he looked at his watch. One-thirty and he could hear the voices and music from the District again. It wasn't going down easy, but it was going down, and here he was, playing his part in the final drama. The thought pleased him as he began walking in the direction of Roman Street, the route that would take him to the hospital.

Though it was still deep night, the stars began to fade against a purple sky that was strung with wisps of clouds turned white by the glow from the crescent moon. The truck topped a rise and he saw a new dazzle of lights, not above but straight ahead. They were moving slower now and on either side buildings and signs appeared in place of the trees.

The man behind the big wheel pointed a finger and said, "Baton Rouge." Then: "You know why? Because back when, there wa'nt nothing here but a red stick in the ground."

The truck was crawling along now and sounds came to him, night birds and machine noises and steady hums, too. A train whistle far off. Lonely figures appeared along the way, this one or that who were not invisible. He understood: city. But not New Orleans. Not yet.

Some time passed and the slowing became a stop and the man said, "Far as I go." He jerked a thick thumb to the road they had just crossed. "What you want is off that way."

After Mr. Blank sent Picot on his way, he walked the streets back to Marais and stood down the block from the saloon, surprised to see that the window he had destroyed had been only partway boarded-up, as if in an act of defiance. He moved closer and saw figures passing back and forth in the glow of a pot-bellied stove. Another few steps and he stopped, again sensing that he was being watched. He scanned both sides of the street but saw nothing.

Now the door opened and the policeman, St. Cyr, and the newspaperman stepped onto the banquette. A quartet of drunkards had stumbled by. The Creole detective surveyed the block, at one point seeming to stare directly at him. The gaze passed on.

They whispered among themselves, walked to the corner, and split up, St. Cyr heading south and the copper and the reporter east in the direction of Conti. So the proprietor, the old man with the pistol that had grazed him, and the dago kid with the shotgun remained inside. He waited a few seconds more before following St. Cyr and was unaware of the bent-down woman in a winter coat and several scarves trailing behind him.

Valentin arrived on Miss Antonia's gallery, but before he could knock, the door opened and three merry fellows tumbled outside and down the steps to the banquette. The madam saw him standing there and said, "I was wondering when you'd show up."

"How are things?"

"It's the last hurrah." She beckoned him inside. "You're looking for Justine."

"Is she here?"

"She was. Not now."

He was incensed. "Not *now*? Where did she go?"

"Out to find you. But…"

"But what?"

"I don't think she wants you finding her right yet."

"Well, isn't that lovely?"

Miss Antonia treated him to a cool glance. "I believe she gets some of her notions from a certain detective."

She waved for him to follow her through the noisy parlor and into the dining room where Lulu White was holding court. "Mr. Valentin," she called over the heads of the men and women gathered around the table. "We meet again."

"Miss Lulu," he said.

"What news?"

"Nothing to report."

Lulu White gave a sly smile. He wouldn't have shared anything of import in public and they both knew it.

"We'll talk later," he said and allowed Miss Antonia to escort him away. "What about Evangeline and Miss Eulalie?" he asked her.

She took his arm, said, "Come with me," and led him to the bottom of the staircase.

After another half-hour downstairs, Miss Eulalie had decided she'd had enough and joined Evangeline in the master bedroom. Miss Antonia had Molly come along behind with coffee, brandy, and a plate of sweets. The voodoo woman closed the door and pulled her own chair to the window. "Anything interesting?" she asked.

"No, nothing." Evangeline sipped from her cup. "You know, now and then, I would hear Valentin and Justine talk about Storyville."

"What you're seeing tonight is not how it was before."

"I thought not." She paused. "Justine."

Miss Eulalie said, "What about her?"

"She was here, wasn't she? As a..."

"Yes. It's where she and Valentin met."

Miss Eulalie hoped the older woman wouldn't inquire further on the subject.

She did not. "She's such a good woman," she said. "A good wife."

Relieved, Miss Echo said, "She is, indeed. He's a lucky man."

At this, Evangeline fell into a rumination that lasted until they heard a tap on the door.

From a hundred feet down the banquette Justine watched Mr. Blank watch Valentin climb the steps to the gallery. The door until opened to disgorge a trio of drunks and then Miss Antonia's stout figure was framed in the light. After she let Valentin pass inside, Mr. Blank moved off and she followed. As much as she yearned to be safe at her husband's side, she didn't want to let the man trying to kill him out of her sight.

Trailing along, she asked herself why she didn't simply wait for an empty space and plunge the knife she was carrying into his neck. She stopped to let the scene play out in her mind, imagining the thrust of her arm, the jolt as the map of red spread down his coat, the mask of rage when he turned to see... her.

She caught a breath and walked on, wondering if she could go that far. Valentin wouldn't do it that way; he'd face the man so he could stab him clean through the heart, the same way Each had been struck, and watch the light go out in those flat eyes. So, no, she was not prepared to commit that final act. Unless it was the only way to save her husband and then she would not hesitate. Because she had done it once before.

When they reached the end of the hall, Miss Antonia tapped with a knuckle, turned the knob, and opened the door. Valentin stepped inside to find the two women regarding him with gazes that were so alike in their gravity that he came up with a dim smile. Miss Antonia closed the door and padded away.

"What are you doing here?" he said.

They both stiffened at his tone and he very much wished he had bitten his tongue.

Evangeline said, "We came looking for Justine. Who came looking for you."

"Because you wouldn't stay at the lake where it was safe," Eulalie said.

None of the three spoke for a moment.

"So you'll be going out to find her," Evangeline said.

He got the message. "Yes, she needs to be inside," he said. "If she comes back, tell her to call and leave a message at Mangetta's." He looked at Miss Echo. "Do you—"

"I know it, yes," she said. "Now, go."

"Please find her," Evangeline said. "I'm worried."

The moon went higher and the road began to move again and this time it was not a lumbering truck but a rusty, creaking sedan and the man behind the wheel was a redbone with freckles on his cheeks and a head of wild hair. Buddy read signs: *Westminster, Duplessis, Gonzales.* That last one was somehow familiar.

The redbone talked as if his passenger could understand every word from his mouth. In truth it was only a few. *Traveling. Dark out here. Blind River, outside of Gramercy.* The rest was a faint hum that rose and fell as he fixed on the stars and the shadows that traveled alongside for a bit and then fell behind. At one point, he recalled that he had been at the hospital and understood that he was moving in for a reason that he did not recall, but it was important that he keep going all the same.

The fellow said, "Just about forty miles now."

Forty miles. *Forty.* The number sounded right. Forty days. Forty days and nights. Forty miles. Forty. And then he would be there.

Before Valentin left Miss Antonia's, he called Union Station to inquire about the Seaboard Limited and the Southern Crescent. The sleepy clerk told him that the first train had arrived in Atlanta and the second had left, both on time. The train carrying Geary's two men and a portfolio of documents would steam into New Orleans at 8:15 in the morning.

Highway 61 was mostly empty in the middle of the night this late in the fall and Baptiste could drive at his own pace, keeping it at thirty and letting the rare automobile or truck whiz past as he lost himself in his thoughts. So say crazy man Bolden made it all the way to the Crescent City. What then? How in the world could he hope to find him amidst the confusion of the last hours before Storyville closed down?

He knew only a few facts about the man: his early life in the neighborhood around First and Liberty streets; making a whole new kind of music for seven years before it all blew up; his long friendship with Mr. St. Cyr, the only one who called or came to visit anymore. It wasn't much and finding him was someone else's business and he had every reason to turn around and go back. But then he imagined how he would feel if something terrible happened and he didn't try to stop it. So he drove on.

As dangerous as the streets were for anyone close to Mr. Valentin, James decided to spend an hour roaming alone, hoping to encounter Mr. Blank, bring him in, or finish him. The St. Cyrs weren't his blood, but like Miss Evangeline, he was the next thing to family and he owed them. And so he sharpened his eyes as he moved along the banquettes, remembering the edge he felt when he and the Creole detective had chased down the Rampart Street and the madman who went by Gregory except that Mr. Blank was far more conniving and lethal than either of them as he used the revelry lighting up the Storyville night to hide himself and his crimes.

The lieutenant steered clear of the mobs swelling with new arrivals and those abandoning the outlying streets to move closer to the center of the District. He slipped through the throng to the corner of Iberville and Villere, hoping to dodge whatever might be coming his way.

It wasn't enough. With the multiple strings of firecrackers dancing on the cobblestones and the boom of 80s, no one heard the single gunshot.

James sensed the threat too late and in a sudden second, felt a sharp blow and then a shock of pain in his left armpit. He lurched back and looked down to see a dark, wet stain flowering beneath his coat. No one in the crowd swirling around him had noticed. He wrenched his revolver from his pocket, made his way into the nearest doorway, and leaned there, taking stock. Blood was seeping down his side, but his body told him the wound wasn't dire. He stared at the red patch with wonder. He had been shot for the first time.

A minute later, he beckoned to a corporal and a private who were passing by on patrol. When they drew close, he lifted his arm to reveal the patch of red. They stepped to his sides and walked him the three blocks to Canal Street and the door of the all-night clinic.

"You're lucky," the corporal said as they started up the stairwell. "He missed."

James stopped and said, "No, he didn't."

Mayor Behrman looked up, startled, and the acting chief came out of a drowse when Major Sont came charging into the office. The major ignored Acting Chief Cook as he crossed to the wide oak desk.

"Major?" Behrman said. "What is it?"

"Lieutenant McKinney was shot."

Cook roused himself, suddenly animated and for what the mayor noted was the second time that night spoke the words, "Is he dead?"

Sont addressed the mayor as if he had asked the question. "Not dead, wounded," he said. "I just got off the telephone with him. He's at the emergency clinic on Canal Street." He touched his hand to the left side of his chest. "Took it right here."

Mayor Behrman mulled for a few seconds, then said, "Wait. Isn't that the same spot where this Mr. Blank was hit?"

"Close, but no," Sont said. "Anderson winged the man. The lieutenant gets shot in the flesh." He paused. "It was intentional. McKinney said he could have killed him, but didn't."

"Well, goddamn," Behrman said. "So he stabs one of St. Cyr's men, shoots another one, lets some poor sot die in a fire, but then he has a clear shot at St. Cyr's partner and doesn't take it." He turned to the acting chief and said, "You have an opinion on this, John?"

Cook had been gazing at the floor. Now he looked up quickly and said, "Sorry. On what?"

"On all this," the mayor said, with a flash of annoyance. "On some fucking felon roaming the District killing and wounding people connected to St. Cyr."

In response, the acting chief's face lost some of its color and he said, "Well, it's...that's a...a mystery, Mr. Mayor."

Major Sont did not move or speak, wondering if the next words out of Behrman's mouth would be, "And what do you know about that?"

The mayor kept staring at Cook. "Well, maybe we'll have an answer in the morning." The acting chief was now listening with glazed eyes, a child caught in mischief. *Oh, you know,* Behrman mused. *You know.*

Valentin got word of the attack on James by way of a telephone call to Miss Antonia's. He had just descended the stairs and was almost to the door when she hurried to intercept him.

"But he's alive?" he said after she told him what had happened.

"Yes. He's at that place on Canal Street with the doctor who stays open all night. What's his name? Rall?"

"Did you say 'Rall'? Are you sure about that?"

"Yes. That's the name."

"Oh, Jesus," Valentin said and left the house, muttering.

Outside, Mr. Blank watched him turn and start for Canal Street.

The address was on the uptown end of the street, over an apothecary. "Well, of course," Valentin said to no one as he opened the street door.

He had first encountered John Rall ten years before when he was investigating the Black Rose murders. Kid Bolden had come under suspicion and Rall had been prescribing narcotics for Buddy and helping himself as well. Valentin recalled visiting a ratty office and instead of a man of medicine finding a shaking wreck of a drug addict.

Even that did not prepare him for what he encountered when he reached the second floor. At first he thought the crabbed figure was a patient lingering on death's doorstep. When he looked closer, he realized it was the doctor himself, hunched over in a spasm of some sort. Rall's attempt at a smile was ghastly, his breath was foul, and his voice creaked like a rusty hinge when he said, "Mr. St. Cyr? You remember me?"

James sat in placid repose atop a gurney, his shirt off and holding a red-stained bandage under his arm. "Don't worry," he said in a low voice. "I'm not letting that old dopehead touch me. Major Sont has them sending someone from Mercy."

Hearing this, Rall muttered something, and Valentin turned around, took him by the elbow, ushered him into the front room, and closed the door. Then he said, "So, did you see him?"

"I didn't," James said. "I knew he was there, but by that time..." He shrugged. "I figure he couldn't have been more than ten feet away. He could have plugged me right in the heart if he'd wanted to."

He had just asked Valentin for a report on his travels when there was a tap on the door and a dark-haired man in his thirties entered, carrying a black bag which he placed on the gurney.

"Gentlemen," he said. "Carlo Gatti. Gunshot, is it?" He began pulling the bandage away. Valentin and the lieutenant exchanged a smile. *A dago doctor, no less.* Gatti opened his bag and set to work cleaning the wound.

"Do you want me to leave?" Valentin asked him.

"You can stay." He produced a syringe. "An anesthetic," he explained and jabbed it into James's shoulder. "I'm hoping I can treat it here and not have you go in for surgery."

"If that's the case, leave it," James said. "I need to be on the streets."

"Let's see what we have first," Dr. Gatti said.

Valentin picked up where he had left off, relating what he learned at Miss Antonia's. "So everyone is accounted for. Except for Justine."

Ten minutes later, Gatti had the lieutenant laid out on the gurney and was working on the entry and exit wounds with a scalpel and forceps. James stared at the ceiling, his left side numbed with a massive injection of tropocaine.

"I'm going back out," he said at one point.

"I heard you," the doctor responded. "And you can. But you won't be worth much. Just so you know."

James mugged at Valentin, then said, "You need to be getting on, don't you?"

"In a minute."

It was half that. The door creaked open and Dr. Rall poked his skull inside. "There's a boy out here," he said. "Looking for you. Something happened. Concerns your wife."

TWENTY

The sky on the north side of the river was spread with glorious white clusters. The redbone pulled out a packet of Wings and offered one. Buddy shook his head and he snapped out a cigarette for himself. When the cab filled with smoke, Buddy rolled down the window and felt a rush of wind that lightened his head. He closed his eyes and drew in the smells of paradise.

"Won't be long now," the redbone said. "Maybe a half-hour until we cross over."

Cross over. They had sung about that in church while he played along on his horn, the one made from the silver plateware that the white folks had melted down to keep it out of the hands of the Yankees. And how did he know *that?* Someone had told him a long time ago.

J. Picot spent the walk to Mercy convincing himself that the violence he was about to commit would be worth being rid of St. Cyr for good. After ten years of the Creole detective hanging about his life like a, it was about time to have it finished. He wouldn't be the one to commit the deed, but he was going to help and by the time he crossed Tulane Avenue, he had braced himself for the task at hand.

At the hospital, he was greeted by a stroke of sheer luck. He didn't know the uniformed officer posted at the front door, but when he went to the rear entrance, he spied a familiar face. It took him a few seconds to recall the name: Berry. As before, the copper displayed the same red, piggish face topped by a thatch of dirty blond hair. His blues were still a sloppy mess. He had never risen above patrolman first-grade due to his stupidity and unsavory habits, good only for duty like guarding a door far from anywhere a true police presence was needed.

Picot stepped up. "Patrolman! Good evening."

Berry peered. "Hey," he said. "Hey. Look." He squinted. "It's Captain... Picot."

"That's right."

"I ain't seen you in a long time."

"I've been on special assignment."

Berry nodded, impressed. "So...what are you doin' 'round here?"

"Chief Reynolds asked me to come check on the patient."

"You mean Cook. Acting Chief Cook."

"Oh, yes. Cook." Picot grimaced the slip-up. "So I'll just..." He gestured to the door.

"Oh, yes, sir." The patrolman grabbed the brass bar and pulled it wide.

Picot spent a moment relishing the slavish treatment he had once known on a daily basis. "Who's on the floor? Third, is it?"

"No, fourth." Berry frowned. Even his dull brain was sensing some-thing off. "You say the chief sent you? Cause nobody said nothing to me about it."

"They want it kept quiet. Don't worry." With a wink, the former captain took quick steps inside. "Keep up the good work," he said and made for the elevator.

Mariette came out of the room and peered down the hall to see the two coppers on guard duty together at the nurses' station instead of at opposite ends of the floor. She understood. It had been quiet and Jane the night nurse was as pretty as Theda Bara. Still, it concerned her.

She had just started down the hall to speak to them when she caught movement out of the corner of her eye. Someone thick of body and huddled in a coat and hat had gone into Each's room. Startled, she called out, "Sir? Sir!" and ran in to find the man just reaching the bed. "Sir!" she barked.

In the next moment, she heard one of the officers call, "What's wrong?"

Mariette got only a quick look at the man as he turned around, pushed her aside with a rough hand, and bolted into the hallway. But she knew she had seen the face before. A quick glance told her that Each had not been disturbed and she rushed out and ran to the top of the stairwell. The two officers arrived right behind her.

"A man," she told them. "Going down."

One of the coppers went after him while the other returned to the room with her. She put a hand on the iron bedstead and let a wave of sour fear come and go. The patient was safe. In the next moment, she was shocked to see him open his eyes.

"What happened?" he said. "Where am I?"

Valentin used the doctor's telephone to call Miss Antonia.

"I have a message for Justine if she comes back. Tell her James McKinney was shot. He'll be fine. But she needs to stay indoors. Do not let her leave," he said. "Strap her down if you have to."

"I understand," the madam said. "Now I have a message for you. From Mariette at Mercy. She said to tell you that something happened there."

Valentin placed the handset in the cradle and threw a curse at the bare wall.

Baptiste saw a sign: **NEW ORLEANS 25 MILES**. He would reach the city in less than an hour. Far ahead, the taillights of a lone Ford sedan were like twin buoys guiding him. His Model T and the other machine were the only vehicles moving through the middle of the night.

Soon enough, though, the farmers' trucks and horse-drawn wagons would take to the road, carrying their goods to the markets and to the sellers, most of them Italian, who would load their hacks and roll down the city streets, calling up to the women lowering buckets with bills and coins to receive their fruits and vegetables in return. How did they say it? *Buon giorno, signora! Chi é la bella insalata! Chi é la frutta!* And his mother would be waiting on the balcony with her bucket and rope.

His thoughts shifted to what he would find when he arrived. The only way he might be able to locate Buddy would be to seek out Mr. Valentin and enlist his help. But just locating the Creole detective would be hard enough in the midst of the commotion—if he hadn't already left New Orleans. Driving on, Baptiste decided that this was unlikely. From what he knew of the man, he would be around to see the District through to its final morning.

Mr. Blank would know that someone was dogging his steps. Justine followed him anyway. Valentin would be furious when he realized how reckless she had been. She didn't care and she trailed the gray coat of Mr. Blank as he zigged one way and zagged the other at his hulking pace, as if leading her through a maze. They passed crowds and women and men wandering alone or in twos and threes. Couples twisted away on each other in dark passages and alleys and doorways. Bonfires blazed on the cobblestones and horns shouted from galleries and open windows. The heat from the flames and the bodies crammed together were raising the temperature to feverish.

Mr. Blank now turned south on Villere and she wondered if he was about to cross over to Canal. If that was the case, she'd drop the chase, find Valentin, and stand still for her scolding. She allowed herself a brief laugh as she lifted her skirts over the gutter, thinking of what she could do to slake his anger.

When she looked up again, her quarry was nowhere in sight. Now she slowed her steps, casting her eyes from side to side but she saw no tall man in a grey coat and black homburg among the random citizens ambling this way and that. When she reached the corner of Iberville she stopped. She had lost him.

Just as she was turning to head back, a rough hand grabbed her bicep and in five dizzy seconds, she was whipped around and dragged off the banquette and into the narrow walkway between two shops, hoisted along at such an angle that she couldn't catch her balance. Her spine slammed against the brick wall of one of the buildings, knocking her breathless as she toppled to the cobblestones.

Looking up at the hovering silhouette, the thought raced through her mind *He's going to kill me now,* and she conjured Valentin's face and wanted to cry out to him. In the next instant, one of the hard hands pulled away her scarves and the other fastened around her throat. Her feet left the ground and now both hands squeezed. She was gasping as he pushed his soulless face and his glass eyes to hers. For an instant, he eyes fixed on the bloody tear on the shoulder of his coat.

"You tell him I got this close." The breath was rank. "Tell him I could have taken you. Tell him I could have finished you. But I don't just murder women. I do worse."

Her brain was in a raw spin from the loss of breath. The words he spoke came out garbled as he squeezed tighter. Then, in a sudden second, he smiled in a hideous way and the pressure eased just a bit. Her mind made a jagged jump that threw her back twenty years to the shack on the bayou and the monster who had called himself her father and a fire rose from her gut and she brought her right fist down on the blood-stained shoulder and then jabbed her knee into his solar plexus.

He let out a gasp and bent over wheezing. The hand around her neck went limp and she struggled until he dropped her to the bricks. She then twisted away and he reached to snatch her back but she was gone, out of the alleyway and onto the banquette. She staggered her way to Bienville Street, pushing people aside and almost falling twice. Ahead, she saw bodies dancing in happy animation against flames and let out a cry at the sight of fierce life.

When Valentin walked in the door, Miss Antonia told him that his wife was waiting upstairs with Evangeline and Miss Eulalie. She related the incident in the alley as Justine had related it to her, keeping to the basic details.

"How badly is she hurt?" he said.

Miss Antonia put a hand to her neck. "She's got some pretty rough marks here, but I think she's all right. She's always been a strong one." She watched him for a moment. "Don't you go up there and fuss at her. I know she's your wife, but I will not allow it."

"I won't. She's alive. And—"

"And that's all." The madam waved a hand. "Go, then."

He opened the door to find her standing with Evangeline on one side and Miss Eulalie on the other, closing ranks, a battlefront if he had ever seen one. Even if he had wanted to berate her, he would not have risked their wrath. As it was, he felt himself all but trembling with relief at the sight of her. He moved to her and she came to him.

Behind them, Evangeline said, "We'll be downstairs," and she and Miss Eulalie left the room.

After the door closed, he laid gentle fingers on the marks on her neck and shook his head. "How are you doing?"

"I'll be fine. I was scared to death, but..." She looked away from him. "I know it was stupid. But do you know why I did it?"

"I do," he said.

They stood thinking their thoughts for a few quiet moments. Then she looked up and noticed an odd light in his eyes and said, "What?"

"Come with me," he said and took her hand.

He led her to the dark end of the hallway and when she realized where they were going, she let out a wild laugh, and said, "Are you.... No!" But when they reached the last door on the right and he produced the key Miss Antonia had given him, she let him draw her inside.

The room had long been kept for special guests. Now she turned her around and put his hands on her hips and gazed at her with a message she knew well.

"Here?" she said.

He pulled her closer. "Yes, now. Everyone is safe. We have this little time."

She met his bright gaze and understood what he wouldn't put into words: that he wasn't sure he would be there in the morning. And so she let him undo the buttons on her dress and push it from her shoulders and then raised her arms so he could pull her camisole over her head. He tugged at the band of her step-in and dropped it to the floor, then took a step back to drink in the sight of the body he knew so well, as if to hold the image in his mind.

She laid back on the bed, hiked her knees, and waited while he undressed. When he came to her, she wrapped her legs around his waist and locked them tight so he couldn't get away.

It was the same and yet different, the way it had always been with him. The moment and the place and the flashing thought of what she had just survived made her tremble more than before. She stopped thinking when the heat rising inside her carried her back to their beginning, when he had first come to her bed in this very house, sweeping into her like an invader and leaving her in sweet rags when it was over. And after that, she never wanted anyone else.

This was like that time and he drove into her with such raw intent that she did care if the bed and her spine broke and her insides were blasted to bits. She went missing as she felt a wave crashing over her and let out a sudden shuddering cry. Before it had died, he groaned and growled and slammed into her three more times before he collapsed. She could not remember him taking her as hard as he did in that place and on a night that had been spikes and flashes with their lives spinning on a thread.

In the wake of the moment of bliss, the words *she* couldn't speak crossed her mind. *I won't let you leave me. You will live and so will I.*

The thoughts calmed her and her vision returned. Now in a luscious heap, she allowed herself a laugh, wondering if anyone had heard the crashing of the bedsprings and her final wail.

"Can we just stay here until the sun comes up?" she murmured. "And then go home?"

"I would like that, too," he said after a moment. "But..."

"But, no."

And yet how sweet it was to muse on this notion. She understood: in a few minutes they would untangle, fix their clothes, go downstairs, and make their way out of the house and onto the street. Where it would all start again. Sometime before dawn he or they would meet Mr. Blank face-to-face. And that would be the end of the story.

His shoulder and chest throbbing, Mr. Blank had come away from the alley in time to see St. Cyr's wife escaping down the street in a dizzy ramble. He let her go. The detective would soon know that he had put hands on her and, if he had chosen, could have ripped away her clothes and ravaged her against the grimy brick wall. The thought gave him a quiver below his belt that grew at the thought of the fight she would have put up. Not that it would have ended any differently, leaving the detective shamed to the last second of his life for what he had allowed to happen.

And what of the copper McKinney, who had again put himself in harm's way, wandering about alone as if he wouldn't be spotted? He could have taken him, too. But at the last moment, he held back, choosing not to add the murder of a policeman to his crimes. For now, he savored the recollection of peering between the bodies, raising his pistol, and seeing alarm in those eyes in that fraction of a second before he pulled the trigger.

The damage done was enough. He stopped to look at his watch. It was time to meet Picot and see if he had finished off the fellow who called himself Each or had lost his nerve and run off. Not that he could ever get away.

Once they had dressed, Valentin spirited Justine out of the room, down the stairs, and out the door before the ladies in the dining room table noticed. They rounded the blocks to Marais Street. She barely glanced at the shattered window. He led her inside.

Frank shouted in Italian when he saw her and stepped up with an embrace. He looked close and said, "*Cosa ti è successo?*" before turning a hard stare on Valentin.

"What happened was she—"

"It wasn't his fault, *zio*." Justine clutched his hand. "I went out on my own." The saloonkeeper's eyes widened. "You tell him."

Valentin said, "He got the drop and grabbed her off Villere Street. Dragged her down an alley and got his hands on her throat. But she got away." He caught the flash of her dark eyes and said, "Sorry. She fought him off and then got away."

Frank's olive features had flushed red and he hissed a string of Sicilian curses. After which, he wrapped an arm around her and led her to the booth where Mr. Tom had settled. The old man regarded her with a faint smile as she sat down. Valentin stepped to the bar to pour brandies for both of them.

"You fought him off, did you?" the King of Storyville said. "Why does that not surprise me?"

"*Voi due*," Frank said, waving his pinched fingers in the air. "You two. Mr. Tom, he shot the man when he broke my window and come through." He mimed firing a pistol, then tapped his shoulder. "Hit him right here."

Justine got excited. "I saw that! I slammed it with my fist. Then I kicked him in his chest and he let go enough for me to get loose."

Valentin placed a glass before her. Anderson treated him to a cool eye, but spoke to her. "First you ran off from Miss Antonia's and came here. But why did you go out alone like that?"

"She did it for me," Valentin said.

"Also no surprise," the old man said. He raised his glass to her and she raised hers in return.

Twenty-One

First came the lights of the freighters plying downriver in slow motion, passing over the distant shapes of buildings. More machines moved along the highway. What number is it? Sixty-one? They made a line like a train now.

He heard the sound of a forlorn horn calling out, a lonesome lover. That meant something to him. Smells arrived from the vehicles passing by and from the farm fields and orchards on either side of the road. After some minutes, the sedan slowed and then came to a halt with two Fords ahead of them. A silent shape approached on the dark water.

"That'll be the ferry," the redbone said. "Gon' carry us to the other side."

Mariette first called Miss Antonia's looking for Mr. Valentin. She heard the chatter and the music in the background and was glad not to be there. There had been far too many of those nights. She next called Mangetta's and found him. She explained what had happened with the man sneaking into Each's and then running off. "But he didn't get to do any harm."

"Because you caught him in the act," Valentin said.

"Maybe so." She paused, then said, "I know who he was."

Valentin was startled. "Who?"

"That copper who used to work in the District. Collect the payments. Make trouble for all the houses."

"Do you mean Picot?"

"That's him. Yes. Lieutenant Picot."

"He became a captain."

"Sir?"

"Never mind."

"About these coppers here..."

"Yes?"

"They're fretting over it."

"I'll bet they are."

"They feel bad they let it happen. So now one stays right outside the room and the other one walks the hall, one end to the other. Ain't no one else going to bother him."

"And you're there, too."

"Yes, sir, and I'm here, too."

He was ending the call when she said, "Mr. Valentin, wait. That ain't all. After that man ran away? Each opened his eyes."

Valentin wasn't sure he had heard her correctly. "He did what?"

"Opened his eyes. Just for a moment."

A few seconds passed before Valentin could speak. "Is he awake?"

"Not right now, no," Mariette said. "He went out again. But this is good news. I seen it before. They start waking up more regular. Most times, it means they're doing better. It ain't for sure, but..."

He couldn't thank her for the catch in his throat.

She said, "It's okay, sir," and broke the connection.

James walked in a few minutes later, holding his left arm out over the bandages that strapped his chest. His eyes brightened when he spotted Justine. "I'm glad to see you here."

She said, "And I'm glad to see you, James."

Out of habit, they gathered around Tom Anderson and Valentin told the lieutenant about Each. Frank ordered Carmine to make sure everyone had food and drink. After Valentin finished, a silence settled.

Presently, Mr. Tom said, "You know, it's not a large place."

Valentin said, "Storyville?"

"Storyville." He produced a wistful smile. "'The District.' 'Anderson County.' Twenty blocks. Less than a half mile square. It's that small." The smile faded. "No one can find this fellow and yet he's found every one of you. And me, too."

Valentin stiffened. "Because it's his game. It's the way these things work."

The lieutenant said, "And it's not a normal night, Mr. Tom."

"No it's not, is it?" The old man took a troubled pause. "He's out there waiting for another chance at Valentin and maybe the rest of us." He turned his hard stare on the Creole detective. "And you won't tell me why that is."

"It doesn't matter why," Valentin said. "Because right now it only matters that he's stopped."

The King of Storyville wasn't pleased. "You know that's not good enough."

"I know. I just want to finish it first."

"And how will you do that?" Mr. Tom didn't add that nothing so far had worked.

Valentin said, "He'll come after me. And I'll be waiting."

Now his wife said, "He means *we'll* be waiting," and James nodded.

Valentin tilted his head to the door and he and Justine stepped outside to spend a few idle minutes in what passed for quiet. It didn't last; Reynard Vernel came hobbling along the banquette and wrestling to manage a heavy black case.

He stopped and wheezed when he reached the saloon. "I heard there was some excite—" He gaped at the window yawning wide. "I heard right."

Valentin pointed at the case. "What's this?"

"My typewriter. I'll be working the rest of tonight's stories from here. A copyboy will be by every half-hour or so to pick up the copy."

Before he could spot the marks that had not yet faded from Justine's throat and start asking questions, Valentin said, "Go on inside. They'll tell you all that's been going on." Reynard opened the door and lugged the case inside.

Justine allowed a moment to pass before saying, "When you go out again…?"

"Yes?"

"I'm going, too."

"We can't take—"

"James has only the one arm. You know I'm good enough. And because I looked in the man's eyes. Twice. Saw what was there."

"Which was what?"

"Nothing, that's what."

"So?"

"So he can't hurt me now."

Valentin did not want to tell her how foolish this sounded. Foolish and dangerous. He knew it was something that she had carried from the deep bayou where she was raised. The city had not washed the beliefs away.

"He *can* hurt you," he said.

She crossed her arms. "And I say he can't. He won't. Not ever again."

"You sound like a voodoo woman."

"Well, maybe I am." She stepped closer. "But whether or not I am, you need me with you."

"I need you alive," he said.

She wasn't giving an inch. "Valentin…"

"The man is going to die. And I'll be the one who kills him."

"How can you know that?"

"Because that's what he came here for. It's him or me."

"Over some papers."

"I have a feeling that doesn't matter to him anymore. He just wants me."

"You mean us." She kept her eyes fixed on his.

"All right," he said at last. "But we're going to have a plan."

"Yes, master," she said and leaned close to kiss his cheek.

Lulu White had been so caught up in the excited chatter of the girls—most of them familiar from years past—and the men who knew her by name treating her like the queen she had once been, that she barely noticed anything else. Laughter rippled through the downstairs as the stories were reeled out. She found herself dabbing her eyes as she recalled those golden days and nights.

So she didn't see Justine and Valentin enter and leave out again or the two older women appear downstairs and then disappear again and it was not until the mantle clock struck five and the house reached a sudden pocket of quiet that Miss Antonia had a chance to tell her what had transpired over the night, from the shooting at Mangetta's to the attack on Justine in the alley off Villere Street.

Miss Lulu sat stunned at hearing what she had missed and of the threats visited on people she cared for.

The madam of the house sat down at the table and said, "I don't believe there was anything you could have done."

Miss Lulu shook her head. "What good am I if after all this time I couldn't help?" Miss Antonia waited while she pondered. "Well, I can," she said at last. "Will your girl carry a message for me?"

"You don't want to use the telephone?"

"That won't work. Not for this."

Miss Antonia knew not to press further. She called for Molly.

Baptiste understood that the banks of the river afforded him his last chance to turn around and he could be rolling back into Jackson by dawn.

At this hour, the ferry only crossed once every half-hour and he had some time to think about it. His musings went to his wife. He could save himself the worst of her ire by finding a telephone to call to say he was on his way home.

Then he pictured Buddy standing amid the mayhem of the city after spending ten years locked away from the world. He wouldn't last, unless he happened to find Mr. Valentin. And what were the chances of that? About the same that Baptiste Marchand would have of finding him?

By the time he heard the faint horn and saw the ghostly shape of the ferry in the middle of the river, he had made his decision and when the last of the three automobiles rolled off, he released the hand brake and drove onto the deck. Once the vessel left the dock, he climbed out of the roadster and found one of the deckhands, an old salt who had likely been on the Mississippi since the end of the War.

"Your last crossing in this direction," Baptiste said.

The deckhand eyed him. "What about it?"

"How many machines?"

"Four, I believe. Three was Fords. One Paige."

"Did you see the drivers and passengers?"

"Did I—" He stopped, puzzled. "They was all driving on their own except for the one sedan. A redbone. He had someone with him. Strange sort."

"Strange in what way?"

"I passed by and caught a look at him. He had some crazy eyes. Kind of glowed, you know? Like a blind man's. You know? I didn't see no more than that."

Baptiste thanked him and instead of climbing back into the machine stepped to the rail to watch the ghosts riding on the waves as New Orleans drew near.

"Christ Almighty." He whispered to the night. "He made it."

The sedan had rattled to a stop. The fellow at the wheel pointed and said, "This here's where you want to be. Decatur Street." Buddy opened the door and stepped out. The Ford creaked away.

He stood very still, letting it in. The lights. The noise of traffic, even at this hour. People out, some walking somewhere with their heads bent down. Some men and women strolling along, walking and laughing.

Faint music. New Orleans.

He wandered with pictures playing in his head until he heard a whisper. Then part of a word. Then it was a name, fully-formed after being hidden for such a long time: *Valentin*.

Molly found her way to the house in what had once been the neighborhood called "Black Storyville," a four-block section on the other side of Canal that had served a colored clientele, though without legal sanction the District enjoyed. In a year's time, the blighted blocks had fallen further into decay and what once were decent houses were closed and shuttered. A single streetlight cast a glow at the corner of Perdido and Lasalle Streets.

Hedging her way through the darkness, she located the address and knocked. A man whose face she could not see but whose bulk she could feel opened the door.

"From Miss Lulu," she said. The man accepted the folded square of paper without a word and closed the door.

Twenty-Two

Mayor Behrman had tried to nap at his desk to no avail. Every time he closed his eyes, the phone rang or Major Sont barged in to deliver a bulletin, like the shooting of McKinney and the assault on Justine St. Cyr. Meanwhile, Acting Chief Cook spent most of his time dozing, staring into space, and then dozing some more. His face kept the same sour frown throughout and from the odd jerks of his arms, his was not a peaceful sleep.

To get his mind off the troubles on the streets, the mayor spent another minute imagining the scene at Mangetta's with a formerly missing-in-action Tom Anderson firing his Derringer at the very character who had come to cut a path of destruction. It sounded like a scene from the wild days before the ordinance and caused the mayor to laugh for the first time all night.

The acting chief blinked awake and sat up. "What is it?"

The mayor had become even more uneasy with Cook as the hours passed and had decided to tell him as little as he could about the attacks on the lieutenant and St. Cyr's wife. If Cook wondered what part of this grim news Mayor Behrman had found humorous, he didn't inquire.

The mayor looked at the clock on the wall over the couch where the acting was perched. A little over two more hours and they'd be seeing dawn. It wasn't a long time, but it seemed that it would go on forever.

J. Picot weaved through the Basin Street crowd, mulling his failure at Mercy and considering what might happen when he reached Eclipse Alley. The botched attack wasn't his fault. He wouldn't have gotten inside at all, save for a dunce of a copper. And then it all went wrong. Only luck had placed a dunce of a copper at the back door who let him slip away again. Had Mr. Blank been expecting him to die trying to kill the already half-dead patient? It wasn't like he was getting paid for committing such a serious crime—or anything else, for that matter.

And hadn't *they* sent for *him*? The voice on the telephone had said: *This will be the time to settle your grudge.* He had been carrying the notion that this meant he would get to do away with St. Cyr and that was enough to entice him.

Right now, he had a larger problem. Berry would have been questioned and of course blurted the name "Picot." After getting over the shock, the duty captain would have put his name on the street with the word to collar him on sight. The cool of the night was his one bit of luck, as he could huddle in his coat and pass unnoticed among the dozens of drunks rambling this way and that.

He now spent some time mulling an escape. The trains would start running again soon and he could hide for that long. After musing on it more, he decided that this time he wasn't going to bolt like a frightened mouse. He also wasn't going to be foolish about Mr. Blank and he crossed over to Union Station and stepped into one of the telephone booths.

Sergeant Maris came on the line, all hoarse and groggy. "God damn it, man. At this hour?"

"It's important." The sergeant grumbled something and he said. "Are you awake or not?"

"I'm awake. So?"

"I want some insurance tonight."

That did it. After a pause, Maris's voice came back clear. "What the hell are you talking about?"

"Mr. Blank. That's what. I found him. Spoke to him." He hesitated. "I did him a service. I mean, he asked me to. I was not able to complete it."

The sergeant said, "Do you want to explain that?"

Picot told him about the encounter in Eclipse Alley and the scene at the hospital.

When he finished, the sergeant said, "Jesus. You know I can't do anything about that."

"I know. But now you have the facts."

Maris said, "So what happens next?"

"Next, I meet him again."

"Where?"

"In Eclipse Alley."

"Wait," the sergeant said. "Isn't that—"

"Yes," Picot said. "There."

"How much trouble are you in, Captain?"

"I don't know."

"Then get out of town."

"No. Not again. I'm going to be here come dawn."

"To see what happens to St. Cyr."

Instead of replying, Picot said, "I just want to make sure someone understands the situation."

"All right, then," Maris said. "I hope you come out all right. Call me in the morning." After a few silent seconds, he heard the line go dead.

Baptiste had not visited the Crescent City in over three years and that time had been only for a day, a matter of picking up a new patient and transporting him to the hospital. He had been born and raised there and had still known where to find a good meal on Tchoupitoulas Street before heading back out of town.

Now he thought about the hours to come. Other than a lucky sighting, his best chance to find Mr. Bolden would be to first locate

Mr. Valentin. He paused to imagine the look on the detective's face when he delivered the news.

He parked at a Canal Street lot and walked to the Western Union office, where he paged through a telephone directory. The only "St. Cyr, V." listed was on Dumaine Street. He stepped into a booth and dialed the number. The fellow who answered was not Mr. Valentin. He said that the detective was not at home and that's all he would divulge.

Back on the banquette, Baptiste decided to cross into Storyville with only a few hours before it would close forever. There was no choice; it was where he would most likely find the Creole detective Valentin St. Cyr.

Four blocks away, Buddy was moving through light and dark as fragments of image and sound visited him. Yes, he had once stood on this corner. Yes, he had once smelled the crawfish boiling inside an eatery no larger than a crib. Yes, he had heard brass bands from doorways, along with the music of lazy talk, joyous laughter, and a woman moaning through her minutes of passion. And the sights still dazzled, even so deep into the night.

He stopped to listen and watch and remember and wait for a sign. When none came, he moved on.

The saloonkeeper offered Mr. Tom better seating than the corner booth, perhaps one of the padded armchairs stored in the attic, but the King of Storyville said, "No, thank you. This right here is good for my back. And I can keep an eye on things." The Derringer was still lying on the table in front of him.

Frank had Carmine fetch candles and light one in the booth, two on the bar, and on two of the tables. With the low glow from the stove, the room was almost cheerful.

The old man pulled the watch from the pocket on his vest and said, "Almost five o'clock. Three hours to the end."

Valentin said, "The sun will be up an hour before."

The lieutenant said, "I guess he could just walk to the middle of the street out there and start shooting." He heard Justine breathe something unkind and immediately wanted to take back the words.

Valentin spoke up to save him. "I doubt it. He wouldn't be able to see if he was hitting anyone."

"Then what's to stop him from wrapping a half-dozen 80s and tossing them in here?" Mr. Tom said.

"He tried for a bloodbath and it didn't work," Valentin said. He felt Justine's stare and said, "It's been one stupid move after another." He looked at the reporter. "Correct, Reynard?"

"Yes, that's correct."

"And your editor still knows nothing?"

"I haven't said a word. Not until you—"

The banging wasn't from a pistol. Tom Anderson had slammed his palm on the tabletop. "Enough. Tell me what this is all about."

Valentin met the old man's stare. "All right," he said. "All right." He sat down across the table and proceeded to tell him about the secret plotting and the graft behind the closing of Storyville, Patrick Geary's investigation in Washington, and the results being carried on a train running west from Atlanta as they spoke.

"My God," the old man said. "And you didn't tell me about this because?"

"Because you showed no interest," Valentin said. "You told the world you were finished with Storyville."

Anderson sat back. "Yes, I did. But it seems that's not the case." He shook his head. "And now there's nothing I can do to help you."

"Yes, there is," Valentin said and waited.

Mr. Tom stared at him for a very long time before raising his hands in surrender. "It's not what I know," he said. "Only what I've heard?"

"Which is what?"

"That they were going to destroy Storyville one way or another. It could not stand as such. I was warned to get out of the way."

"And you did."

"I got old. And I was tired of it. Even New Orleans couldn't escape America forever."

"Who told you this?"

"Gentlemen I did not know. They appeared at the Café and asked to speak to me in confidence. They said they represented 'important concerns.' And that they were extending a courtesy." His eyes went cold. "They informed me that I needed to stay out of the way. And then they left."

"And you never saw them before?"

"Or since. In any case, I got the message. I could retire or I could die."

Valentin looked at James, who was studying Mr. Tom with narrowed eyes. He didn't buy all of this either.

Justine said, "So the proof of all this is coming on the train?"

"Yes. And those 'important concerns' are going to be nailed. Courtesy of me."

The calm way he said it gave Justine a chill and she pulled her shawl over her shoulders. "We could all just leave," she said "Disappear. All of us. Let someone else deliver the papers." After a few moments' silence, she said, "I'm sorry. I know that's not possible now."

"Not after what he did to you," Valentin said. "And to Each and James and Black Jimmy. No. I'm going find him. Corner him. And kill him." He looked from face to face with a dim smile. "Unless someone gets there before me."

Picot reached the mouth of Eclipse Alley and stopped to peer into where the passage made a bend to the left. Once small shops had lined it on either side. Now they were all closed and boarded. He could hear voices from over on Franklin Street, but nothing else.

He caught movement and saw two rats lifting their heads to stare back at him with their black eyes before skittering out of sight.

He called, "Hello? Mr. Blank?" and heard only his own echo.

After a few seconds, he wondered if he had let his imagination get the best of him. Blank needed an ally and so there would be no reason to do him any harm. So what if he hadn't finished Each? He was half-dead already. How long could he last? He would explain about the nurse and the two coppers, but change a few details. Running away would only make him look guilty of something and who knew who Mr. Blank might have waiting and watching?

He walked into the alley and reached the bend to see that it was empty right through to Liberty Street. More minutes passed and it dawned on him that the game was more dangerous that he had surmised. It was one thing to visit violence on others, another to be exposed. This was beyond him, He could just as well see what happened and deal with St. Cyr himself, if need be. That way, he could—

"Picot."

He gave a start and turned his head. Mr. Blank didn't reply. The figure he glimpsed over his shoulder taller than before? He wheeled around and saw that Mr. Blank's homburg was pulled so low that he could barely see his cold eyes. All his other features were lost in shadow.

"Did you finish the work at the hospital?"

Picot said, "I couldn't. It was bad luck. A nurse came into the room and started yelling. And there was coppers there."

"And so?"

"And so...I...uh, left. Got out of there. Before—"

"Before you got nabbed." Mr. Blank nodded, considering all this. "But you could have finished the work before the police got to you, correct?"

Picot sputtered out a tense laugh. "Well, yes, but then I would have been caught in the act. Arrested. What good would that have done?"

Mr. Blank didn't reply.

"I can go back. Tomorrow or the next day. And get him for sure." Picot wondered if Blank heard how hollow it sounded.

"No, that won't be necessary. We won't worry about it."

Picot was relieved. "Good. What the fuck does it have to do with St. Cyr, anyway? It don't make sense. There's other work, ain't that so? We got, what, three, four hours left? And I'm ready to go."

Blank nodded, taking the point, and Picot relaxed further, pleased at how he had managed the situation. He was about to ask what was next when the revolver appeared out of the pocket of the gray coat and the barrel was jammed beneath his chin. Before he could utter another word, Mr. Blank pulled the trigger.

Though Baptiste was less than a block away, the crack of the pistol was lost in the commotion. He had walked the four blocks of Franklin Street, saddened at what he saw and heard. Storyville was not what he remembered from seven years before, when it had been alive with new electric streetlamps and painted women in camisoles and chippies perched on every gallery and in most of the windows. Now the lights were dim, only every fourth house showed signs of life, and he picked out at most a dozen trollops and the women filling the banquettes were not on parade in their finery but careening in whatever they had thrown on for the night.

He peered down Iberville, Bienville, Conti, and St. Louis streets as he passed them, witnessing more antics set against the light of the bonfires. Though his odds of stumbling upon Bolden or St. Cyr were slim, he went about questioning random citizens, hoping someone might have seen the private copper who had worked these same streets for the better part of ten years. He laughed at the thought that now *he* was the detective.

The first two men he stopped—both drunk, of course—gave him blank looks when he spoke the names St. Cyr and Bolden. He was encouraged when the next man he asked knew of St. Cyr, but only because he had the read the crime stories in the *Times-Picayune* where he was mentioned. A broken-down sot who happened to be passing by overheard his next encounter and came to a halt.

"Did you say *Bolden*?" He was a mottled and white-haired man, a shaking wreck who now became animated, his smile going wide and bloodshot eyes lighting up. "*King Bolden*? Oh, hell, yes!"

Baptiste was forced to stand and listen to a jagged history of what they had first called *jass* and now *jazz*, a colorful rendition that placed

Buddy at the inception, the mad genius who snatched gutbucket, second-line, church music, and anything else that could fit into something that no one had ever heard before but had then broken apart.

Baptiste interrupted before the tale could wind on longer. "So have you seen him?"

"Seen him?" The red eyes went fiery. "I used to see him at Long-shoreman's Hall. Toro's Saloon. Funky Butt Hall. All them places. He would—"

"I mean have you seen him tonight."

"Tonight?" The old sot stopped and blinked. "What, is he back? Where? I want to hear him." Baptiste walked off, as he yelled, "Where's he at, goddamnit? I want to hear King Bolden just one more time!"

Mr. Blank spent only a moment staring into the dead eyes. He had been told that Picot could be counted on, but the man had failed to perform a simple task, then failed to grasp that there would be a consequence if he didn't, and that punishment would be something more than a lecture. He had guessed wrong. But he had never considered that he had been chosen only to be brought in, used, and then erased.

Mr. Blank couldn't see his pocket watch in that darkness, but he guessed it was close to four o'clock. So a little over three hours to get the detective where he wanted him. The game was his and St. Cyr and his crew in that saloon didn't know from what direction he'd be coming next. He counted on that.

With a last glance at late New Orleans Police Captain J. Picot, he exited the alleyway.

Buddy gazed across the tracks, surveying the street as if it was a painting in a frame. He had been there. He had been everywhere in New Orleans. The house at First and Liberty. The Saint-something School for Colored. He stopped to laugh over a vagrant memory. His half-dago friend Valentin had been put down as Colored, too. They were children and then they were not. The houses he had painted while he was learning his horn. The dark little rooms and the saloons and dancehalls. He crossed the rails and let the city surround him.

For years, dreams had inhabited his nights and days, and as he walked the banquettes, he began to feel that he was waking from one. The noises and sights sharpened as if his ears and eyes were opening even as the frantic movement around him slowed. The shimmering figures brought to mind how women gyrated on the dance floor, some down to their chippies and now and then, one of them lusciously naked. They did that for him. For his music.

He continued on, keeping to the edge of the banquette and sometimes stepping into the gutter to avoid the bodies moving past. When he reached Bienville Street, a distant sound called to him.

He crossed Liberty and then Franklin as if being drawn by a rope. Then he saw the sign at the corner of Marais Street. He knew that one, too. Near the end of the block, he came upon a lone man, up in years, dark and ragged, wearing in an ancient suit and a derby that was dented and scuffed. His features weren't clear, but the golden horn he held to his lips was as brilliant as a star. The fellow caught sight of Buddy and stopped and stared, his eyes going wide. A long few moments passed before he shook his head, raised the horn again, and began to blow.

Frank got Reynard and his typewriter settled at a back table. The reporter asked Tom Anderson about shooting Mr. Blank and Lieutenant McKinney recounted that same character stepping from the crowd to put a .32 slug through his side.

Valentin noticed that Mr. Tom was taking just a bit too much delight in the tale. It had been a lucky shot and the old man was just as lucky that *he* wasn't dead. Though he likely would have been happy to have gone out that way.

They moved to the bar. Reynard said, "How am I going to cover all this?" He looked between Valentin and James. "And there's going to be more?" He pushed back from the bar. "I'm calling in to ask two more inches." He looked at the clock. "There's still four hours to go."

"So what do we do now?" Justine said after he walked into the hall.

"Go out and see if we can hook a fish. We can bring Carmine to run messages."

She came up with a light smile. "Thank you for including me."

"He'll see that he hasn't taken you two out of commission."

"And then?"

"And then we put an end to him."

She was just about to add something when Reynard reappeared and James took his place at the hallway phone.

Mariette heard the lieutenant's voice through the telephone all the way down the hall at the nurses' station. First one officer and then the other got on the line and they each came away as pale as death. Neither one spoke a word to her, so intent were they on their duties now. One of the janitors told her that the copper who had let the man inside had been whisked away in a police sedan.

It was quiet on the floor and she stepped into the room to stand over the bed. She had been consumed with joy at her patient's revival, and now she wept, at last releasing the fear that he wouldn't survive. He was not yet safe, but the doctor had come by and was pleased. It was all good news.

She crossed to the window and looked out over the city. She could pick out Storyville, where she had once sold her favors for cash, and wondered if the man who had stabbed Each and likely sent the other character to finish him, was still on the loose. And what of Mr. Valentin and Justine and James McKinney?

She watched the fires and said a small prayer that for the rest of the night and beyond, there would be no more harm visited on any of them.

TWENTY-THREE

The French Quarter and at its center the Vieux Carre, the old city. He remembered the names. But in his recollection they were never places for the likes of him, with their ornate iron balconies draped with flowers and vines, the tidy cafes and fine stores, and the elegant folk who passed up and down its narrow streets in promenades of good fortune.

They did not see him back then, just another dark shape moving by. They did hear, though; once the sounds of jass rose up and their children began venturing to risky parts of the city and into saloons and dance halls where the music blasted until dawn.

He crossed Royal Street and stopped at a storefront with a wide window and saw a tall and gaunt man dressed in odd clothes. A sick person's clothes. He drew closer to find the image still unclear, a half-shadow, a haint. Yes, the face was familiar and the eyes that swam in the glass were not unkind. His, both the young sport's and the older man's. Now he remembered: *King Bolden*. They had called him that. He moved on.

After six blocks, he heard the sound of a chugging engine and saw a plume of smoke, gray against the night sky. The steel monster wheezed into silence. Trains were always good for rhythm and anybody who couldn't play like a locomotive picking up steam was good for nothing except maybe a cakewalk or Sunday concert in the park. White men, in other words. Negroes could do it. Mulattos, quadroons, and dagos could do it. But not the white men; at least few that he had ever heard.

He didn't know where these notions were coming from. It was only a few minutes ago that he had crossed the river. And a few minutes before that, walking off the grounds the way no one but he knew. And now he was looking up at the sign. Rampart Street. Where the music had begun. Not right there, but far to the dark, bloody south end.

By the time the bells struck five-thirty, Mr. Blank decided that he was done with the foolishness and was simply going to take out whoever crossed his path, whether it was St. Cyr, his wife, the police lieutenant, or another member of that little circle. If any chances arrived before the dawn that Mr. Smith had deemed so magical, he'd tell the man that he had been confronted and that there was no choice in the matter. He would get paid the rest or he would not. What mattered now was finishing the Creole detective. If his employer wanted drama, he'd leave St. Cyr's dead body in the Basin Street gutter.

This would also upset any plans Mr. Smith might have to remove him once his work was done. With that settled, he began his last prowl.

At the very moment that Mr. Blank was entertaining his raw notions, his prey was leaning on Frank Mangetta's bar, sipping a chicory coffee laced with a half-shot of brandy. James, Reynard, and Justine had only coffee, Frank drank brandy, and Carmine a Chero-Cola.

Valentin wasted some minutes with a study of the clock on the back wall, imagining the long hand advancing one more sweep. If there was a choice, they would all remain inside while he went out to face the man so intent on killing him.

Neither his wife nor the lieutenant would stand for that. James, because it was his sworn duty and because Valentin was his friend and Justine, because she didn't want to be his widow. As he was considering this, she stepped up to say, "Everyone's waiting."

———

Valentin had Frank check the *lupara* and Carmine the Bisley. He looked to the booth in back. Mr. Tom said, "Yes, I know," and took a few seconds to inspect the chamber of the Derringer. The old man snapped the pistol closed, poked a thick finger to his forehead, and said, "Next time, right between the eyes." The moment of levity came and went.

"Now we can go," the detective said. Justine and James followed him to the door. He turned and said, "Carmine? *Andiamo*."

Outside, the four made a slow walk along the banquette to the corner of Iberville Street, where Valentin stopped.

Justine regarded her husband for a moment, then traded a glance with James. "Well?" she said. "What now?"

"Now we start moving until he spots us," Valentin said.

"That's your plan?" Justine said.

"I know it's not perfect," Valentin said.

"It's not even close," she said.

James and Valentin smiled at her tone. The Creole detective said, "Do you have a better idea?"

"Maybe," she said. "If we stay together, he could just shoot the four of us right down." At this, Carmine swallowed so loudly that they all heard it.

"Yes," Valentin said. "Except he—"

"What?" she said.

"He's planning something more...*personal*." James looked at Valentin. "Correct?"

"Correct," Valentin said. "He could have shot any of us a half-dozen times and didn't. That's not what he wants. He's been told to make a show of it."

Justine said, "So you're going to leave it up to him? That's not like you."

The cool light in her eyes gave him pause and he said, "What, then?"

She became quietly animated. "Sometimes we would trap animals or fish by closing in on them from different sides."

Valentin knew that the "we" meant the children, their father, and whoever else they could wrangle from nearby cabins. "So...you want us to do that now?" he said and turned to James, who gave a shrug. "All right," he said. "But that would mean we'd all be alone."

"That's right."

"*You* would be alone."

She said, "Yes."

"But I'm the bait here."

She watched him for a moment, then shook her head. "Not just you."

He crossed his arms and stared down at the banquette, then raised his head again to say, "All right. I would like you in the open. On Basin Street. Carmine will go with you." He looked to the young Sicilian and received a nervous nod.

"And I'd like to change the plan a bit. He's going to follow the first one of us he sees. So we'll—"

"Lead him to the others," Justine said.

"We hope."

"And what then?" James said.

Valentin looked his way. "You think you'll be able to arrest him?"

"Not likely."

"You remember what Major Sont said about what to do if we find him?"

"I remember," the lieutenant said. "I'm still a police officer."

"Yes, I know," Valentin said. He didn't want an argument. "I don't believe he has any interest in the crib alleys. So you and I will start at the north and south ends of Villere and work our way up and down the blocks until we get to Justine and Carmine on Basin Street."

"And with some luck, he'll join us," Justine said.

Valentin said, "Lieutenant? Any thoughts?"

James said, "I'm concerned about..." He offered a vague gesture in Justine's direction.

Valentin understood. But the Colt would be heavy for her. "Do you have something?"

James reached inside his coat, produced a Remington .25, and handed it to her.

"Don't use it unless you have to," Valentin said.

She turned the pistol over in her hand. "I won't."

"There's one more thing. We need to be either moving or out of sight. So we'll work our way to the colonnade at Anderson's." He nodded to her and Carmine. "You two go. James and I will watch until you get to the line and then we'll split up," he said. "If something goes wrong or you get a bad feeling, make your way to Miss Antonia's or back to Frank's and stay there."

She said, "We will," and stepped close to embrace him and whisper in his ear before turning to walk away. Carmine hitched his shoulders and followed along behind her.

Valentin and James spoke for a hushed few seconds, then moved off in opposite directions, Valentin crossing to the north, the lieutenant retreating south in the direction of Canal Street. For the rest of his years, the lieutenant would remember Valentin saying, "He gets me. Only me. You make sure, Lieutenant."

The two detectives had just walked away from the intersection when Baptiste turned the corner from Liberty, on his way to asking more citizens about Buddy and Valentin St. Cyr. Almost every one of them knew Bolden—or knew of him from long ago. Some puzzled over the "St. Cyr," and then delivered some version of "Well, I think I know... Naw, I guess not," before ambling off. Another came alert at the mention of the name and said, "Well, of *course* I know him! Used to work at Union Station."

Some minutes later, a dapper gent stopped, listened, and replied with a pronounced British accent. "Yes. I knew Bolden. Know Mr. Valentin. Saw him a couple hours ago. Don't know where he was headed. Maybe to Fewclothes. Maybe Mangetta's. Maybe some other saloon." He tapped a finger to the brim of his hat. "If you find him, tell him Prince Albert sent you." He strolled away.

Baptiste walked back to Basin Street and stopped in at Fewclothes Cabaret to find it only a third full. The customers who remained wandering about, pushing little eddies of sawdust. He overheard some mutterings about an assault that had taken place the previous morning. Harry the bartender told him he hadn't seen St. Cyr all night. When Baptiste asked about Mangetta's, Harry tilted his head and said, "Marais Street."

He had a vague recollection of the saloon and made his slow way there, feeling the sleepless hours weighing on him again. He arrived to find the front window had been smashed in and the place appeared to be deserted. But as he was moving away, he heard voices from inside. When he stepped closer, he made out the figures of two men, one large and the other smaller. He opened the door. His eyes adjusted to the dim light and he was startled to see both holding weapons, the big man at the table a Derringer and the Italian behind the bar a shotgun.

Holding up his hands, he said, "My name is Baptiste Marchand. I came from Jackson. I'm looking for Valentin St. Cyr."

No more than a couple dozen people were scattered ahead of Justine and Carmine and the streets were much quieter than before. Random shouts and laughter and small rags of music came and went from the east and west, the very air seeping away as if the blocks of Storyville had heaved a sigh before surrendering.

Justine understood that Carmine would rather be back at Mangetta's, so as they made their way along, she tried to buck his courage. At one point, she whispered, "We all know you'll be fine, whatever happens," and was immediately sorry. The words puffed his pride and she saw the troubling gleam in his eyes that told her that he might do something foolish if trouble came. She sighed over the rash minds of men in general, young men more specifically, and young Italian men in particular.

Carmine wasn't the only one unnerved. The echoes had shifted from joyful to something that hinted at menacing. She surveyed the street in a casual way so as not to worry her companion. And yet she wasn't sure, either. The bodies that were gone left shadows where someone could be lurking. They continued on.

Baptiste did not recall ever meeting Frank Mangetta, but who didn't know the name Tom Anderson? As he settled into a chair with the cup of strong coffee the saloonkeeper offered and began his story, he found himself at first abashed and vexed to be in the presence of the man they had called the "King of Storyville." This was no "king," but a quiet old man. Even so, there was an electric glint in those aged blue eyes—and a loaded Derringer on the table before him.

Baptiste's hosts listened, astonished, as he related the tale of Buddy Bolden managing to walk off the grounds of the hospital undetected and make it all the way to New Orleans overnight. He told them about the deckhand, the redbone in the rusty sedan, and his odd passenger that could only have been Buddy.

When he finished, Frank and Mr. Tom sat back, both wondering how many more bizarre episodes would come to pass before the night broke into day.

The crowds were thinning as men and women walked or stumbled away, so many of them bent, weary, and hankering for rest. Buddy understood the feeling.

He had heard enough. Seen enough. It was beginning to break into pieces around him, the same way the world had cracked when he did something awful and they carried him off to the hospital. He couldn't let it happen again.

His footsteps led him on. He had walked the same route so many times for so many years that he didn't have to think about it. He laughed at the thought that they used to run all the way, the first time when they were kids and it was Saturday and the world was bright and they caught sight of a sporting woman standing in a doorway and smiling at them, her yellow dress and scarlet lipstick shocking against the dark flesh that all but spilled out of her chippie. And he and...and...he and *Valentin* stopped and stared until she called to them, and they ran the whole two miles back to First and Liberty.

Canal Street was as broad as a river, but there was little traffic and the streetcars weren't rolling yet. As he crossed over, he heard a sad horn and stopped to see the tall lights of a freighter drift by at the bottom of the boulevard. He remembered where he was and where he needed to go. Before he could take a step, he sensed that a lone passerby had stopped and was now staring at his back. The eyes were like those of the man in the hospital, the one in the stairwell, Big-Something who had committed murder. It was not him, but someone with bad intentions.

Whatever it was that had caused Mr. Blank to stop and glance back when the crazy-looking fellow passed was gone when he crossed Canal Street. He had just started down the first block of Villere Street into the District when he saw a figure that by now he knew well crossing the intersection.

Was St. Cyr such a fool as to stay out in the open and chance walking into harm's way? The answer was no. The detective either thought his hunter had given up, had come to some misfortune, or was still lying in wait somewhere. Most likely, the last.

He had been the fool when he agreed to stalk St. Cyr and those close to him through the long night when it could have been handled so easily any time after the sun set. Now it was going to come to a showdown and on Basin Street, no less.

Mr. Blank walked at a quick pace to the intersection at Iberville and peered around the corner to see his quarry just turning onto Marais Street at too casual a pace. He understood; St. Cyr was hoping that he'd see him and follow along, right into whatever trap he had set. Like a squad of coppers with their pistols drawn.

He decided to turn it around and instead of tracking the detective, he continued north so that he could make a loop, scan the street, and perhaps pitch a net of his own. After which he would walk into Union

Station, call Mr. Smith, and buy a ticket for the next train leaving in any direction.

Justine was tending to the private hope that Mr. Blank would show his face so that she could dispatch his evil self on her own and have his carcass waiting when Valentin and the lieutenant arrived. So it took an extra effort to keep her eyes—and make sure that Carmine kept his eyes—straight ahead, so as not to alert Blank or let anyone else surprise them.

This was not to be. Seven slow minutes later, they reached Basin Street. She allowed Carmine to peruse the banquettes in both directions. He took it seriously and was no longer so interested in examining her figure.

They stood quietly for some moments. There was no more music and no signs of bonfires, only the smell of burning wood and wisps of smoke. Presently, Justine said, "He's not near."

Carmine said, "How you know that?"

"It's just..." How to explain it? "I've been with Mr. Valentin for most of the last ten years, that's how. Anyway, there's no danger close by. That's all I can tell you."

"So do we go to Anderson's?"

She said, "Yes. Lead the way." As they walked the two blocks to the corner of Iberville, where the famed establishment had once stood, she remembered to cast glances over her shoulder. She wasn't good enough to see something beyond her powers of sight, no matter what she had told Carmine.

Now standing below the roof of the colonnade of the most important address the District had ever known, she allowed herself to think about the next hours. That she and her husband and the others would all be alive when the sun came up was all that mattered.

To curb her jitters, she stepped to the corner, as raindrops appeared on the banquette. Looking west, she saw a figure crossing at Iberville and for a moment thought it was someone she knew. Or had known.

But how foolish to think that she recognized someone whose face she couldn't make out two hundred paces away.

It's the last scenes of the last act, she told herself, *and I'm seeing things.* She turned around and walked back to duck under the colonnade once more. Carmine was watching her for a sign. She said, "It won't be long."

Valentin had reached his corner and he guessed that James had done the same on the far side of the District. Justine and Carmine would be waiting on Basin Street.

The streets had fallen almost silent this far back. A slight drizzle was moving in from the gulf. The feathery rain would be tamping the few bonfires that were still burning. Wisps of wood smoke hung in the quiet air.

And so it all passes. It seemed sad that for all the bedlam that had animated the night, the District had not been retired with more fanfare. Surely, after twenty years since the ordinance had made it legal and the sixty years that it had thrived before that and the tens of thousands of people on both sides of the scarlet equation who had been born or passed through or died there, the place deserved a proper wake.

And what of his role in the spectacle? Half of his adult life had gone by with him either in the center or on the fringes of Storyville. He had only found the woman who became his wife there and a case that began on those blocks had led to the other woman living under their roof. For a few moments, a parade of faces drifted by and he realized that most of them were dead and a half-dozen of those thanks to him.

And, he told himself, in a few short minutes, he could be joining them. It could be so and yet he didn't truly believe it; because he was never one to surrender and because even entertaining the thought might tilt his chances of staying alive. Storyville would just have to die without Valentin St. Cyr. The notion roused him and he began walking north.

Fog had entered the lieutenant's head, which he knew meant he could make a mistake, which meant he could end up a fatality, and yet he was certain that he would survive. He wasn't so sure about Valentin. They both had leave to shoot Mr. Blank dead on sight, but it was not the lieutenant's way. He was a police officer and that meant something. The late Chief Reynolds understood that and so did Major Sont. Too many, like that bastard Picot, did not. He stopped to wonder where the former captain had gone after failing at Mercy Hospital. Back the way he came, if he had any sense.

When he felt the first drops of rain, he took his slouch hat from his pocket and after donning it, began his walk toward Conti Street. As he moved along the banquette, he spotted police vans creeping across intersections on their way to taking up positions. The officers would soon fan out and clear the houses. Where the madams and the trollops went next was no one's concern, as long as they were gone. James mused on the city's reaction on waking and realizing that an amputation had been performed overnight, as promised. Except that for him and a small group of others, there was a final scene to play out.

Ten minutes later, both detectives set foot on Basin Street, Valentin at Iberville and James at Conti. The lieutenant raised a hand and Valentin did the same. Between them were some later stragglers, but no Mr. Blank. James turned south.

He was fifty paces away when Valentin saw the lieutenant stop and stare and in a flicker of an instant, he realized that he had made a terrible mistake, and that his brain had stopped working from fatigue and he had slipped and been duped. He felt a blow in his chest as if someone had slammed into him and took a staggering step to one side, then reeled around and started down the block.

He came to a sliding halt on the wet banquette at Anderson's Café. Justine was standing with Carmine beside her. Mr. Blank stood in the shadows under the other end of the colonnade holding a pistol aimed directly at her head. Carmine gave a start when he saw the detective and Justine turned his way.

"I've just been speaking to your wife," Mr. Blank announced in a voice that was now dark and sugary. "Explaining the situation."

Valentin felt a raw catch in his throat that meant he was ready to do murder. He steadied himself and said, "You don't know the situation."

"Then tell me."

"It's all about papers."

"What papers?"

"Information. The kind that will ruin some people. And it's too late to do anything."

Mr. Blank said, "None of that matters. It's not my affair." He waved his revolver. "You're my affair."

Valentin took a careful step forward and he thrust the weapon a few inches in Justine's direction. "You want her to die?" he said.

Without moving her eyes from him, Justine made a motion with her hand and Valentin stayed where he was. "You came for me," he said.

"Yes, but she put herself in the way, didn't she?" He produced a ghastly smile. "Is her life with you so unpleasant that she'd risk suicide?"

Valentin said, "She's just brave."

A shape that became James McKinney approached from the north. When he was halfway to Iberville, Mr. Blank, still lost in the shadows, called out. "You can stay right there, Lieutenant." James stopped.

"You have some skills," Valentin said.

Mr. Blank said, "As good as yours?"

"I doubt it."

"But you'll be gone soon."

"Isn't your arm getting tired?" Valentin said.

"You're right, it is," Mr. Blank said and switched the pistol to his left hand in one sharp motion. "Let's make this simple. You come with me. She stays. And lives. The copper and the boy, too." He turned slightly. "And I'll be watching. Any one of you moves, he's dead on the spot."

Justine said, "No..."

Valentin gazed at his wife for a lingering moment, then said, "Which way?"

They crossed a set of tracks and Valentin was overtaken by a sudden airy feeling, as if a weight had lifted and everything had been peeled away, and he wondered if he had just died. But then he heard the scraping of shoes behind him and realized that he had only found the place where he went quiet and nothing could touch him.

It was something that had lingered with him since childhood, a sense that the fate that had claimed his brothers and his sister and his father had been waiting over all the years to make the boy and then the man pay for not saving them. For not saving Buddy Bolden when another demon came to claim his soul. Call him Mr. Blank or by some other name. Clothe him in a dark coat and a black homburg or paint him naked with horns and a pitchfork. The end was the same, as he carried the sorrow that lurked in the midst of the madness.

He walked on. Dawn was less than an hour away, but he knew for him it might never come, that the first pale light would stay forever out of reach. And it might be easier to die, save for letting Mr. Blank win. No; he'd drag them both to the bottom of the river before he'd let that happen and take the evil and his sadness to a watery grave.

He glanced over his shoulder at that moment and caught a slight shift of motion in front of the Café. Mr. Blank noticed and aimed the pistol at Valentin's skull while he turned for a quick look of his own. The three figures were standing still and he waved Valentin on.

"You know how many times I've taken this walk with someone?" Mr. Blank answered the question when Valentin wouldn't. "More than I can count, that's how many." His soles were grinding through the cinders. "And do you know how many go along without a fight? Most of them."

They crossed the next pair of rails. "You know why that is? Because they come to believe that I'm Death himself. And that they deserve me."

Even with every nerve on edge, Valentin fixed on the preposterous notion and said, "You flatter yourself."

"Well, for them, I am."

Valentin kept moving. An early train emerged from the station, all grinding wheels and huffing steam, and in a flickering of pictures, he imagined what might transpire in the moments to come.

Mr. Blank raised his voice over the rumbling locomotive. "And just like you, I never know why. It's none of my business. I just do the work." He stopped for a moment. "But this time, it's different, isn't it?" Valentin said nothing. "I have my own reasons."

"You don't scare me, sir," he said.

"Maybe I should," Mr. Blank said. "So we're here. And now, after all that you put me through, you're going to die on your knees."

"I don't think so," Valentin said and drew to a sudden, stubborn stop.

Mr. Blank gave a hard shove and he went down between the tracks, feeling the gravel cut into his hands. The train was drawing closer.

Blank had stolen a final glance toward Anderson's and was turning back when a shot cracked. He jerked in a move that took just enough of a split-second for Valentin to come off his knees, holding the stiletto he had pulled from the sheath on his ankle. He shoved the blade into the side of the thick throat and Blank's eyes went wide as he clutched at the wound with one hand and struggled to raise his pistol with the other. He began to sway and the revolver tumbled between two crossties. In the next moment, he toppled and landed face down, the blood spreading in a dark pool. More bloomed from the hole in the back of his coat.

Justine was standing ten feet away, the barrel of the .25 still smoking. She stared back at her husband and then stepped up to bend over the dead man and hiss in his ear. "*This* is how it ends."

James appeared from the shadows, holding the Navy .45 in his good hand. Behind him came Carmine and two hard-looking characters Valentin didn't know. He stopped and holstered his pistol. Justine seemed to have drifted away from the violence, gazing past him at the lights of the train.

Valentin said, "How did…?"

"First person who walked by," the lieutenant said. "Some sot. He was Miss Justine's size. So we pressed him into service and she slipped away."

Valentin looked at his wife and then back at James. "You let her do that?"

"It happened fast. And Carmine wasn't ready. So…"

"He couldn't have stopped me," Justine said.

She moved to him and he felt the shudder that ran through her bones. The sob that rose to her throat did not leave her mouth. "How close?" she said.

"Close enough." It was true; Blank could have shot him in the back at any moment, but instead chose to make a speech. His mistake.

James had bent down to pat the dead man's pockets. "Nothing."

"Someone was thinking ahead," Valentin said, then tilted his head toward the two silent strangers and hiked an eyebrow.

"They just showed up," James said. "Miss Lulu sent them. For whatever use we might have."

Valentin said, "They can get rid of him."

James turned and raised a beckoning hand and the men stepped forward.

TWENTY-FOUR

James had sent Carmine back to Mangetta's and he was standing in the doorway when Valentin and Justine rounded the corner. He ran to escort them to the saloon as if it was his designated duty. Once they were inside, Mr. Tom waited for them to take off their coats before saying, "Well?"

"Dead," Valentin said. "In the train yard."

Reynard had been typing. Now the clatter stopped and he stared across the room at the detective.

"How?" the King of Storyville said.

Valentin tilted his head to his wife. "By her hand. And mine."

Frank heaved a relieved sigh and murmured something in Italian.

"He had no identification of any kind," Valentin went on. "And we found nothing in his room at the Crescent. So that finishes him. Whoever he was. James has some help getting rid of the body. Courtesy of Miss Lulu."

Frank had Carmine pour two cups of coffee and two short brandies and place them on the bar for Justine and Valentin.

"So now what?" Anderson said.

The detective looked up at the clock. "The train gets in at eight-ten. What they're bringing will come here first. James will hold it until we see the mayor this afternoon."

Reynard stood up and began placing his Underwood back in its case. "I'm heading in to finish my stories," he said.

"Valentino?" Frank said, "There's somebody to see you. He come from Jackson. I had him wait in the grocery." He waved a hand and Carmine disappeared into the hallway, then returned with the visitor in tow.

"Mr. Valentin?"

Valentin said, "Baptiste. Did you find him?"

"I don't, but he's here. I just don't know where."

"I might," Valentin said.

James thought it odd that he knew most of the characters downtown but did not recognize either of the two who had walked up as he was crossing into the yard, the shorter one saying, "We're from Miss Lulu." And that was all.

After the steam from the passing train had drifted into the night, the lieutenant was relieved beyond words to see the St. Cyrs standing there.

Valentin and Justine started back to Mangetta's, with her clutching his arm to steady herself. James and the two men studied the body for a few seconds before the taller one walked away. He was back in five minutes with a heavy canvas tarp from one of the loading carts slung over his shoulder. By now, Mr. Blank had lost most of his blood and they rolled him onto the tarp, folded it over, and dragged him away, all without speaking. Which suited the lieutenant just fine.

Now he heard a deep whistle from far off. Another morning train was arriving. He walked out of the yard and crossed a mostly empty Basin Street on his way to the saloon.

Mr. Smith paced as he waited to hear from Blank. Six o'clock sharp was the appointed time.

The hour came and went. He had already heard from the man he had assigned to track him through the night and he had lost him. So he made a call of his own to police headquarters to ask his friend to request a report from Storyville, and specifically news of any bodies found. He understood that Blank might have murdered St. Cyr and disposed of his remains, though he had been told not to go to that extreme. They had agreed that proof would be provided. But Blank—whoever he was—had shown himself a rogue, so who knew what the man would do once the Creole detective was finished and his part in the matter of the papers from Washington discarded as so much false news?

So he was now waiting on two calls, one from headquarters and one from Blank. He sat for a half-minute, then got up and paced some more. After more time had passed, he began packing a valise, just in case.

James arrived back at Mangetta's, offered Valentin a quick nod, and sat down for a cup of coffee. No one was talking much and he was struck by the calm of the room. He saw a stranger seated with Mr. Tom. Valentin bent to whisper that he was an attendant from Jackson and, yes, Buddy had managed to escape the hospital and make it to the city.

Valentin caught his stare and shrugged. What else *could* have happened this night? He pondered for a moment, then moved to the center of the floor.

"Well, it's daybreak," he said and smiled at the small rise of applause. "And it's over now."

"For us," Mr. Tom said. "Not for some others."

"Yes, sir, that's true. For them, the trouble is just about to begin." He paused. "All right. Baptiste and I are going to go find Buddy. James will wait for the delivery from Washington." He turned to Justine. "If you would call the house and ask Eloi come collect Evangeline and Miss Eulalie. You can meet them at Miss Antonia's."

"What about Each?"

"Yes, after it's all done," he said. "And Mr. Tom..."

"I'll tend to him," James said.

Valentin took Justine aside for a few moments and then raised a hand to beckon Baptiste.

Long ago, they had stood in short pants and ragged shirts as the fat, heavy drops of an afternoon shower pocked the dry earth. The showers became gray downpours. Thunder and lightning and whipping winds did not signify. They were drenched and delirious, bare feet slapping the dirt as it turned to glorious mud.

The memory of those hours brought to mind the brazen blur of lights strung around a dancehall, the shouts and laughter that swept up in waves but were still no match for the brass, the oceans of motion as the bodies swirled and splayed. Did the floor quake and the earth shift? During some of those wild seconds, it seemed so.

Now the noise and the music faded and his mind cleared as he continued along the quiet streets. He didn't need to read the signs; he could name them without looking, even after so long away: Felicity, St. Andrew, Josephine, and so on and so on. It was funny that the street that he followed to arrive there was called Liberty and he had stayed on it until he reached First Street. Where he stopped.

Now all the nights when they had stood in an empty lot while the fireflies flew sorties around their heads came back to him. Hot summers, a neighbor would put out a block of ice that had somehow fallen off a wagon and set it next to his back steps, so anyone on the street could come around, pull out the pick, and chip off a chunk to suck or rub on a nappy head. One night, a fellow grabbed the pick and stabbed the man that had been visiting his wife while he was at work and there was blood on the ice and everywhere else, too.

Had the moon been full every night? Could that be? The dancing lights were fireflies and the careening bodies had been the children gathered on the corners, those who had managed to survive the Bronze John running in hysterics that didn't end until a father bellowed or a mother called sweetly from a kitchen doorway. And everywhere was the blessed music that was New Orleans. He was hearing and seeing this, dreaming this, when a voice called, "Buddy."

———

Baptiste had followed Valentin's Ford out of the District by way of Liberty Street. Faint glimmers of daylight were appearing between the buildings and early risers walked the banquettes.

The detective pulled to the curb after they crossed Jackson Avenue and waited for Baptiste to stop behind him and climb out of his Chevrolet.

"You sure about this?" the attendant said.

"No," Valentin said, "I'm hoping."

"And if he's not here?"

"I'll have James put out a report. And hope someone spots him. It's all we can do."

He paused to look over the streets that had once been so familiar. Not much had changed. Here and there a house had been abandoned. Some of the empty lots remained. He could see the back of the Bolden house at number 2309 First. A block to his left was St. John de Sales School for Colored, where they had been students. He could make out the spires of Holy Light Baptist Church, where Buddy had spent his Sunday mornings, and St. Angelo's, where he had spent his. They would meet after services, free themselves of their coats and ties, and rush out into the day.

Another street on and he would come upon his childhood home, but he had no desire to visit it and wake up the ghosts that would surely be lurking there. He had spent thirty years almost leaving them behind and he had—

"Mr. Valentin."

He came alert to see Baptiste pointing his finger across the way. Valentin looked to see a tall figure standing on the next corner. Even in the darkness, the silhouette was unmistakable and he half-expected to see a horn raised and hear notes pour from a bell.

He didn't realize that he had moved until he found himself on the other side and gazing at the face he still knew well. He said, "Buddy."

Buddy turned, not in a sudden motion of surprise, but as if he had been expecting to hear the voice. He regarded the two men, first Valentin, then Baptiste, then Valentin again. His gaze remained there and a slow smile brightened his features. A long few seconds passed. Then he said, "Tino."

Baptiste glanced at him and said, "That's you?"

Valentin nodded; it had been Buddy's nickname for him from the time they were kids. Now he studied the shadow of the face he had once known so well. But it was still dark and he was exhausted and so the visage seemed to float like a wandering memory. He steadied himself and said, "Buddy. What are you doing out here?"

"I've been trying to find this spot for a long time," Buddy said. "Forever, almost."

"And now you have," Valentin said.

"I haven't forgotten everything," Buddy said. "No. I remember." He waved a hand. "Used to be parades down on Lasalle. First lines, second lines." He turned toward First Street. "I would sit on the back steps. Play my horn. Kids would come around."

Valentin said, "You always drew a crowd."

Buddy said, "I sure did, didn't I? Anywhere I went. And anytime I started to blow, they'd come running."

His eyes shined as he took delight in the memory and for those brief few seconds, Valentin shared the images swirling through his head. He saw Buddy in front of a dance floor crowded with sweating bodies and shifting like the sea and the man on the stage was the captain of a ship that was rocking on the waves, blowing his life out through a silver bell with the lights burning over his head and he floated above the crowd, a wizard with a cornet for a wand. He had left it behind. Buddy had stayed.

As if reading these memories, Buddy produced a wicked smile so startling that Valentin took a step back, feeling the fierce heat that he had known so well so along ago flash on him. Then Buddy's face closed and it was gone.

Valentin and Baptiste waited out the moment, until the glow that was enveloping him began to fade. Now he peered over his shoulder at the azure streaks that had begun to touch the end of night. "But morning always came around again," he said. "Didn't it?"

Valentin couldn't think of a word to say. The rising dawn had turned the tableau stark and whatever recollections he had been holding began a slow retreat. Soon, he knew, there would be only the sad, broken man and the two who had come to find him standing there. Machines would begin passing on the streets. More citizens would appear from their houses and not one of them would recognize the one who had been born and had lived there until he was taken away. Buddy Bolden had gone missing a long time ago.

Baptiste let the silence linger and said, "Buddy? I come to take you back."

Buddy had been looking fretful. Now he calmed. "Back?" he said. "Yes. I believe it's time."

Baptiste said, "This way, then."

Buddy took a step to follow, then stopped, extended a hand to Valentin and said, "So long, friend." His grip was strong but lasted for only a second before he let go and walked off. Baptiste waved farewell.

Valentin stood where he was and listened as the Chevrolet's cylinders rattled to life and the machine rolled off. He didn't move until the bell on the first streetcar on Napoleon Avenue gave out a happy clang.

An exhausted Mayor Behrman was watching the sky lighten to the east and pondering the call from Lieutenant McKinney who was back at Mangetta's Saloon. The man who went by Mr. Blank was dead, with nothing to mark his true identity. His body had been "removed," McKinney's word for weighted and dropped in the river or carried off somewhere to be burned or buried. So that was over.

The lieutenant also reported that the documents they had been expecting had arrived on the morning train from Atlanta. He had them in his hands and St. Cyr would bring them to City Hall later that afternoon.

"All right," Behrman said. "We can all get some sleep now."

He placed the handset in the cradle and looked out over his city, trying to imagine what the day would bring now that the last few denizens of Storyville were vacating the streets. Some half-hearted scuffles would ensue and a few more cells at Parish Precinct would be occupied. Much to the dismay of the gentlemen who had worked so hard to see this very conclusion reached, come morning, the scarlet trade would resume elsewhere in the city.

The mayor looked around as Acting Chief Cook returned from the men's room, his eyes flicking about.

"There's news," Behrman said. "That fellow Mr. Blank is no longer a threat." He allowed time for the acting chief to make of these words whatever he wished.

Cook said, "Well, then, that's a good thing, isn't it? What about...?"

"St. Cyr? He's fine. Worn-out, like everyone else."

The acting chief did not appear to know what to do next. "All right," he said. "All right. Then the vigil is over."

"It is," the mayor said. "You'll want to get back to your office. It's a new day."

Cook peered at him, unsure if this last comment was serious or some sort of joke. He was almost to the door when Behrman called after him. "Please be back here at five o'clock." The response was a nervous nod.

Behrman summoned Mr. Pettibone. "Get the commissioner on the phone," he said. "And I want to see Major Sont."

Carmine escorted Justine to Basin Street. She had shared a tearful good-bye with Frank and bestowed a grateful kiss on Mr. Tom's cheek. Now she and her young companion walked along as stragglers ambled here and there. Police wagons had pulled to the banquettes and the coppers lounged and smoked and watched her handsome figure pass by.

"I don't understand a bit of it," Carmine said. "Why did he want Mr. Valentin dead?"

"It wasn't him. Someone hired him. Sent him here."

"What someone?"

"We don't know. Yet. Maybe we'll know today. And maybe never."

They had reached the steps to Miss Antonia's gallery and she now enveloped him in a hug that pulled him to her bust and she laid a fine kiss on an olive cheek that was flushed red when she let him go. His eyes were swimming with pleasure.

"*Tu sei bravo*," she said and turned to climb the steps.

At about the time that Baptiste's sedan was rolling off the Algiers ferry and starting on the highway north with its silent passenger on board, Valentin was arriving back in Storyville. He had decided on one slow tour before returning to Mangetta's and first rolled down Claiborne and then back south on Robertson, counting memories as he passed empty doors.

When he stopped at the corner of Conti and Villere, heard the faint sounds of a clanking piano and rough trumpet. He looked left and right and then turned in the seat, but saw nothing, so he steered to the curb and turned off the engine to listen. Then he remembered.

He climbed out and crossed to the other side and stepped into the walkway between the first and second buildings. The door creaked when he pushed it open and the groans of the steps when he descended were lost in the tapping of the keys and the deep notes from the horn.

With all the shadows, it could have been the middle of the night. The room was one of the few in Storyville that was below ground. Valentin couldn't quite recall the history, something about someone hiding contraband. The ceiling was low, the room was damp, and a single bulb hung down from a rafter. Shapes huddled at the tables.

The music didn't stop when he reached the floor. The man at the piano, who went by Tall Bob and was the only pale face in the room, smiled when he saw him. His partner Joe Juignet followed his gaze and raised the bell of his horn. Valentin began to pick out faces and some of the people nodded as he crossed the floor to drape an arm over the box of the old upright.

They were playing what was called "gutbucket," but everyone now knew as "blues." It was sweet and sad and Valentin heard the longing carried on in lowdown melody. There would be no second lines this day.

He looked around at the resigned expressions of the sporting girls and rounders, most of whom he knew from his years in the District, and realized that this was truly the last of it, that these were the soldiers surrounded at the end of the final battle and would soon be gone, not dead but scattered. Each one of them would carry away a tiny piece of Storyville and then only skeletons and empty shells would be left behind.

The duo began a lowdown version of "Careless Love" and a trollop Valentin didn't recognize rose on unsteady legs, made her way to Joe's side, and began to sing along.

> *Love, oh love, oh careless love*
> *Love, oh love, oh careless love*
> *You caused me to weep, you caused me to moan*
> *You caused me to leave my happy home*

Buddy had played that song. Not with melancholy but with vigor in spite of lyrics of betrayal and loss. And wasn't that something to remember?

> *Well, it's sorrow, sorrow to my heart*
> *Sorrow, sorrow to my heart*
> *Sorrow, sorrow, sorrow to my heart*
> *Since me and my true love had to part*

If he could only hold this moment in time or even turn back the clock, just long enough to grab one more fragment of that strange, dangerous, dirty, marvelous place. But that could not be. It was over now.

> *Well, I wish the Lord my train would come*
> *Wish the Lord my train would come*

Wish the Lord my train would come
And carry me back to where I belong

Her voice faded away and she stood there until the musicians picked up a meandering tune and she drifted back to her table. Valentin knew that soon, in mere minutes, in fact, coppers would come to rapping on the door with their nightsticks and shouting, "Everyone out!" Then the occupants of this room would climb the stairs and scatter like leaves tossed about in the gray autumn wind. He had no wish to witness that, so he left to climb the steps back to the street on his way to leaving Storyville behind.

He drove the three blocks to Basin Street and pulled to the curb in front of Miss Antonia's mansion. Before he could climb out, Justine came down the gallery steps. He let the engine idle and circled around the front of the Ford to help her to her seat.

"Eloi came to collect the ladies," she said. "Eulalie invited Miss Antonia and her girl to the lake. So they went."

"What about Miss Lulu?"

"She made a call and some fellow came for her."

"What fellow?"

"Don't know him. He looked like a dandy, though."

Valentin produced a weary laugh at the thought that some things would never change.

"I telephoned Mercy and spoke to Mariette," Justine went on. "She said Each came awake a few more times, but mostly he's been asleep."

"And so?"

"And so we can go back home," she said.

TWENTY-FIVE

At three-thirty that afternoon, Valentin left Justine and Evangeline at the house and drove back downtown and parked in the lot next to City Hall. James was waiting in the lobby. He looked at the Creole detective and said, "Did you sleep?"

"Some. Enough, I guess. You?"

"About the same."

He came up with a dazed grin and Valentin said, "Did Anna Mae require some attention first?"

The lieutenant laughed. "She did. And I obliged."

Valentin saw the leather portfolio tucked under his arm. "The papers?"

James nodded. "Did you get a look at them?"

"Oh, yes." He was smiling. "Your man did well."

He pointed to one of the marble benches and they sat down. The lieutenant opened the portfolio and withdrew some twenty typed pages. Valentin read through until he arrived at one that contained a short list of names. He kept his voice low as he read aloud.

"Alonzo Moran, Deacon, St. Patrick's Church. John Wales, President, Gulf Bank and Trust."

"I know that name," the lieutenant said.

"Charles Flowers, President, Cross Shipping. Garth Gainey, President, G&O Steel. Elmer Lassiter, Chief Officer, Lassiter Holdings."

"And I've read about those last two in the paper."

"They're all very important men. And they're about to become very unhappy men."

He skimmed the final two pages then tamped the sheets into a neat stack and handed them back. "Jesus and Mary," he said. "Hearing a report over a telephone line is one thing. These are the real goods. It's all there."

They stood up. James replaced the papers in the portfolio, then said, "Are you ready?"

Before they reached the elevators, he bent his head to whisper, "So you know, the mayor called Cook in. He'll be waiting outside." He snickered. "And shitting in his pants."

They walked down the hallway to find Acting Chief Cook sitting stiffly in a chair next to the outer office door. He gave a small start at the sight of the two visitors and his stare went directly to the portfolio. No one spoke as they passed inside.

An aide who on this morning was not Mr. Pettibone ushered them into the office, where they found Mayor Behrman dressed more carefully than they would have expected. He wore a fine dark suit, his shave was clean, and his hair oiled nicely. It appeared that he had also managed to get sufficient sleep and his eyes were clear. He rose to his feet at their approach.

When James stopped and held out the portfolio, he said, "This is it?"

"It is, Mr. Mayor. Valentin and I have already been through the pages."

"Sit, please," Behrman settled into his chair, unclasped the flap, and drew out the sheaf. "Well?" he said. "Was it worth our trouble?"

"Oh, yes, sir," James said.

"But it got here too late."

"Yes, I'm afraid so."

"All right, let's hear it."

James said, "I'll allow Mr. Valentin to explain, if it's all right."

"Yes, of course." The mayor plucked a pen from his holder, "Go ahead, sir."

"It was a plan of opportunity," Valentin began. "Six city leaders have been casting greedy eyes at the District for years. All that land sitting right there. With Union Station on its doorstep."

The door opened and the mayor held up a hand. They waited for the aide who had greeted them to deliver cups of coffee and a plate of sweets from a tray. Valentin stirred cream and sugar into his cup and then waited for the mayor's assistant to exit.

Mayor Behrman caught the curious glance that passed between Valentin and the lieutenant. Neither of them had ever been in the office when Pettibone wasn't hovering close by.

"He left the building this morning. On an errand, he said. He hasn't come back. Mr. Golar is taking his place for the moment."

He watched his two visitors spend a moment staring at nothing.

"I missed it," Valentin said. "It never occurred—"

"I know," Behrman said. "I hope it's not the case, but if it is, it would be one hell of a coincidence. For now, we have people looking for him." He shook his head. "Continue, please."

Valentin gathered his thoughts. "Yes, sir. Those blocks were already producing wealth. Millions. As you said. Month after month, year after year. For almost a century and especially in the twenty years that Mr. Tom ran things. It's true it had been slipping down some, but it was still valuable revenue for the city."

"Indeed it was," Behrman muttered.

James said, "And the scarlet trade was contained. Controlled."

The mayor said, "So..."

"Their problem was that none of them owned any of the properties. Of course, they knew who did. And had influence with them." Valentin sipped his coffee. "One or two of them might have had moral objections to Storyville. The others didn't. In any case, they had been talking about the potential there for a long time. Completely in secret, of course."

The mayor said, "And how did you first find out about it? You never said."

Valentin's eyes shifted enough for him to see James barely hiding a smile. "It was from...from a young lady I know. The daughter-in-law of one of those gentlemen. She overheard it being discussed in her home. And she passed the information along to me. Confidentially, of course."

Behrman hiked an eyebrow. "I see. I thought you were a happily-married man."

"Oh, I am," Valentin said. "This was a person I knew some years ago."

"The former Miss Benedict?" Now the mayor shared the lieutenant's smile. "Go on," he said.

Valentin was pleased to do so. "Then the Navy came along. They had been considering a base at Belle Chasse, starting about ten years ago. But there were other sites in the running."

The mayor eyed him. "Do I smell bribes in the air?"

"Yes, sir. That started with the announcement that they made about the new base. Certain individuals who represent our fair city were blessed with bundles of cash. As were certain officers at the Department of the Navy. There's no doubt that the bribe for some of these gentlemen was simply to ensure that the District would close. They thought it was a blight." He shrugged. "The wheels were set in motion and it was moving along."

"Until I had you in the way."

"Yes, sir. And that's when things went off. Word got around New Orleans and then Washington that Mayor Behrman was raising doubts about the arrangement. And he put a man on the job. Me."

At this, the mayor came up with a cold laugh. "Son-of-a-bitch," he said. "So they hired someone to try to put the fear of God into me. Actually, hired someone who hired someone."

Valentin said, "It does make a certain sense, Mr. Mayor. A person on the inside who—"

"Who was it?"

"I don't know that," Valentin said. "We might find out when we see who leaves the city in the next couple days."

"Yes, yes, I see that now. But what was the goal of all this?"

"To take over Storyville. Or what was left of it. Demolish every building right down to the ground. And turn the twenty blocks into real estate that would be bought out and carved up between them."

The mayor said, "And do what?"

"To create a new French Quarter."

The mayor stared at him. "A new...?"

"Quarter. Without the Vieux Carré. All modern. Hotels. Ten or twelve stores. A new opera house. A casino. And no homes."

"Would that even be possible?"

"They thought so. Because they had cover. It was true that the Navy didn't want the District so close. But it wasn't all that important. Because most of the sailors would be out to sea most of the time." The detective smiled. "Out to sea and visiting ports a whole lot more sordid than the one we have here."

The mayor turned his chair to face the window and didn't speak for a long minute as he gazed out at the lights glowing as evening approached. Finally, in a tone of regret, he said, "All right, I suppose I need to hear the names." He swiveled back around.

Valentin stood up, said, "May I?" and flipped through the sheets of paper, drawing out the third from the last. He remained standing as he read.

When he finished, the mayor held out his hand and perused the list on his own. "I guess this proves that you don't have to be smart to get rich." He pushed the sheet aside. "What the hell were they thinking? And maybe adding murders on top of it?"

It was not a question that required an answer. They all knew how greed could turn sober men into fools.

"And all this came into your hands by way of your man in Washington?"

"That's correct."

"Who had a girl pumping some fellow on the inside." A second passed and he laughed at how the words had come out. Then, sobering, he said, "So what happened to him?"

"He went back to his wife," Valentin said. "And was told to keep his mouth shut forever."

"What about the girl?"

"She's taking her talents elsewhere. Geary helped her with that."

James glanced at Valentin and then said, "Mr. Mayor? What will happen now?"

"Now?" Behrman said. "Now I take over. And make these gentlemen and whoever was in cahoots with them face consequences." He stood and held out his hand. "Thank you both. We'll speak again soon." He called out, "Mr. Golar?" The door opened and the aide appeared. "Please escort our guests out. And tell Acting Chief Cook that I'll see him."

Eloi drove Justine into town and she met Valentin outside the hospital. They were not surprised to find Mariette waiting, even though it was her day off.

She led them to Each's room and they stood around the bed. Justine dabbed her eyes. Valentin stayed silent for a few moments and then said, "Emile Carter." He waited. Then: "Each?" He waited again. Finally: "Beansoup?"

The eyes fluttered and a whisper came from his mouth. Valentin bent closer to the bed. "What was that again?" He listened, smiled, and straightened.

"He says no one calls him that anymore."

Twenty-Six

The following morning saw New Orleans return to an oddly sudden kind of normal. The workday began as any other, with the rousing of citizens going off to their labors, children to school, wives to market, and the pious to mass.

Only a handful of the Storyville saloons like Fewclothes Cabaret and a few shops like Mangetta's Grocery opened in their usual fashion. The small army of sots who had for years made daily treks to spend their waking hours on those scarlet streets and in any of a dozen watering-holes arrived to find a ghost town and so had nothing to do but to amble about the banquettes muttering to each other.

At the same time, there was no shortage of curious citizens who pulled their machines to the curbs to gaze at the empty avenues. After the school bells rang that afternoon, gangs of boys went roaming about, alert for anything wicked that might have been left behind. Other than that, it was all very quiet.

This was in contrast to the flurry of activity at City Hall that began with Mayor Behrman's appearance at eight a.m. sharp. He had called for an early-morning meeting with three councilmen he trusted, the City Attorney, and Police Commissioner Williams. The five men sat in stunned silence as he spent an hour describing what had transpired in New Orleans and Washington over the prior three months and then through the night before.

He answered the questions that he could, deferred the rest for another time, and went on to explain what he planned to do next. There were no protests. He asked for a few days' secrecy and sent them away, asking the commissioner to stay behind.

"You couldn't have told me all this before?" Williams said once the door had closed.

"It wasn't a matter of not trusting you, Arthur. I just didn't know what we had. It wasn't clear until the end. I still don't have all the details."

The commissioner was not pleased with the explanation, but chose to let it go. He was still struggling to grasp what Behrman had divulged to him and the others. "Well," he said at last. "I have a personnel matter to attend to."

"We might never know if he was in on it. Mr. Pettibone, either." He sighed. "I'm still stunned at the thought that he..." He waved a vague hand.

"Whatever the case, Cook doesn't have what it takes to serve as chief," Williams said. "I'll see that he's tucked away where he can't do any harm."

"Good enough," the mayor said.

"When will you start your...?"

"Interviews?" the mayor said. "The first one will be at noon. Then as quickly as I can get them all in here."

The commissioner stood up. "Holy hell, Martin," he said. "How did it ever come to this?"

The mayor thought about it but had no answer to offer other than, "It was Storyville."

Rather than summon Anderson's man Louis so early, Lieutenant McKinney had called ahead to Lucy and then drove Mr. Tom to Annunciation Street. The maid was waiting on the gallery and together they helped him up the steps and into the house.

James waited until Lucy got him settled in his Morris chair. She stood before him with her hands on her hips. "You can't go back," she said. "Storyville ain't no more."

"Because I'm not there," Mr. Tom said. "But I always was when it mattered, wasn't I?" He leaned his head back and closed his eyes.

On the stroke of twelve, Mr. Golar ushered Charles Flowers of the Empire Shipping Company into the mayor's office. The message that had summoned him expressed the "extreme gravity" of a matter of import to the city. So Flowers showed no surprise when Behrman asked that he leave his assistant in the outer office. He was the cool sort in general and did not show anything as he settled his large frame into a chair.

The front didn't last long and it was the first of six times over that day and the next that Mayor Behrman watched the face of a wealthy and respectable citizen go pale and the lawyer from the diocese sit frozen as the evidence was stacked up and the realization dawned that all the money and power he held was not going to save him.

The mayor gave each gentleman time to mull the situation before delivering ultimatums, offering a way to keep their bodies out of Parish Prison and their good names in exchange for keeping the shameful and damning information of their misdeeds from the police and the newspapers.

"I'll be clear," he said first to Flowers and then to the four other businessmen, using exactly the same language. "Going forward, you will be a reliable benefactor for the city. You'll give me no reason to question you or your company's practices. You will not touch one inch of real estate on the blocks formerly known as Storyville. You'll pay every cent of your taxes. And you will give strong support to all my programs, no matter how repellent you find them. For that, you'll not be exposed." To the lawyer he said, simply, "Tell your clients to tend to God."

The reactions were some variation of Flowers', who dabbed his lips and his white brow with a handkerchief before rising to make a shaky exit.

That evening, Valentin received a telephone call from James McKinney. He had just come from the morgue where he viewed a body that had been discovered in Eclipse Alley.

"Our friend J. Picot," he said. "Shot once below the chin."

"Mr. Blank," Valentin said.

"I suspect so," the lieutenant said.

"And another story ends." Valentin said good-night.

Whether or not Mr. Pettibone had been "Mr. Smith" was never ascertained. He disappeared from New Orleans, which many saw as a clear indictment of him as that character. Suspicious eyes were also cast at Acting Chief Cook. That officer was assigned to manage an administrative department of the N.O.P.D. and would leave the force during the winter.

The world went on. Without the lights and the bustle and the hundreds of warm bodies, the blocks faded by slow degrees, like a photograph left out in the sun. Now and again, a traveler who had somehow missed the news would step from a train in his best country clothes and gaze dumbfounded at the bleak tableau that was Basin Street. His queries would bring only blunt replies: "Gone."

Gertrude Dix's calls to local voodoo women to lay curses on Judge King had not worked to change the outcome of her lawsuit. However, several years later and under odd circumstances, the judge was struck and killed by a car on St. Charles, and not a few counted it as a hex delayed. The former madam claimed a second victory when, a year later, she and an aging Tom Anderson were married.

For the rest of New Orleans, there was satisfying news. Unexpected investments from a number of the city's larger companies and cooperation from the diocese allowed Mayor Behrman's agenda of improvements to move forward.

By the time December arrived, Valentin was only one of the thousands of citizens who had to be reminded that Storyville was no more. It was also true that he went nowhere near the District as he lived his days in peace, waiting for whatever was coming.

Each made a slow but steady recovery and was released in time to spend the holidays on Dumaine Street. It was there, as the sun was going down on a

Friday afternoon, that Justine and Evangeline arrived back at the house. Valentin and Each were in the kitchen. The detective had been hovering between the stove and the icebox, working up his courage to cook dinner. He had made no progress when the women appeared, back from shopping. They both laughed at the sight of him, standing in fright of actually preparing a meal.

He had somehow managed not to ruin the chicken and rice and beans, though Evangeline saved him by hovering at his shoulder.

After he had cleared the dishes, he came back to the table, sat down, and said, "I think we should move."

Justine said, "To where?"

"To the lake. Where there's more room. Maybe close to Miss Eulalie."

She was quiet for a moment. "Then I want to start a family."

Valentin stared at her, then looked at Evangeline and saw a smile lighting that kind face. He turned back, took Justine's hands in his and said, "Well, I do, too."

"You do?"

"Yes." He sighed. "And I think it's time for me to be done with detective work."

She laughed, even as tears welled in her eyes. "But what will we do for money?"

"I don't know. I'll find something." He brightened. "Maybe I'll write a book."

"A book?" Evangeline said. "About what?"

"I've had some adventures. About those." He leaned forward and clasped his hands before him. "Whether I do that or not, I'm going back to my true name. It's been too long. I'm going to be Valentino Saracena again."

At this, Evangeline let out a small sound of surprise and stared at him. He said, "What is it?"

"Saracena," she said. "I know that name."

THE END

Thanks are due.

To my publishers Joe Phillips and Susan Wood, cover artist Kerrie Kemperman, and to typesetter extraordinaire Geoff Munsterman.

To Sansanee Sermprungsuk, who brought first-rate skills as editor of this work, along with the far more difficult task of being my wife.

To Michael Allen Zell, who started me on this last leg of the journey. And as this series concludes, to all those named and nameless readers who went on this journey with me, offering kind words along the way. You have supplied the other half of the equation and for that I am deeply grateful.

As the author of twelve novels and a novella, David Fulmer has won a Shamus Award and a Benjamin Franklin Award and has been nominated for a LA Times Book Prize, the Shamus Award for Best Novel, a Barry Award, and the Falcon Award. His titles have been selected for numerous "Best of" lists, including *New York Magazine*'s "Best Novels You've Never Read" and *Atlanta Magazine*'s "Best of the Shelf," and have received superlative reviews from *The New York Times, USA Today, The San Francisco Chronicle, The Washington Post, The Times-Picayune, The Detroit News, The Boston Globe, Kirkus Reviews, The Minneapolis Star-Tribune, Publishers Weekly,* and *The Christian Science Monitor.* In addition to audiobook versions. his books have been translated into Italian, French, Japanese, and Turkish. A native of central Pennsylvania, David Fulmer lives in Atlanta with his wife Sansanee Sermprungsuk.

The Day Ends at Dawn is the seventh and final installment in the Storyville series.

CRESCENT CITY BOOKS
New Orleans, LA
www.blackwidowpress.com

The Sound of Building Coffins by Louis Maistros

Stay Out of New Orleans: Strange Stories by P. Curran

THE VALENTIN ST. CYR MYSTERIES by David Fulmer

Chasing the Devil's Tail

Jass

Rampart Street

Lost River

The Iron Angel

Eclipse Alley

The Day Ends at Dawn

CCB is a premier publisher of new and reprinted works that celebrate the culture of New Orleans, promoting diverse narratives that deliver New Orleans to the rest of the world. CCB distributes both nationally and internationally through NBN, a division of Rowman & Littlefield Publishing.